BACKBENDS

A MEMOIR

TIMOTHY DYKE

HIGH FREQUENCY PRESS

In *Backbends*, a filamentous work of autotheory, Timothy Dyke is discomfited by the possibility—no, certainty—that narrative distortion is inevitable. Whether these distortions are attributable to personal flaws (a botched eye surgery, for instance) or generic ones (like "trauma dumping"), though, are at the philosophical core of this book. Through vivid encounters with cigarette-smoking ghosts, a predatory yoga teacher, a metaphysical mango expert, and a revolving door of characters at his beloved Makiki Park, Dyke joins—and destabilizes—a genre inhabited by Brainard, Myles, Bellamy, and Lisicky.

—Lawrence Lenhart, author of *Backvalley Ferrets: A Rewilding of the Colorado Plateau* and *Experimental Writing: A Writer's Guide and Anthology* (co-editor)

It is well worth your precious time to spend some quiet hours in Timothy Dyke's perceptive, sensitive, and full-hearted world.

—Pamela Rotner Sakamoto, author of *Midnight in Broad Daylight: A Japanese American Family Caught Between Two Worlds*

Reading Timothy Dyke's *Backbends* is like dancing. Or like watching dancing. Or like watching beautiful dancing while a firework display of philosophical revelations goes off in your own brain. It's powerful. You will want to read this book.

—Frankie Rollins, *Do You Feel Like Writing: A Creative Guide to Artistic Confidence*

*For Aurelie Sheehan, an inspiring teacher and writer.
In Memoriam.*

*

Poetry lies. That doesn't stop it from being poetry. We sit down to lie. To craft a lie we hope will reveal truth—generally not in spite of the poem, but because of the poem.

—Douglas Kearney, *Mess and Mess and*

*

Creating a narrative from real life requires some element of misdirection. No piece of literature or documentary is a 100 percent faithful encapsulation of reality. In memoir, the author creates a gap between their true identity and the version of themselves depicted on the page. They become a character.

—Alex Sujong Laughlin, "You Never Get the Full Story"

*

ONE

MY NAME IS TIM, AND I REVEAL TMI: TOO MUCH INFOR-
mation. I over-share at least in part because I want to apply the same
storytelling gaze to myself that I apply to other people. Is it possible,
though, to view myself through an objective lens? If pushed, I'd admit
to being a person who doesn't believe in objective lenses. In order to
function, lenses need light to pass through them. All eyeballs process light
differently. My left eye has been plagued by flawed biology and surgical
error. Everything I see is cast in shadow. No one can look at themselves
directly. To see ourselves, we humans depend on the subjectivity of
reflection. What we see is what is in our heads more than what is there.
If I'm trying to tell a true story, how should I handle the inevitability of
narrative distortion?

I've been thinking about another specific question for a long time
now: how does confession lead to absolution? If I wanted to disclose
shameful truths, I wouldn't even have to write about the actual worst
thing I've ever done. Small stories have the potential to reveal as much
as big stories. I can write down some anecdotes about shitty behavior,
and from these little confessions, readers glean the kinds of harm I'm
capable of inflicting on others. The worst things we do are sometimes
the things we don't do.

My friend Sharon Smith called me in the early 1990s. I listened to
her cry on my answering machine. Her cat had died. I stood there and
listened to her sob. I had just come home from work and smoked some
weed alone. I didn't want to talk to Sharon with a foggy brain, so I didn't
pick up. I stood there and listened to her cry until my answering machine

tape filled. I checked in with her a week later. At that point our friendship was permanently diminished and altered.

When I was twenty, I was hiking in the woods behind my grandparents' house with my little brother in Tennessee. We had been fighting about something. I can't even remember the point of conflict. We mutually decided to separate on the trail. We had enough sense to stay within shouting range in case one of us got lost. About a half hour after walking alone, I heard the faint sounds of my brother's scream. I didn't answer. I let him believe he was lost in the woods alone.

One of my fifteen-year-old students recently told me about the phenomenon of "trauma dumping." They learned the term on Tik Tok, a digital platform I've never used. We were reading *Maus*, Art Spiegelman's Holocaust memoir. The graphic novel is about a writer who coaxes genocide survival stories out of his father. *Maus* is about other things, too. In a wide-ranging class discussion, a sophomore named Cully zeroed in on their version of the confession/absolution question. This is when they introduced me to the term, "trauma dumping."

Cully writes poetry. They didn't always want to hear about their friends' problems, so why should they expect their friends to read their troubling poems? Cully stayed after class with their friend, Shawn. I told them I don't consider confessional poetry and trauma dumping to be the same. I told them everyone gets to figure out when and how to tell their own story. Maybe what I told Cully and Shawn wasn't 100% true; maybe there is an area of overlap where bad confessional poetry veers toward the dumping of trauma. If that notion rings true, then so does its opposite. Good confessional poetry makes me feel connected to other human beings through alchemic language that turns shame into art.

I didn't talk to these two tenth graders about Robert Lowell, but if they were poet-friends my age, and if we were talking about the confession/absolution question, I might have brought up Lowell's poem, "Skunk

Hour." I love "Skunk Hour." I'm struck by his image of the lonely queer man, going to bed alone at three in the morning after an in-the-wee-hours bout of furtively watching other humans connect and touch. The solitary, self-hating man ends his night gazing upon some skunks in his trashcan, the mother skunk's head stuck in an empty carton of sour cream.

I come from a family of four children. My parents are still alive. They divorced when I was in college. Up until his recent incapacitation, my dad continued to have "girlfriends" who he respected and disrespected at various times, in various ways. Mom went on her own journey. She has lived with the same woman for the past thirty years. My mom's "friend," Wanda is a better husband than my dad ever was. My brother, Caleb is two years older than I am. I'm the second child. My sister, Hattie came along two years after me, and then three years after that, my brother, Dmitri was born. I've always referred to Dmitri as my little brother. He was fifteen when I abandoned him in the woods. I was twenty. He was calling my name. I sat down under a tree and let him scream. If I could hear his voice, then it stands to reason that he would have heard mine if I yelled back. I stayed silent. Eventually his voice faded away. I kept hiking. When I got back to my grandparents' house, Dmitri was still missing. My grandfather gave me a look of utter disappointment, the kind of disappointment that could last a lifetime. And has. He headed into the woods and found my little brother. When I think of the worst things I've ever done, I think mostly of things I didn't do. Neglect can be benign, but neglect can be malignant as well.

Attention isn't always better than neglect. Attention can be malignant, too. Think of the attention of a murderous stalker as an obvious example. Or the malignant attention of the identity thief. In her poem, "The Summer Day," Mary Oliver writes, *I've learned how to pay attention.* My very first poetry teacher said something similar. On the opening day of a community class I took when I was 19, this teacher,

Valerie Nash wrote on the chalkboard, "I write to save my life." At first, I assumed she was saying something hyperbolic and dramatic: writing is my rescue. It's possible that's part of what she was implying. But now I also understand that she was saying something about writing to pay attention. "Save" can mean rescue. "Save" can also mean preserve.

I write to save my life. I write to save and preserve my memories of what I've paid attention to in this life. If I write about people I know with a critical eye, then it is only fair to cast that same critical gaze back at myself. Maybe that's not true at all. Embedded in the nuances of the confession/absolution question, are even more questions about attention and neglect, how one can feed the other, how it's not always easy to separate the malignant from the benign.

This book, which I think of as a memoir, is not a story as much as it is about stories. I consider how much I should interrogate a statement like that. Aren't all tales concerned not only with content but with form? Don't all stories ask us to examine how the tale is told? A Buddhist notion: there is no such thing as a true narrative. Am I irritating? My story is not about Buddhism, and my story is not about notions. My story is about truth. I won't always tell what Tim O'Brien names in *The Things They Carried* as "the happening truth." I aim to tell, as O'Brien puts it, "story truth." When I make assertions like this, how derisive will your laughter be?

From my rocking chair in my fifth-floor apartment in Makiki, the most population-dense residential district in Honolulu, Hawai'i, I look out the window at other windows. Light bounces and memories float. Thirteen years ago, at the beginning of the second Obama term, I was a 47-year-old student in a graduate school program full of brilliant fiction writers in their low-20s. I noticed, not so much that my younger classmates hardly ever wrote stories with characters over 35, but that when they did, their characters were always sitting on porches, drinking whiskey, reminiscing from rocking chairs about life's lost luster.

In Makiki, at the nexus of the aqueduct and the alley, there is a patch of grass where a group of people work out on Saturday afternoons. I have come to expect these weekend warriors. I mark time by them. I never see any faces. I've listened to their voices from my rocking chair. I hear friendly sounds, a mix of gender possibility, some grunting. I hear limbs hitting hard foam. Perhaps the people in the alley learn some kind of martial art together. One Sunday during football season, I hear one of the fighters in the alley say that while he has no problem with gay people, he doesn't like to have gay friends because "they always end up hitting on me." Do his women friends say that about him? I consider getting up from my rocking chair to yell something off my balcony like, "Stop talking nonsense about gay people in a world full of gay people!" Then I remember he is down there across the parking lot working on a martial art. I hesitate to spark up a ruckus. I wonder if he is wearing a shirt.

I am inclined to go on a digression about body positivity. This one person I know referred to the upper body of Carlo Valdes, the Olympic bobsledder, as a Dorito. She made a wide-to-slim, shoulder-to-hips triangle with her index fingers. She told me my body was a Cheeto. She waved her hands into a puffy shape. I figured I should probably laugh. My mask slipped off my face. Most Covid masks don't fit me. I must have a huge face. Perhaps this contributes to my Cheeto shape. I wonder if I'm baked or fried. I wonder which I'd rather be. I try to appreciate my lumps and puffs. Could I possibly be a Flaming Hot Cheeto? I guess I shared a body positivity anecdote after all. I am exhausted.

My name is TIM, and my mode is TMI. Any kind of shame experience tends to conjure in me the competing impulses of disclosure and withholding. As a practice, I opt to let shame move through me. I notice it. I think reflective thoughts at some point. Then I try to get on with my day. For years I hadn't wanted to think about a series of bad experiences I had after I first moved to Hawai'i in 1992. At the time, I lived in a different apartment in Makiki. A coworker and I shared a two-bedroom in the same building Barack Obama lived in with his mom and grandmother when he was a boy. My housemate and I decided to try yoga, so we signed up for some free introductory classes at the Makiki YMCA down the road.

The teacher was about ten years younger than my mother. This yoga teacher was nice to me and invited me over to her home studio for a free private lesson. I was very naïve. I had no idea she was going to ask me to lick chocolate off her fingers. There was not such a yoga craze back then, no internet, and I didn't really know what yoga was supposed to be. I'd taken mushrooms in college. I thought yoga might foster the same kind of hallucinatory intimacy. It was only after my bad yoga teacher asked me to take a bath with her that I started to get suspicious.

My bad yoga teacher convinced me to moan while I stretched in public. I had no one to tell me that orgasmic moaning during forward bends is not typically part of the yoga routine. I felt the glow of her attention whenever she chose to be my partner. She pressed down on my thighs. She lifted me at the hips. She placed her hand below my navel and ordered me to breathe deeply. I didn't have enough experience to understand that yoga was not necessarily designed to be a two-person activity. My bad yoga teacher said that by vocalizing my breath, I would relax more. I was in my late twenties. I had seven more years of the closet ahead of me before I would come out as gay. I had a couple of decades to go before I would routinely and comfortably refer to myself as queer, asexual, attracted to love removed from romance and penetration. In one of her classes in the YMCA activity room, my bad yoga teacher coached me through a half-wheel pose. Prone, pushing from the souls of my feet, hands gripping my teacher's ankles as she stood behind my head, and lifting from my hips as if the drawstring of my yoga pants was tied to a system of pulleys, I'd moan into a backbend.

In retrospect, I'm aware other people in the class laughed at me. My teacher put me in a position to be ridiculed, perhaps for her own pleasure. I was deeply closeted in 1992. Twenty-eight, newly relocated after working in a suburb north of Houston, Texas, I had just been hired to teach *The Lord of the Flies* and a textbook called *Multicultural Perspectives* to high school students in Honolulu. I had rejected my conservative and Christian upbringing about ten years prior, then passed through a phase where I made fun of people with New Age ideologies. Terrified I might be gay, I tightly regulated my inner monologue. I turned off parts of myself. I walked through my days with a muted sense of sexual perception. I didn't know what yoga was. I trusted this teacher enough to do as she instructed. I couldn't read vibes. I still can't read vibes. After my yoga teacher stuck her tongue in my mouth during the private lesson, I stayed for cat/cow pose. I left after downward-facing dog. As I walked into my apartment, my roommate told me I looked weird. I said I was fine, then walked into the bathroom where I threw up.

Old joke: why don't Baptists have sex standing up? Punchline: they don't want people to think they are dancing. Why haven't I written about this incident before? I didn't want people to think I was bad at yoga. I've attempted to forget these stories. A famous poet once told me that every poem is about place unless it is about time. Then she said time is a place. Memories ground themselves in time and place. Could we agree that all poems are also about memory?

Another famous poet taught a seminar I enjoyed on Contemporary Poetics. Like a gameshow host, she'd shout out big questions. "Post-modernism is dead," she proclaimed. "What's next?" A man with shoulder-length hair said "Post-post-modernism." The famous poet, refusing to acknowledge the long-haired man, emphatically answered her own query. "NEO-CONFESSIONALISM!" Under what circumstances does confession bring absolution? There was that night in Burlington when the man at the ATM asked if I wanted to be his friend.

The bad yoga teacher and I are still acquainted, thirty years later. Before Covid, we would hug when we ran into each other. I saw her walking her Golden Retriever in Makiki Park a couple of weekends ago. We fist-bumped. She asked if I had any interest in buying fresh eggs from her. I lied and told her I don't eat eggs. That wasn't even the most awkward thing that's happened to me in Makiki Park this year. At the beginning of football season, I was reading *The Overstory* under a monkeypod tree. This is admittedly an on-the-nose way to read this novel about trees. I was enjoying myself in the shade on a bench until a man walked up to me and asked about the number on my shirt. I was wearing the NFL jersey I'd ordered the previous weekend. The shirt displayed the name and number of Carl Nassib, the first active player in National Football League history to identify openly as gay. I bought the shirt on a whim, inspired by his bravery. Looking up from my book, I told the park stranger that 94 was the number of Carl Nassib, a gay NFL defensive lineman. The stranger in the park crinkled his face. He stammered something about how he supposed a guy had to be what a guy had to be. He wore no literal mask.

If you are a queer person who grew up in America, you understand how deeply and consistently young children have been taught that gay kids should be punished if they try to play sports. Trans kids are shunned—literally legislated against—for athletic aspiration. When officials with power stoke fears of the queer teen locker-room predator, bullying becomes sanctioned. Most queer kids have been beat up in the showers at least once.

The park stranger said he also had a favorite football player, and then he named the third string quarterback on the worst team in the league, C.J. Beathard. Was this park guy trolling me? Was he hitting on me? Was he about to ask me for cigarettes? He pointed to a blooming flower at the community garden. After some deft segue, he was talking about how God had a plan for everyone. He said God's plan for me was beautiful.

I grunted, stared at my book. As I have had more than one bad experience with unsolicited God-talk, I've come to resent any kind of non-consensual spiritual meddling. I sensed that this park stranger was about to get on his knees. My anxiety rose. I was going to need to be rude on purpose. As a conflict-averse person, I don't like to do that. He stood over me as I sat on the bench with *The Overstory* in my lap. The man said he wasn't religious: he was spiritual. He was in a relationship with Jesus. I think he saw me as some sad park dude who would receive his patient attention. I saw him the same way.

I am wearing my #94 Carl Nassib jersey as I write this. A friend told me I shouldn't put Carl Nassib on a pedestal because, according to this friend, Nassib is a Trump supporter. I told my friend that human beings are complex creatures, and I wasn't putting anyone on a pedestal. I was putting this gay football player's name on my back. I had a Martina Navratilova poster on my wall when I was twelve. My father made me take it down because he said the world-class tennis champion looked like a man. He told me Billie Jean King was immoral. During the time I've been writing this story, Carl Nassib has been cut from his football team. I'm not sure he is in the league anymore. Oops. I take that back. He plays for the Buccaneers now. He just had a big game last week. Okay, never mind: he's retired now. As for Martina Navratilova, I've read statements she's made dismissing the rights of trans women. She's not my hero anymore.

When it comes to making stories out of real experiences, I suppose that on some theoretical level it would be best to narrate the events in chronological order without interpretation. This is not possible. The other day at work, the eighteen-year-old English students in my Identity and Fiction class were talking about stereotypes. Without meaning to, I indicated that I was recalling a dormant memory. One young woman asked me to tell the story. I stammered through a recollection of a Christmas Eve in my twenties.

As soon as I finished narrating the anecdote, I felt regret for telling a tale that should have remained a personal memory. An experience separates from reality as soon as it is recalled. A story can never be one-hundred percent true. I'm also aware that real humans are not side characters in my story. Folks don't exist to teach me lessons. Actual humans are not archetypes. As I continue to write about this bad yoga teacher, I don't even pretend to be telling the tale with objectivity. Even calling her "bad yoga teacher" is an interpretation. The moniker reduces her to a single identity. The character in the memoir is not the person I know.

When two people share an experience, they each tell a different version of the event. Everyone sees through distorted vision. For me this is literally true as my sight is impaired in the left eye. Light enters through a torn retina that has been reattached twice. My brain fills in when my vision draws blanks. Two people can stare at the same red wheelbarrow, but so much depends upon the eyes they look through. You and I would take in the scene, and if I had my right eye closed, I would not see the white chickens. You would. We'd look at the same scene and tell two different stories. Which is not to say that objective truth doesn't exist, blah, blah, blah. After I'd been taking classes for six months from the bad yoga teacher, the woman who taught me to moan while I stretched, she invited me to a weekend retreat at an old monastery by the sea.

Inner monologue from 1992: I go to the retreat because I want to learn more about yoga and meditation. Inner monologue from 2025:

I went because I was new in town and not yet out of the closet. I was lonely. Someone cool and beautiful was inviting me to a cool and beautiful place to do cool and beautiful things. I gave her my check and booked the weekend. We sat in natural volcanic steam vents naked. We smoked weed on the beach at sunrise. I kept saying to myself, "This must be what cool people do."

This simple and bewilderingly stupid acceptance of my teacher's worldview made sense to me at the time. All day on Hawai'i Island we did yoga. I enjoyed the walking meditations after Morning Fruit. On the last night, my bad yoga teacher introduced a channeler named Dewi. Dewi sat cross-legged on a wooden platform surrounded by plumeria blossoms and candles. She croaked in the distorted voice of a medieval cleric named Epiquo. She seemed to be performing rehearsed material. I knew all of it was ridiculous, but everyone around me seemed sincere. I was high on joint smoke.

Just because an act of faith is meaningless to me, that doesn't mean there is no meaning in the act for other people. A mother and her late-teenaged daughter sat on a woven mat between Dewi/Epiquo and me. As the young woman cried, the older woman hugged her with both arms and gently swayed. Who am I to say that the channeling session wasn't transcendent for them? When faced with an apparently ridiculous ritual, I ask myself whether the practitioner is sincere. If the practitioner sounds sincere, I listen. I suppose this makes me susceptible to cults.

By the sea, we made raku pots and fired our creations in the sand. My bad yoga teacher led this mud-molding activity. With her hands deep in clay, she challenged us to make pinch-pots in the shapes of our souls. I bent a slab into the form of a cup, narrow at the top, a small oval vessel. To be honest, the shape of my soul pot was decidedly vaginal though I couldn't recognize this at the time. I didn't really know what a vagina was shaped like. With the obvious exception of birth, I have never seen a live vagina up close.

The proselytizer in Makiki Park tells me God doesn't hate me. He tells me God thinks I'm pretty rad. I lean into the book on my lap. I stare at an open page of *The Overstory*. I aim to perform the act of disappearing into a novel. He sits down next to me and bows his head. I spring up. I'm sure he is about to start talking to Jesus. Would it be true to say that any queer adult who grows up in a conservative religious environment knows how uncomfortable it can get when people pray for your salvation? I don't want him to touch me. I don't want him to shout about my demons. I have not given him permission to speak to me with words of love.

From my rocking chair in my apartment in Makiki, I look out the window. I am TIM, and my tendency for TMI grows out of some misplaced belief that confession will lead to absolution. I have become the old man on the porch, searching for lost luster. I see evening light bounce off hundreds of panels of glass. I have become the Jimmy Stewart character in *Rear Window*, except when I look out the window, I don't imagine that I'm looking at other people. I imagine other people looking back at me.

I do backbends by myself now. Alone on the floor next to my bed, I lay prone, breathe in and rise into a half wheel. In memory, I hear the voice of my brother, Dmitri, as he screams for help in the woods. I hear the sobs on my answering machine as my friend, Sharon Smith with the deceased cat, asks for support I never provide. Exhaling deliberately, as silently as possible, I aim to quiet my thoughts. My inner monologue whispers suggestions for ways to seek truth in Makiki moonlight. From bed, I stare out the window. I'm not looking for lost luster. I am not *not* looking for lost luster. Time is a place. I fish up a question from the stream of my consciousness. Which hurts more: the story I can't remember or the story I can never forget?

TWO

MY LEFT EYE HAS BEEN RIPPED AND INVADED. MY LEFT eye's vision reveals very little. Since 2017, I've had three cataract surgeries and two retinal procedures. "Procedure" feels like an ineffective euphemism. Fifty years ago, standard practice would have been to replace my biological eye with a prosthetic one. Had I lived two centuries ago, would I have been like the victim in Edgar Allen Poe's "The Tell-Tale Heart?" Poe's murderous narrator is freaked out by the old neighbor with neglected eye trauma. I feel sorry for the old guy, his eye protruding and discolored like a blue crab's.

Let's use that crab image as a point of transition, a segue—deft or not. There could be several starting points for this story about my haunted Makiki condo unit. To me this ghost story begins when I have dinner at La Hibiscus on Waialae Avenue with Brit Takano, my eventual real estate agent. The crab enchilada at La Hibiscus was less than delicious. I picked at the food on my plate and wondered if the crab inside the tortilla came from a can. Was it even really crab?

I was casually listening when Brit mentioned this condo in Makiki her in-laws were trying to sell. She said it was unusual, even frowned upon in professional circles, for one real estate agent to represent both buyer and seller. She wanted me to allow an exception. Brit knew this place would be perfect for me.

My writer friend Regina says you don't have to believe in God to believe in ghosts. I have a hard time agreeing with her. If you believe in ghosts, then you believe in a world beyond empiricism and science. If you believe in a world beyond empiricism and science, you allow access to magical possibility. Unlike nature, supernature invites discussion of good and evil. Discussion of good and evil invites consideration of the existence of God or gods. Regina would say that two pillars of the human condition are discomfort and alienation. Regina would ask this: how hard is it to believe that human discomfort and alienation would extend past death? God. She has a point.

A writing teacher once told me all ghost stories are grief stories. The year of my first retinal detachment surgery, I was cast in a community theater production to play a lead role in *Mothers and Sons*, one of the last plays written by Terrence McNally. *Mothers and Sons* is a grief story. I played Cal, the husband of a younger man in the earliest days of marriage equality.

Cal's first love, Andre, died of AIDS in the early 1990s. The plot follows the consequences of the unannounced arrival of Andre's mother at the ritzy apartment Cal now shares with his husband and son. During the production, I started to perceive an anomaly in my vision. At first, I thought my eyes were strained from staring into theater lights. I played the character opening weekend, but then I had to drop out of the production for emergency surgery. My friend Leilani replaced me in drag.

This would have been 2017. Or 2016. Somewhere in there. I had been renting one side of a duplex in Manoa from my cousin. I don't want to talk too much about my cousin. We had always been close growing up. For six years, it made sense to live with him as my landlord. After he got divorced, his drinking took an even more dangerous turn. I believe that he crashed my car into a tree on Tantalus so he could refill a Vicodin prescription. You can see already I am starting to tell my cousin's story more than I care to.

The vision in my left eye is so impaired that when I close the right eye, I can't see the chart in the ophthalmologist's office. I'm not saying I can't see the gigantic E. I'm saying that with my left eye, I can't see the eye chart. I can barely see the wall. The first reattachment surgery of 2017 was successful enough to let some light in. I learned to live with impaired vision.

In the summer of 2022, on the advice of my retinal surgeon, I underwent another surgery to remove a cataract on the same eye. The surgery went so poorly that I had to have three more. As a result of all this eye trauma, the retina detached again. Before the second retinal surgery, the surgeon told me my best-case prognosis was that I would always have blurry vision in my left eye. The worst-case scenario involved organ removal, stitched lids, an eye patch.

One story folds into another. My cousin went to rehab. I went looking for a new place to live. This led me to the shitty enchilada. Eventually I moved into that condo in Makiki. Brit assured me I would be happy there. Questions of happiness can be confusing, of course. I did some formal research into the topic for a professional project.

I moved to Hawai'i to work for a newspaper that no longer exists. For a while I had a regular column, and then I moved on to freelance work. I began supplementing my paycheck by writing public relations stuff for a local hospitality company. It became harder and harder to make a living in the newspaper business. Eventually that supplemental P.R. money became my primary source of income.

I keep going off on tangents. I was talking about happiness. I wrote a series of pieces for the in-flight magazine of Hawaiian Airlines. After interviewing a professional surfer, a woman who runs a non-profit for the homeless, and a social worker who teaches a course on happiness at the University of Hawai'i Hilo, I put together a collection of pieces that had titles like "Ten Ways to Be Happier, Starting Now" and "Is Gratitude the Secret to Lifelong Fulfillment?" Answering that last question, I'd probably say yes. Or at least mostly. To achieve happiness, it's also important to rid one's life of harmful ghosts.

I was molested by my pediatrician when I was fourteen. There is no appropriate time to bring up this story, so I might as well mention it now. During my adolescence, I saw a pediatrician who had spectacles and a salt-and-pepper beard. It never occurred to me to think of him as anything other than a nice doctor. I had been seeing him for two years, since I was twelve. During a routine checkup, he cupped my balls without a glove.

I remember giggling. He screamed at me to shut up. I complied. He didn't take his ungloved hands off my genitals until after he asked me if I menstruated. I didn't know what menstruating was. Continuing to touch me, the doctor told me about periods. I felt shame for not being well informed. After the appointment, I didn't tell anyone what had happened. I wasn't sure what to tell.

Five years after the troubling pediatrics checkup, my grandfather and my mother were reading the local paper in the den on a summer morning. My mother sighed as she narrated a news story about the arrest of that same doctor. He'd been caught molesting a teenaged girl. My mother seemed shocked. She asked if he had ever done anything "suspicious" to me.

At the table in the den where we were all eating breakfast by the window in front of the cactus garden, I told them about the time the doctor asked me if I menstruated while he fondled my genitals. My grandfather pounded his fist on the table. He said the doctor was not right in the head. My mother looked down at the newspaper. I returned to my breakfast burrito.

This brings me back to that crab enchilada. Brit told me that her dead husband's sister owned what might be the perfect place for me. The apartment had belonged to Brit's mother-in-law who died from lung cancer. Brit's deceased husband's sister was eager to sell the place. I picked at my mediocre Mexican food and told her I'd be willing to take a look.

I moved into the Makiki condo on Halloween. The walls were beige. I painted them green. I was looking for some way to distance my new apartment from its history. Any new living situation is going to come with a unique set of noises and surprises. The condominium building had a couple of huge exhaust fans on the roof. They gave off a hum as I attempted to go to sleep the first night, October 31st. While the walls of the building were mostly thick and concrete, I could hear toilets flush in other apartments on the fifth floor. I heard the revved-up engines of motorcycles on Nehoa Street. None of what I heard sounded supernatural. At least not for the first half-year or so that I lived there. Ghosts have a way of blending in for a while. They don't always make themselves known right away.

Remember my cousin with a drug problem? His name was Marco. I must use the past tense because his addictions got the better of him. He died on October 3rd, 2019. Again, I hesitate to tell his story here. He didn't exist for the purpose of providing backstory in my ghost narrative. That said, it's hard to tell of the haunting without telling something about my relationship with my cousin.

Marco was my mother's brother's kid. I grew up in Texas, and he grew up in Vermont. We'd see each other every other summer at reunions and whatnot. Marco and I were exactly the same age, born on the same day in 1979. We unironically called each other "cousin twins." For the rest of my life, I will feel an emptiness when he doesn't call me on May 5, our shared birthday, a day that will not be fun for me ever again. Cinco de Mayo be damned.

Is Marco the ghost I am haunted by? Yes, in a metaphorical way. I wish the ghosts in my story were only metaphorical. Until he was fired for passing out drunk in the seat of a bulldozer, Marco made his living as a site manager for a construction company. He divorced his wife, Emalia, the year after their son was born.

There is an alternative universe where those years of Marco's life would have been his most joyous. If reality hadn't been so punishing, Marco could have been one of the people I looked to when I wanted to understand happiness. Instead, Marco lost his job, his money, his family, his friends, his health, self-respect. All of it. He traded in everything good so that he could feed his raging demons. Again, I'm being metaphorical. Again, I am about to get literal.

Before I get literal, though, I want to say something about alternate universes. I don't understand anything about theoretical physics. When I think about alternative universes, I think about the worlds fiction writers build for their invented characters. In realistic fiction, characters on the page cannot walk into the writer's room. The writer cannot step into the page and interact with the invented characters. Walls between writer and character are impenetrable in realistic fiction. The writer and their creations exist in simultaneous and parallel worlds. An author of realistic fiction will never meet their created protagonist in the aisles of the Safeway on Piikoi Street. This is how I conceive of alternate realities from the fiction writer's perspective. There is the reality of the character, and there is the reality of the character's creator.

In this ghost story, I am writing about a version of a version of myself who is haunted by the memory of a dead loved one. The character who eats the crab enchilada is a freelance journalist. The writer character who had eye surgery is a high school English teacher. We have both eaten at La Hibiscus, the bygone Mexican food joint in Kaimuki. The writer knows his character is a fictional creation. The fictional character may or may not know his creator is a writer.

Recently in English class, I asked my students to write down philosophical questions they cared about. More than one student asked, "Are we living in a simulation?" The characters in a story live in their creator's simulation. I wanted to say this in class. I wanted to ask my writing students if we are living in the stories we've invented for ourselves. Are we living in the stories we've been subjected to by the people, systems, and structures that have power over us? Are we living in stories written by fate or God? I wasn't sure if my point would be clear, so I deflected the students' inquiry about simulations.

Before I came out of the closet at the end of the 20th century, students would sometimes ask me if I had a girlfriend or a wife. The closet was a simulation I had created for myself in the earliest days of my teaching life. I would tell anyone who asked that I'd just not met the right woman yet. In order to occupy the space of my false heterosexuality narrative, I found it necessary to make up former girlfriends. I invented women in other states who I would have sex with on vacations. I entered alternate realities.

I watched my TIM character inhabit a story. When I first started teaching teenagers in Hawai'i in the early 1990s, I met a teacher who kept pictures of a fake family on his desk. He woke up each day on a mattress he shared with the same man for thirty-five years. If anyone at school asked him who his partner was, he would point to a photo of a pretty woman. It was the picture that came in the package when he bought the frame.

On the one-year anniversary of the day I moved into my Makiki condo, I found the stuffed rat behind the water heater. Halloween, 2018. I have always enjoyed Halloween, but as I've aged, I haven't felt the need to party. I like solitude. I accept a scary movie and a seasonal sweet treat as my Halloween celebration. Recognizing that I had moved in exactly a year ago, I resolved to be productive before I settled in for the night. It was time for a Halloween edition of "spring cleaning." If I worked hard for two hours, I would reward myself with *Psycho* and an orange and black Foodland cupcake. I began with the basics. I scrubbed the sinks, vacuumed the floors, and bleached the toilet bowls in each of the bathrooms.

Then I opened the closet with the water heater. I'd opened that door one or two times since I moved in. The heater was only a couple of years old. I didn't store anything in that tiny room, so mostly I ignored the space. On this day of not-really-spring-cleaning, I found a stuffed rat. I don't mean that it was a product of taxidermy. It was a plush toy.

Maybe it had been the kind of thing someone would have purchased for a child who loved *Ratatouille*, that animated movie from Pixar about the rodent who cooked French food. I thought of my cousin, Marco. His son was barely out of infancy, but maybe he would like to have this toy. When I called Marco, he asked me how the stuffed rat got there.

"Wasn't the previous owner an old lady?" he asked.

It's true that she was old. The previous owner would have been the mother of my realtor Brit's deceased husband. Brit had never said anything about any children who lived in or visited the apartment, but it didn't seem impossible that this toy could have belonged to some grandchild in their family. I told Marco as much.

"Okay," Marco said over the telephone. "The reason I'm asking is because I bought a *Ratatouille* toy for Ethan last Christmas. I found it at Goodwill in mint condition. I put it in my closet at home, and by the time I went to wrap it, I couldn't find it. I never did find it."

I see spots in my vision. Ever since I have had my fifth surgery on my left eye, I have known there are differences between what we see and what we think we see. At times the spots float like orbs. Other times they explode into tiny dots. The dots connect into patterns that make me think of tree roots. Then they might disappear. The doctor tells me that my brain must learn how to filter out the visual impact of my eye damage.

Though he's talked to me about these vision anomalies five or six times, I still don't understand if the dots are really there or if my brain thinks they are there. When the dots disappear, have they really left my field of vision, or has my brain learned how to unsee them? Am I seeing more clearly, or am I becoming accustomed to the delusion my brain provides for me?

One problem with having a drug addict for a loved one is that you often don't know how much to believe them when they say anything. That sounds cruel, but I mean it in a non-judgmental way. Addiction is a disease. The disease does whatever it can to feed itself. The disease made Marco say things that weren't true.

Sometimes these falsehoods were intentional, and sometimes they were the result of a confused perspective. When I stopped trusting my cousin, it wasn't because I didn't trust the person inside his body. It was because I didn't trust the disease that had taken over my cousin's mind. I told him this was most likely not his baby's stuffed rat. The thing was not in mint condition. It was kind of dirty. I apologized for calling him. I would throw the stuffed rat away.

On the day after Halloween, I threw the *Ratatouille* doll in the dumpster. On November 2nd, I found it under my couch.

"What the fuck?" I said out loud.

I thought about calling Marco again. At that point every communication with him felt somewhat labored. He had stopped going to his 12-step meetings at the end of September. When I told him I didn't think that was a good idea, he became hostile. He told me all the reasons I was the one who should see a therapist.

I didn't want to get into it with him over the stuffed rat again, so I threw it away a second time. This time I deliberately snuck it into the trashcan at the Brew Spot Cafe. Three days later when I found it in my car trunk, I started to get seriously worried that maybe I was losing my mind. Initially I attributed my confusion to work stress.

Writing inflated prose about shitty hotels was no fun at all. It never occurred to me to blame the appearance of the stuffed rat on anything demonic. I didn't start thinking about evil spirits until I started to notice the cigarette smoke. My building is a no smoking building when it comes to hallways and elevators. If I understand the condo rules correctly, the building association cannot tell people they can't smoke in their own apartments.

Brit, the realtor, the woman with whom I shared two orders of bad enchiladas, looked embarrassed when I told her I smelled stale tobacco smoke in her dead mother-in-law's apartment.

"Is the smoke smell constant?" she asked.

"Comes and goes," I said. "It wafts in and out."

Memories also waft like smoke. Even though the pediatrician who molested me when I was fourteen went to jail, and even though I noticed how the adults in my life avoided discussion of this incident, (which suggested to me that the incident was something I should feel shame over) I didn't really understand that I had been sexually violated until years later. The story has been floating back to me during pandemic times.

In the early period of Covid quarantine, I spent day after day alone in my Makiki apartment. I read Russian literature, streamed free opera from the Met site, and baked loaves of sourdough. This makes me a cliché of a certain kind of person. That is what I did. I filled my solitude with mental activity, chasing scary thoughts away. Like cockroaches, the scary thoughts came out at night. I'd step on one on the way to get a drink of water and pee.

During one of these confrontations with my inner-monologue, I realized that that doctor had used my fourteen-year-old body for sexual pleasure. I don't want to write about this. Though to be honest, there is catharsis in writing about bad experiences. The real anxiety comes from reading what I've written. That's one of the biggest problems with this whole autofiction or memoir-with-lies-in-it storytelling project. How can

I write something anyone else would choose to read if re-reading my own work gives me diarrhea?

And again, the crab enchilada comes to mind. Or more specifically, my real estate agent, Brit Takano, comes to mind. Brit said her mother-in-law died in what is now my bedroom. The old woman had been a smoker. She loved Marlboro cigarettes and would buy them by the carton. Brit explained this to me the first time she showed me the unit. One of the conditions of the condo purchase was that the seller would pay for a deep cleaning. By the time I moved in, I didn't smell smoke anymore.

I hadn't smelled any smoke for months. A couple days after Halloween "spring" cleaning, I nearly choked on the smell of stale tobacco. I asked around. The folks who lived in the apartments above me, below me, and to either side all swore they hadn't smoked in years, if ever. The woman in 404 implied that maybe I was the smoker. She implied I was deep in denial.

This is not a book about denial. This is sort of a book about emotional avoidance. This is at least a story within a story, or if it is not a story within a story, it is a mosaic of a picture of a rustic farmhouse on a river made of little bits of glass. I meant that the mosaic was made of little bits of glass. I didn't mean that the river was made of glass, though of course it would be if it were in the mosaic.

I imagine my story as a picture made from shards of memory. The picture is of a thing, and the thing may or may not be what the story is about. I tried to write this ghost story in a straightforward way, but I burned that version down. This is not a story about not being straightforward, but then again, my memories always seem to involve some kind of tension between emotional nakedness and emotional avoidance, so maybe this is a story about not being straightforward.

The smoke smell persisted throughout my apartment, and then one day it stopped. The day after that, I found an empty Marlboro box behind the plant underneath my TV. When I moved in and set the flatscreen into the wall, there definitely was no cigarette box in the spot where I put a plant. I threw the container away and tried to forget about it. A day later, I found another Marlboro box under my bed. Two days after that, I found another stuffed rat. I called Marco.

"How's it going, Cousin?" I asked. I was trying to sound casual. I knew he was not doing well. One of the reasons I'd moved out of the duplex was because he would enter my place without my permission to drink. I found him passed out on my couch more than ten times. "Hey," I said casually. "You started smoking again, right?"

After silence he said, "Are you judging me? What a shocking surprise."

I thought about asking Marco straight-up if he somehow had a key to my place. I didn't want to get into a fight, so instead I said, "I'm not judging. I'm writing something for Honolulu Civil Beat about smoking trends during the vaping era. I just wondered what your brand of cigarette is."

Marco sounded dubious. "Marlboros," he said. "I've always smoked Marlboros, Cousin. You've seen me smoke Marlboros literally hundreds of times. You've bought me packs before."

The events of those pre-pandemic days all blend together in my mind. Sometimes at night I heard coughing noises and heavy wheezing, but other than that, nothing weird happened for months. On the day of the 2018 summer solstice, I found another stuffed *Ratatouille* doll in my desk drawer. A few days before the Fourth of July, I opened a closet in my hallway where I keep seasonal decorative supplies. I found a small wreath made from Marlboro boxes. It was the ugliest thing I'd ever seen. I knew it hadn't been in that closet at Easter, the last time I checked. I threw the Marlboro wreath in the dumpster. For a month or so, I opened that closet door a few times a week. Nothing strange appeared. On Labor Day morning, I was searching for some party plates for this potluck I was going to in Makiki Park. I never found the party plates, but I found the wreath made from cigarette boxes. I never made it to the potluck. Two days later, I opened the drawer in the kitchen where I keep sauce packets and chopsticks. There was the stuffed rat toy.

The story about the cigarette boxes and the stuffed rat toys may not be as interesting to the reader as the stories around the story. The simulation is only compelling when no one knows it's a simulation. The ghost story serves as a delivery vehicle for these more confessional stories I'm telling about my own violation and transformation. At age 36, I came out as gay. When I turned 50, I decided to come out again. This time, the first day of my sixth decade, I was coming out as asexual. It felt important to claim my lack of interest in sex as a part of who I am. It felt important to define that lack of sexual interest, not as a consequence of abuse, but as a factor of identity. It felt important to stop telling myself a story of brokenness. It felt important to start telling a different story.

As October approached, I knew I didn't want to be alone on Halloween. I lived in fear of receiving unsolicited, perhaps supernaturally supplied, artifacts. I texted Brit, my realtor. I hadn't seen her for a while. After my third text, she responded. Texting back, I asked her if she wanted to have dinner on Halloween evening. We made plans to meet at the mediocre Mexican place in Kaimuki again. La Hibiscus was not good, but it was familiar. I knew I would never reorder the crab enchilada. I would order the cheese quesadilla. How badly can anyone mess up a cheese quesadilla?

It was Halloween night. I didn't wear a costume. As I waited outside La Hibiscus on the corner, I watched a kid in a vampire cape shoot baskets at the municipal courts near the old Kaimuki Camera shop. I had a sudden fear that Brit might show up for Halloween dinner wearing a racist sombrero. When she arrived sporting a tasteful set of cat ears, I felt bad for my assumptions. We did the cheek-hug thing and went inside. It took me most of the meal to tell Brit the truth about why I wanted to see her.

When she asked me how I was enjoying my new place, I responded with pleasant vagueness. Or maybe vague pleasantness. She told me about the first apartment she and her husband rented in Waikiki in the 1990s. I had heard the story before. Richard Chamberlin's driver makes an appearance. Halfway through my third Tecate, I blurted out that I thought her dead mother-in-law was haunting me. I told her about the *Ratatouille* dolls and the Marlboro boxes. Though a bit defensive, she didn't seem shocked at all.

"Damn," she said between sips of her margarita. "My mother-in-law's presence is strong. It's not my fault. I saged the place before you moved in."

Inwardly I rolled my eyes. Brit and I: both white folks living on island land stolen from indigenous people. We had no business saging anyplace. Brit believed that her dead mother-in-law was lingering in my apartment. She wasn't sure what the significance of the rat toy was, but she was pretty sure the old woman had been a fan of animated movies. I told her I suspected the involvement of Marco and gave her as much of his story as she needed to hear.

"Marco and my mother-in-law both connect to the stuffed rat and the Marlboros," Brit said. "I wonder if my mother-in-law is trying to tell you something about your cousin."

I was wrong. It is possible to mess up a cheese quesadilla. The La Hibiscus version was almost as bad as their crab enchilada. The oil in the cheddar had separated and oozed from the tortilla in unpleasant ways. I sensed the presence of Velveeta, which I'm not even completely opposed to as a melting/facilitation agent in cheap food, but if you are going to mix Velveeta with real cheese, you have to get the proportions right. And you probably shouldn't call it Mexican cuisine. And. The quesadilla at La Hibiscus wasn't even that cheap.

Brit had begun to repeat her story about meeting the psychic in Puerto Vallarta who predicted her first husband's death. I had heard that story more than twice. Tangents to our conversation became our conversation. I was not going to learn anything about what was going on in my Makiki apartment from this realtor who may or may not have been my friend. After splitting the check, we said our goodbyes in the parking lot. Brit told me to call her if I thought my place needed another saging. In the darkness of the Honolulu evening, I really did roll my eyes that time.

A year after that last meal at the crappy Mexican restaurant in Kaimuki, my cousin Marco was dead. He had moved to Colorado, ostensibly to find work. Three weeks after he arrived in Denver, he died in room 212 at a cheap motel on Broadway called The Metlo. In his body was a mix of narcotics and alcohol. Nobody knows what specific chemical killed him. The police called it an overdose. I think of it as suicide, although maybe I shouldn't.

We said prayers for Marco at Kaimana, his favorite beach in Honolulu. As we walked to our cars, his ex-wife, the mother of the child who called Marco "Daddy," asked me if I wanted to keep some of his possessions. I didn't. She said she had taken everything she and her son cared about. There were only a few things left. I said I'd take them, mostly to help her get them out of her house.

Ever since my fifth eye surgery, I've been having these piercing headaches. I have been told that this is to be expected. My doctor told me that the eye had gone through trauma. Obviously, some pain would result. My doctor talked about pain without any specific expression on his face. I've seen physicians do this before. My brother is a heart surgeon in North Dakota. I shadowed him at his hospital during a busy workday in the 1990s for a writing project. I watched him tell a woman that her husband died. He had instructed me to stand in the background and look like an orderly. I watched him display a professional demeanor as he spoke of sad things. I suppose this is something a physician is trained to do.

I opened the shoebox about six weeks after Marco's kid's mom gave it to me. I was standing in my bedroom by the window. When I opened the box, I saw a stapler, an Operation Ivy CD, and a bandana I recognized. I took them out of the box and moved them onto a chair. The shoebox contained two other items: a stuffed Ratatouille doll in mint condition and two unopened boxes of Marlboros.

My stomach clenched. If someone was playing a joke on me, I didn't get the humor at all. That night, I fell into a fretful sleep. I usually don't recall my dreams, but when I woke up the next morning, I knew I had been visited by Brit's mother-in-law, the woman who used to own the place. I showered, got dressed, and fetched the shoebox from the living room couch.

After my most recent eye surgery, my left eyelid drooped perpetually. Coworkers at lunch would ask me why I was squinting. I would tell them I wasn't squinting. Most people at that point would stop talking about my face. Not everyone. I've been in conversations with people who couldn't quit their inappropriate inquiries. A social studies teacher asked me, "You mean you are going to look like that for the rest of your life?"

Opening the shoebox, I prepared for another surprise. The box was empty. The stuffed rat was gone, and so were the cigarettes. The other items—the stapler, bandana, and CD—remained on the chair where I'd left them. I wish I had a better ending to this story. I don't know what my cousin's addictions had to do with the old lady who died in the place where I now live. There must be a connection.

We all know what happened in 2020, 2021 and 2022. Disease hovered over the world like a cloud. We were all forced to spend more time in our living spaces. My apartment became my sanctuary and my prison. I still have the shoebox. It has remained empty. I haven't had any more visitations in my dreams. I haven't spoken to Brit for over a year. Marco's still dead. La Hibiscus closed down. That's not what the restaurant was really called. That's the name of the place in my simulation.

The job with the hotel company dried up when tourists stopped visiting the island during peak Covid travel restrictions. I still write for money. I'm trying to carve out a niche in digital media associated with culture and the sciences. I wrote about the coronavirus. I wrote about ways people coped during lockdown. I did write a piece for Honolulu Civil Beat about smoking in the vape era. So far, no one has asked me to write any more think-pieces about happiness.

I withdraw from the persona of the paid feature writer. That simulation ends. I become my English teacher self again. I wish I could end a story like Edgar Allen Poe. The very first time I ever heard "The Tell-Tale Heart" I was in sixth grade. Our teacher read it to us in class on Halloween from a stage inside the room where they had piano recitals. She turned out the lights and lit a candle set up on a table by a fake skull. I am easily scared by horror and ghost stories. "The Tell-Tale Heart" was my first Poe story. Our teacher didn't explain to us what kind of eye condition the old neighbor endured.

When my teacher read the story, the words came to my ear from the madman's point of view. I pictured the glassy growth on the eye of the menacing old neighbor. Then I thought about the glassy growth on the eye of our family basset hound. In the night, the mad narrator stalks his victim. I used to read the story as an unreliable narrative from a demented protagonist. As a sixty-year-old, when I read the story to my students, I perceive it to be the tale of a man who dies because of his abused and neglected eye. His disability. The victimized man has spent his entire life hoping to avoid acknowledgement of his imperfection. He is unlucky in that he rents his spare room to a killer. The murderer dances to the rhythms of a delusional drummer. The old man's imperfection leads to his wrongful death. The plot concludes when the madman's heartbeat becomes audible.

THREE

MY TENDENCY IS TO CALL EVERYTHING I WRITE A WORK of fiction. This is true even when I head in the direction of memoir. As I write from memory, I conflate characters. I compress time. I speculate. As I don't want anyone else to tell my story, I can see how someone else wouldn't want me to tell their story. I don't exist to be fodder for someone else's fiction, so why should someone else play such a role in my narrative life? Memoir refers to a genre of writing that emanates from memory. If I call my writing "memoir," am I allowed to make up plot threads? Am I allowed to say something happened with one character when it really happened with another character? Is it okay to admit I'm writing a memoir with lies in it?

I was supposed to see Tig Notaro perform a comedy show at the Hawai'i Theater in Honolulu's Chinatown. My friend, Leona Chao, invited me. We didn't find out the show was cancelled until we were already on our way to dinner. Apparently, the ticketing company sent an email. Leona hadn't read it. We went to O'Kims, the fusion Irish/Korean place next to Hank's bar. Everyone in our group has lived long enough to have had bad experiences in Hank's bar. The gochujang-Guinness salmon at O'Kims was topped with seaweed and pickled potato. During dinner, Mathias Worthington, Leona's partner, asked me if I was writing anything. I told Mathias I was working on something autobiographical. Some would call it "autofiction." I said it was taking a long time to pull together.

Leona asked if it was about cars. It took me a moment to understand her question. She was reacting to the term "autofiction." I said no, my book was not about cars. I told her "autofiction" was just one of those writer words. I'm not even sure what the term means. I have been told by some that I'm writing it, a mixture of autobiography and fiction. On the other hand, maybe this is memoir. It's hard to understand these genre differences. I told Leona that my latest project aimed to figure out how to write truthfully about things that have happened in my life. She asked what my new book was called. I hesitated before I said, *"Some Deft Segue."* That's what I'm thinking of calling this manuscript, but I'm not sure. I have other titles in mind. *"Freaky Makiki?"* I'm the only one who seems to like that one. I told my dinner companions the first chapter explores my recollection of the day an aggressively religious man tried to convert me to his version of Christianity in Makiki Park. He deployed some deft segue to move the conversation from weather to Jesus.

I didn't tell Leona Chao, Mathias Worthington or any of my other O'Kims dining companions that the manuscript had anything to do with my bad yoga teacher, a person everyone at the table knows. I still haven't told any of my friends I'm writing about them. Even though I'm doing it, I honestly don't think I should write stories about people I love. I'm pretty sure it's generally a bad idea to write stories about any of my associates. Then again, they say we should write what we know. My thinking becomes convoluted.

I've written stories about friends and family members before. Without exception, when they recognized themselves on the page, my loved ones became angry for a while. I don't blame them for objecting. When I read through what I've written in my narrative about the bad yoga teacher, I worry about unconscious misogyny. I don't want to shame women for having sexual feelings. I'm trying to interrogate the way I'm telling this story without ruining the dramatic momentum.

A teacher friend, Rhonda Saragucci from Sacramento, was in Honolulu last year during Spring Break. We met at Makiki Park on a

Friday to catch up and share anecdotes. On a bench under my favorite monkeypod tree, Rhonda told me about her daughter. She asked if I was seeing anyone. I told her I had trouble seeing anyone with my left eye after my unsuccessful retinal surgeries. She didn't think that was funny. She asked if I was dating. I told her I was defining myself these days as asexual.

I told her that while I wouldn't say I never craved intimacy, I would say I've never really wanted people to climb on top of me. Rhonda Saragucci thought that was funny. She told me she runs the Aces club for the youth group at her Unitarian church. I understood that "ace" is a young person's term for those who express asexual identity. I am not writing about sex, but to write about not having sex is to tell stories about my relationship to sex. I do have a relationship to sex. I wouldn't call myself sexless. I have panted over nude pictures of men before. Nude pictures of women prompt me to wonder if those women pose for these photos willingly. Then, if my prurient side takes over, I imagine other men having sex with these women. I've never felt compelled to have sex myself. I've always assumed this was a weakness, maybe a response to trauma. Now the concept of a spectrum of sexual desire makes sense to me. I am on the asexual side of the spectrum. I seek to find the beauty in living without the same relationship to sexual attraction that most people seem to have. This subject might best be approached by writing poetry. To me, poetry is the art of using words to do what words have trouble doing.

If an artist wanted to convey a color to an audience, they probably wouldn't use words if they had paints or tinted lights. If musicians wanted to convey a tune, they probably would hum or strum rather than break lines and create stanzas with only black marks on a page or noiseless pixels on a screen. Note, though, how excellent a great poem about color or music can be. If you consider how difficult it is to write about what love is, you can understand how poets would be attracted to the subject.

You can understand why humans have always chanted, sung, written, and waxed poetic about this spiritual force, love, this thing no words can contain. Poetry is the art of using words to explain what words cannot explain. Poetry is a loving artform. Memoir as a literary form might be a little more hateful.

Or maybe that's not true at all. Maybe I'm worried that writing about violation can be a violation. The toughest trick in writing a truth-seeking memoir is knowing when to surrender to allegory. I've been writing ghost stories, probably because I've been thinking about addiction, death, grief and family legacies. I've been writing butterfly stories, probably because I've been thinking about transformation and metamorphosis. I've been writing about supernatural mangoes, forbidden fruit. None of these metaphors are original, but I am drawn to them as avenues into the uncanny and unfamiliar.

I will contrive a story about that time I spent the night in an abandoned mental institution. This happened. My friend, George Shim, worked for a law firm that gave its attorneys access to a beach house out by Wailua for a weekend. The property stands next to an old children's hospital, abandoned since sugar plantation days. Long out of use, the buildings are targeted for demolition in order to expand a parking lot. George Shim invited me to a party at one of his swank, work-related getaways. After too much mezcal, I allowed George and three men from his litigation team to take me to the abandoned children's hospital. They said we would share an adventure.

We climbed a lava rock wall. We shimmied through a tangle of invasive weeds. The attorneys locked me in a room with rows and rows of rusting twin bed frames. A ghost child told me how I was going to die. The drunk lawyers were trying to scare me in a fun way. They scared me in a scarring way. By the time George Shim, my so-called friend, unlocked the door, I was curled up in a ball on the floor.

I made up that ghost child part. There is no abandoned children's hospital in Wailua. I made up that whole story. I don't know anyone named George Shim. I don't think I have any close friends who are lawyers. My point is that sometimes when it's too uncomfortable to write about friends or trauma, I'll contrive something supernatural. As I've been inventing stories of hauntings, I've considered whether or not I believe in ghosts. Or God. I believe in history's ghosts. My family on my father's side goes back to anti-Semitic Dutch businessmen who may have been on the wrong side of the Hitler question. There are white slave owners from South Carolina in my mother's family tree. I believe that secrets haunt families over time. If one generation of a family fails to acknowledge complicity in harm, the next generation of the family will probably be complicit in harm. I am not a specialist in any of this. I am one who would rather read a book than see a therapist.

When I read for fun, I don't think too much about the author. It would be hard for me, hypothetically speaking, to read the delightful, witch-related children's books of a hypothetical transphobic author if I knew her initially as a transphobe. If I had encountered the delightful novels first? I probably would have fallen into them. If I must, I can see a story as a reflection of the author, but my favorite way to read is to tumble into the tale. I watch the Hutchinson family gather for the lottery without considering Shirley Jackson's motives for crafting her allegory.

I listen to Holden Caufield call out phonies without wondering if J.D. Salinger would have tried to sexually manipulate my sister. When I read a novel, I aim to stay within the walls of its fiction. When I write, though, I can't stop thinking about my intention and my purpose. I want to write about everything, bordering on compulsion. There is the narrative; there is the purpose for constructing the narrative; there is the effect of the narrating. I want to write about the thing and the implication of the thing. I want to write about the origin of the thing. I aim to write about all of it.

FOUR

IN THE EARLY 2000S, I TOOK AN IMMERSIVE, TWO-WEEK class sponsored by the National Endowment of the Humanities on James Joyce's *Ulysses*. Our cohort of teachers from around the country read the Molly Bloom monologue in public at a bar in College Station, Texas. On the day we studied the "Circe" chapter, our leader, Professor Ikaika Bondumon from Texas A&M, invited us to his house for dinner. He and his wife, Pamela Wykowski-Bondumon self-identified as animal rights activists. We lounged in their backyard as Professor Bondumon grilled bean burgers and tofu dogs. Before serving her non-dairy, gluten-free, vegan, sugarless, no-soy rice pudding, Pamela Wykowski-Bondumon formally introduced us to each of their animals. They had two rescue dogs, a speckled cat, and an Amazon parrot named Rodrigo. The dogs were eager to greet each of us. The cat wriggled out of the professor's arms and ran back into the house. Rodrigo, the Amazon, never left his cage.

Professor Bondumon said that if he had to do it again, he would never get a parrot as a pet. He said he and his wife were mammal people. As if he were listening, Rodrigo the Amazon interrupted the professor's commentary by imitating the sound of a police siren at ear-splitting volume. Professor Bondumon winced. He said that parrots didn't make the best human companions. As soon as I heard this, I wanted a pet parrot. Admittedly, contrarianism is not the best reason to bring an animal into one's life. When I returned from the *Ulysses* seminar, I purchased a copy of *Birds for Dummies*. I enjoyed reading that book more than I enjoyed reading the James Joyce novel. I went back to Borders Books and Music and found *Parrots for Dummies*. That was even better. I completed the trilogy with *Cockatiels for Dummies*. That comment about not liking *Ulysses* was a joke. I bought a year's subscription to the now-defunct *Bird Talk* magazine.

From all of that reading, I gleaned this salient point: dogs and cats are predators while parrots are prey. To live in harmony with an animal predator, the human convinces the pet that they, the human, are the alpha. Dogs and cats need to view their human as master, the leader of the pack. It's not like this with parrots. To live in harmony with a prey animal, the person must prove that they, the human, will not eat their pet. Birds are frenetic, given to flight. To make a bird calm, a human must be calm. I have lived with parrots for over twenty years. I appreciate how they have conditioned me to practice stillness in their presence. A pet bird is a mirror. A mellow human sees a mellow animal. An anxious human fosters parrot anxiety. Some caged birds pluck out their own feathers. To live peacefully with parrots, people must live peacefully with themselves.

My first pet bird was a cockatiel, a member of the hookbill parrot family but smaller and less behaviorally complex than an Amazon like Roderigo. Her name was Cindy. She taught me how to live with a bird. Parrot cultivation is controversial. Even the most enthusiastic parrot keeper would admit that such beautiful birds are not suited for lives in cages and apartments. Parrots should fly and forage. I have come to accept that wild birds belong in the wild. If a bird is born into a pet shop, it can't be released into the open skies of the city where it dwells. In cold climates, parrots would not survive outside. In my hometown of Honolulu, an infusion of parrots into the natural environment would change the natural environment. This has already happened.

Feral cats. Feral pigs. Feral roosters. Feral goats. Feral red ginger clusters. Feral colonizers. All of these non-native invaders have caused devastation to the indigenous flora and fauna, and to the people and culture, of Hawai'i. Excluding humans, this destruction is not the non-native animal or plant's fault. Parrots have become part of this invasion. When I first moved to Honolulu in 1992, one banyan tree near Central Union Church was known for its family of green conures. These birds had descended from pet birds that had been released. In the early 90s there were seventy to eighty green parrots living wild on the island. Seventy or eighty sounded like a lot to me. Occasionally people would talk about what to do with these birds. Thirty years later there are thousands and thousands of green parrots on Oʻahu. Each morning and each evening, green parrots flock across the sky toward the trees in Nuʻuanu. To me these birds are beautiful. I don't deny that they are harmful. Parrots strip plants with their beaks. Parrots shit everywhere. Parrots eat the seeds and berries that would help native plants and animals thrive.

I can't choose whether there will be invasive parrots in Honolulu. I can choose what I will do about the birds in my care. I have dedicated myself to giving my pet birds a decent home. I haven't been one hundred percent successful. When I left my apartment in Makiki for two years to go to Arizona for graduate school, my house-sitter accidentally let my cockatiel fly out the window. That left me with three other birds: the two Red Bellies and a Pionus named Luna. The Pionus parrot is a midsized bird from Central and South America. They are about the size of a large street pigeon. My bird was green and blue with a white splotch on her head that looked like a full moon. That's where her name Luna came from. Pionus parrots typically live for thirty years. Mine lived for twenty. I'm not sure what killed Luna. One morning I took the night-cover off the cage as I always do when I wake up. There she was, lifeless and still at the bottom of her wire home.

Several of the bird books I read said that because parrots are prey animals, they are genetically conditioned to hide signs of illness. If a flock roosts in a tree or across the top of a wooden fence, a predator is going to go for the individual in the group who displays weakness.

To look sick is to invite disaster. This makes sense theoretically, but in practical terms the propensity of house parrots to hide illness makes it hard to know when they are ailing. I had no idea that Luna was near death. One day she was fine. The next day she wasn't. For a month or so, I worried that she may have had a disease that would spread to the other birds. The Red Belly parrots never got sick. I still live with each of them, going on twenty-plus years.

The Red Belly subspecies is native to Tanzania, about the size of a large baking potato. Take your average Russet, add claws, wings, and a beak, and that gives you some sense of the proportions of these birds. Each has a silvery grey topside, some bright green leg markings that resemble feathered bloomers, and a big splotch of reddish orange on the chest and stomach. I named my first Red Belly parrot "Rothko" because the coloring reminded me of one of Mark Rothko's big clouds of colored canvas. After I had Rothko for almost a year, I went into a pet shop on Piikoi Street to buy some bird food. I noticed a sad looking Red Belly in a cage behind an aquarium display.

The bird looked so scrawny and shy. The proprietor told me this bird had been returned after the family who first purchased him decided parrot care was not for them. Maybe the pet shop owner was being honest, or maybe the pet shop owner was manipulating my emotions. For whatever reason, he told me this Red Belly parrot had been abused. I came home with the bird, determined to give him a good life. The bird seemed scrawny yet clever which made me think of my favorite character from *Watership Down*, my treasured book from childhood. Honoring the clairvoyant runt from that Richard Adams novel, I named this second Red Belly, "Fiver." Fiver and Rothko and I have become friends across the species line.

I finished writing the last sentence in that last paragraph and went into the kitchen to get started with dinner. Fiver and Rothko are out of their cages. When I am at work, they live inside their metal structures. When I am home, they fly freely around my apartment. Mostly they stay at the high altitudes in their environment. They fly to tops of bookshelves. They hang from the tops of window screens. Occasionally, they walk on the ground. In Hawai'i, most people leave their shoes off inside their homes. I follow that tradition. In the kitchen, I am slicing sunchokes and okra. The parrots recognize the kitchen as a food source. I chop. I feel a sharp pain on my third toe. This happens often enough that I am not surprised. I don't drop the knife. I set it down gently and jump up at the same time. I bark out some expletive. Rothko has beaked my toe.

In general, I don't like using nouns as verbs. To gift and to journal have been phrases I've resisted. Why can't we say, "to give a gift" and "to write in a journal?" I'm coming around, though. Language is fluid. I don't want to be inflexible, so I will say that Rothko has beaked my toe. He does this when I am cooking in the kitchen. I think he wants me to drop food. A beaking is not the same as a biting. He didn't draw blood. He got my attention. Some people who live with parrots clip their wings. This makes sense. By trimming the ends of a parrot's longest wing-feathers, the human assures that the animal can't attain liftoff. I don't clip my birds' wings. I guess I want their experience in my apartment to be as birdlike as I can make it. In one of my bird books, I read the following argument: a bird will never be a human or a cat or a dog. A bird can only be a bird. If a pet owner hopes to train a bird to live in a housed environment, that pet owner needs to let the bird perform functions that come naturally. Even indoors, birds need opportunities for foraging, for acquiring nest materials, and for socially interacting. Birds need to chew, squawk and shred. Telling them not to won't make them stop.

If someone witnessed my interactions with my birds, they might infer that I make a lot of compromises. Because Rothko and Fiver fly around my apartment, I have to assume they could shit or pee at any time. I cover surfaces in my condo with towels and old blankets that I launder constantly. I wear crappy shirts around my house. I mean this literally. I am pretty sure my parrots know I am not a bird, yet they think we live in a large nest. My birds have chewed my ceiling, poked holes in my clothing, and torn through any plants I bother to bring home. A month ago, I was peeling raw shrimp on my cutting board. I left the kitchen for two minutes to pee. When I returned, Rothko stood on the cutting board with a shrimp in his beak. Three other shrimp had been flung to the floor. I can't get mad at my parrots when they are just being parrots. In exchange for my tolerance for their chaos, I get to live with creatures most humans never get to know.

If folks walk around outside, they see birds from afar. In some kind of scavenger situation, birds at outdoor malls and food courts will get close to humans for breadcrumbs and leftover French Fries. Those connections are purely transactional. I get to know what Rothko and Fiver are like as individuals. When I recline on my couch to read, Rothko will stand on my shoulder which rests against the couch pillow. Fiver stands on my chest where my pulse registers. It's possible these birds think of these positions as matters of conquest: they have pinned me on my back, and they stand on my heart. This doesn't seem like dominance to me. This seems like intimacy. Rothko lifts his beak and lets me scratch him on the underside of his chin. Fiver arches his back and lets me scratch between his wings. Any house-parrot comes from an ancestral lineage of no more than ten generations of captivity. For a dog or cat that lineage of domestication goes back thousands of generations.

I'm friends with wild animals. Occasionally we hurt one another.

When I left for graduate school for two years, my friends, Grayson and Rylie Dunlap, took care of my birds. I left my apartment one day and didn't return for two years. Upon my return, my friends watched me interact with my flock. "They recognize you," Rylie Dunlap said. When

I put Rothko to bed, when I put him on his perch by hand and covered the cage with a cloth for the first time in over 700 days, he said, "Night, night." Grayson Dunlap told me Rothko had never said that to either of them. My birds know me. We are companions. I have friendships with the descendants of dinosaurs. My parrots say, "Hey there!" and "I love you." Parrots are feathered angels. If angels shat and chewed wood with impunity. Which, you know what? They probably do.

FIVE

I WROTE A PROSE POEM AND SUBMITTED IT FOR publication. I called it "Gentle Tool." Though I was aware of the obviously phallic implications of the title, I didn't really think of "Gentle Tool" as a penis poem. I don't really write about penises. It may be unethical to mention Woody Allen in any positive way, but if I were going to mention Woody Allen, I would say that I often laughed at that line in *Manhattan*—a movie I never need to see again—when Diane Keaton's character says she has always been simultaneously attracted to and repulsed by the male organ.

My parents sent me to a New England boarding school, an all-male, mostly white enclave of Elite Education on the wooded site of several Indian massacres in what is now known as Western Massachusetts. During the four years I was there in the late 1970s and early '80s, I was never comfortable. In tenth grade English, the son of a Rockefeller said that Blanche Dubois from *A Streetcar Named Desire* was a slut. I watched the current King of Jordan wrestle when he was sixteen against teenagers from Andover. I developed a raging crush on the son of a key Watergate conspirator. Maybe raging crush is a confusing term because I have already identified myself as asexual. I was confused too. Sexuality is a spectrum. Somewhere on that spectrum, I identified emotions that left me addled and ashamed. I didn't want to have sex with this Watergate conspirator's son. I wanted him to like me. I wanted him to tell me his stories of seduction and sexual prowess. My parents wanted me to meet children of elite society at this school. My parents wanted me to accept as normal an association with wealth and a proximity to rule. That expectation did not end well for me. At age seventeen, I existed within a bubble of ambiguity and fear. Desire was part of the mix too. I wasn't sure how.

Forty years after I graduated from that all-male, mostly white enclave of Elite Education, I attended a conference in Potomac, Maryland. The three-day seminar focused on supporting transgender, non-binary, and gender-nonconforming high school students. At the gathering, I met the diversity coordinator of the prep school I graduated from. When I was in high school, people would have laughed at the idea of a diversity coordinator at that enclave of Elite Education. This woman made it clear she was quite good at her job. I learned through our conversation that two of the most popular teachers when I was there had been convicted of child molestation. I googled and read the revelatory, sickening articles from *The Boston Globe* whose writer used the phrase "nest of pedophiles" to describe these specific teachers who I had been expected to revere when I was fifteen. I went to a boarding school that had been corrupted by abuse, hushed silence, arrogance, and shame.

You would think that when I was a new tenth grader at this enclave of Elite Education, I would have been comfortable with the three or four boys in the high school poetry club. I wasn't. They knew more about poetry than I did. One of them was too pretty to look at without staring. In one of the only poems I ever shared, I rhymed Juliet with sopping wet. I rhymed baked ziti with oh-so-pretty. They basically shamed me out of the club at my second meeting. I never returned. It took me decades to feel comfortable showing anyone my writing again. Eventually I learned how to handle ridicule and rejection as a writer. A fine, queer literary journal based in San Francisco accepted "Gentle Tool." It is not a poem about penises. At least, not so much.

I read something funny once by a fiction writer who said that whenever she worried that a man in her life might accuse her of basing a character on him, she would give the character a small dick. She knew no man would claim such a diminished character for a doppelganger. I did publish "Atoms of Muses", a prose poem about my penis a few years ago. I described it as micro-tiny. Why not poke small holes in some myths about how we must talk about masculinity? Why not try to write into that fine line between accepting one's body and making fun of the ridiculousness of all bodies?

"Atoms of Muses" was also about gay teen suicide. When "Gentle Tool" was published in a San Francisco literary journal, a guy I used to work with wrote a comment on Facebook telling me he didn't understand what I wrote. He congratulated me for the publication. Did he think I cared more about publishing than making sense? The poem was my first public assertion of asexual identity. I wasn't sure if my friend didn't understand my writing choices or if he didn't understand how a person could be asexual. Which kind of misunderstanding bothered me more?

Perhaps I've already said this, but one thing that I find forever ironic is that I can't talk about not having sex without talking about sex. Not having sex is not exactly a kind of sex. Zero is not exactly a number. Zero sits alongside numbers. Discussions of asexuality sit alongside discussions of sexuality.

The absence of one thing can be the presence of something else. I began "Gentle Tool" after I worked with a high school student on her short story project. She defined her protagonist as asexual. This was before I would ever apply the term to myself. At that point in my life, asexuality sounded to me like an insult. In the movie *Ferris Bueller's Day Off*, Ferris makes a joke at his biology teacher's expense. The teacher asks for an example of asexual reproduction. Ferris says, "Your wife."

My teenaged creative writing student did not seem to be using "asexual" pejoratively. There was no shame in her description. She accepted her difference. I had been conditioned to associate asexuality with cracked and unformed vessels, a busted capacity for love and desire.

My student seemed to regard asexuality as a gift of self-awareness. In the first draft of my poem, I ended with a sentence about how a gentle tool was what I wished loved could be. I remember the editor said the line was too summative. I understood the criticism. Sometimes I try too hard to provide closure. I reflected upon the pitfalls of summation.

When "Gentle Tool" was published in its final form, the last word on the page was "fuck," but that is not what I originally wrote. I have mixed feelings about swearing. Sometimes I like dropping F-bombs, and other times it seems like a cheap way of communicating. I know a playwright who loves having his characters say "fucking." I told him that my mother used to say people curse because they have limited vocabularies. My playwright friend has no time for that argument. He insists that curse words are vital tools in anyone's language arsenal. I told him I don't like to swear in my classroom or in my writing because I don't want to be one of those aging adults who drops F-bombs in order to cling to spent youth. He asked me why I assume the word fuck belongs more to younger people than to older people.

The year after I graduated from creative writing school, I visited Austin, Texas and stayed in a motel. I carried paper travel guides back then. Looking for food joints, I found a listing for Franklin Barbecue. The guidebook suggested that Franklin might smoke the best brisket in the country. Taking my cues from the book's pages, I arrived at Franklin two hours before it opened. It turns out the lines at this particular barbecue joint are legendarily long. It became apparent that if I stayed in line, I was going to miss the checkout time at my motel. Not wanting to pay for an extra night, I bailed on the line and never got my BBQ.

Five years later, I realized that in choosing to leave the brisket line, I had made the wrong decision. The lost opportunity to eat perfectly smoked meat remained in my mind far longer than that one hundred eighty dollars of hotel money would have stayed in my pocket. I vowed to return to Austin. On this second trip, I gave myself six hours to queue up at Franklin. I met a man in line who asked me to eat with him once we got our food. Intoxicated by smoked loin and spice rub, I accepted his invitation to go swimming at Barton Springs after our meal. At the state park, he asked me to hold his towel while he took off his pants. With his jeans at his ankles in the Barton Springs parking lot, he told me he was a top and asked if I was a bottom. I stared at his penis and tried to be excited by it. I didn't feel disgust. I didn't feel the same kind of longing I felt when I finally got my plate of Franklin barbecue. I'd ordered brisket, links, pulled pork and smoked turkey. Feeling the weight of all that meat in the center of my gut, I smiled at the naked man's face as he replaced his blue jeans with swim trunks. I felt embarrassed for both of us. Then I chased those feelings of shame away and went swimming. The poem I wrote floated through my mind. I didn't remember every word, but for sure that last line was, "I am not trying to fuck."

SIX

TO BEGIN A RECENT ENGLISH DEPARTMENT MEETING, the department head went around the circle asking every teacher, one at a time, to name their childhood happy place. Most named spaces in nature. We live in Hawai'i, so beaches and rain forests led the way. I could not come up with a better answer than a movie theater. Ever since I was young, I have felt most relaxed sitting in the dark watching a story unfold on a screen in front of me. When I was a child, I loved family movie occasions, whether we'd load up the station wagon and drive to the mall cinema or turn on the television at home on Sunday afternoon with blankets and popcorn for a low-key scary Hitchcock movie. My dad enjoyed sharing his favorite classics with me. Unlike other events involving my father, if he was beside me during a showing of *The Birds* or *Rear Window*, I felt safe.

Perhaps the scariest movie I've ever seen was *Willy Wonka and the Chocolate Factory* in second grade. Dad wasn't with us for that one. My mother took me and my brother, Caleb to see it in the theater in Birmingham, Alabama when it first came out. We had been reading the book at bedtime. I had no idea what I was getting into when we settled into our seats for a Saturday matinee. Nothing had prepared me for Oompa Loompas. They scared the crap out of me. I don't know if it was their eerie theme music or their blue hue, but to this day I choose not to revisit the movie because Wonka's minions terrified me so much as a child. And what exactly was their relationship with Willy? Did he keep them as captives? Did they have freedom of movement? Were they paid a union wage? As a seven-year-old, I could not handle the Oompa Loompas, conceptually or aesthetically.

The second scariest movie I saw as a kid was the original 1933 version of *King Kong*. If I watch that movie today, I am struck by how racist it is. The indigenous islanders are portrayed as savages. The fear-of-the-exotic-ape stereotype is ugly at best. I first saw that movie on television. I spent most of my youth living in a media landscape that offered fewer choices for entertainment compared to today. Movies came to the theater, and then they came to TV. Reruns of the newer films played on one of the three major networks. Reruns of older movies from the Golden Age of Hollywood appeared at random hours of the day on two or three local channels. Every Sunday when the thickest edition of the newspaper was delivered to our house, my dad would extricate the TV listings from the bundle and sit down with the weekly schedule and his red, felt-tipped pen. For an hour or so, he'd thumb through the guide and underline all the movies he wanted to see that week.

We didn't have cable. Neither did many people I knew. Most everyone who watched TV watched the same six or seven channels. There was a good chance that if I watched *King Kong* at home on a Sunday afternoon on Channel 13, half of the kids in my class would have been doing the same thing. I learned a lot about movies by listening to what my friends were talking about on the playground. *Planet of the Apes. Soylent Green. The Towering Inferno.* I heard about these movies from the cool kids in elementary school before I ever saw them. When I was twelve, my parents took my friend and me to see *The Sting* at a strip mall. We would have been living in East Grand Rapids, Michigan at this point. We stood in a modest-sized line. The adjacent queue for some other show was four times as long.

"Mom," I asked. "What movie are they going to see?"

My mother looked at the marquee. She frowned. "They are going to see a very bad movie," she said. "You should never watch that movie."

"What's it called?"

That's when I first heard about *The Exorcist*. I didn't see that one until I was in high school. By the time I reached adolescence, horror movies were trending in the direction of demonic possession. Devils were the most common horror movie villains, at least in the scary movies I was hearing about. The summer after ninth grade, my parents sent me to Los Mochis, Mexico for a month to live with a family as part of a scholastic exchange. My hosts owned the local cinema. Javier Martinez was my age, fourteen years old. For three days in a row, we watched *The Omen*, another devil movie, by ourselves in private afternoon showings at the family theater. In Spanish that movie was called *La Profecía*.

Javier had an uncle named Jorge who used a wheelchair and lived in a studio apartment in the back of the Martinez compound. One afternoon when we didn't go see *La Profecía*, Javier invited me to Jorge's apartment. Jorge produced a photo album full of pornographic pictures. I first saw photos of spread vaginas in Jorge's apartment in Mexico when I was fourteen. The disgust I felt can't really be described as disgust. The word implies moral condemnation. I felt something like shocked repulsion, as if I bit into an onion thinking it was an apple. In a room with another boy my age and his uncle, fifteen years older, in a situation where I couldn't understand the dominant language, I perceived that I should see this porn album as titillating. I tried to act cool, across the language barrier, across the boundaries of my understanding of what was going on.

I first saw *Jaws* in a drive-in in San Bernadino, California with my entire family. As the movie began, my sister, Hattie and I sat on top of our burgundy Buick station wagon watching the big screen and listening to the tinny drive-in speakers we'd affixed to the edge of the passenger window. We lasted outside the car until the scene in the movie where the severed head pops out of the sunken boat. At that point we leapt off the roof of the car and joined our parents in the front seat. That was probably the last horror movie I saw under the protection of my family. By tenth grade, I was living at boarding school. I saw *Halloween* with some boys from my dorm. We'd taken the bus into town and walked over to the theaters at the Greenfield Mall. I watched the movie. I watched my hall-mates watching the movie. Everywhere around me was a source of anxiety.

I've only had two panic attacks in my life. The first came that night after we watched *Halloween*. I woke up alone in my dorm room. I'd had a nightmare. For the first time in my childhood, I didn't have any adult I could go to for comfort. My parents were thousands of miles away. It would have been wildly inappropriate and uncool to walk down the hall and pound on the door of the Corridor Master to tell him, Mr. Zolotnovich, a Russian language teacher with a wife and three children, that I had a bad dream after seeing *Halloween* with Dan Martinson and Huey Gussault. I lay in bed and felt my heart race. I couldn't breathe. For some reason, I felt an impulse to do exercises on my dorm room floor. It must have been something about regulating my breath. After ten pushups, I felt better.

The second panic attack came when I was a first-year college student at Wesleyan University in 1985. I had been trying to date this woman from my Cultural Anthropology class. I was trying to be normal. Her name was Wendy Scudder. I asked her if she wanted to go with me to the movie they were showing on Saturday night at the student center. Wendy said yes. She told me she had heard it was a good film. I told her I had heard that too, but I didn't know anything about it. This is technically not 100 percent true. I had slept through this movie years earlier.

One Friday during my second-grade year, our parents told us we would be going to the movies as a family. We packed ourselves into the car and headed to the drive-in. My parents took us to see a double feature of *Alice's Restaurant* and *Midnight Cowboy*. Years later I asked Mom what she and Dad were thinking. Why would they take a carload of young children to see those movies? My mother said she knew we would all fall asleep. She explained that if they could get us to sleep in the car at a drive-in, my parents could go out on a weekend night without having to pay a babysitter.

When Wendy Scudder and I made a plan to see *Midnight Cowboy* at the student center during our freshman year of college, I knew that the movie was supposed to be good, but I didn't have any idea what it was about. I may have thought it was a Western. *Midnight Cowboy* tells the story of Joe Buck, a young man from a small Texas town who moves to New York City and becomes a sex worker. When the movie first came out in 1969, it received an X rating. To this day it's the only X-rated movie to ever win the Oscar for best picture.

I had no idea that I was taking a potential girlfriend to a movie where a good-looking stud from Texas would beat an old clergyman from Chicago to near-death with a phone as the man screamed about shame. I had no idea there was a scene in this movie where a young teen boy played by Rick Moranis would pay money to give a blowjob to a guy in a movie theater. When I sat down in my seat in the student center, I thought I was going on a date. By the time the lights came up, I was shaking, literally quaking with panic. Wendy Scudder asked me what was happening. Tears rolled down my cheeks. I was having trouble catching my breath. I was having an attack.

"Was it because of the movie?" she asked.

"What?"

"Was the movie too intense for you?"

"Yeah," I said. I was wheezing and talking at the same time. "I think the movie was too intense for me." That was the last date I ever went on with Wendy Scudder.

By this point in my life, I've seen most of the major touchstones in cinematic horror. I love the old Val Lewton version of *Cat People*. I've seen all the Vincent Price must-sees. I've watched the Universal Pictures classics like *Frankenstein*, *The Wolf Man*, and *The Mummy* dozens of times each. I've seen *Rosemary's Baby*, *Diabolique*, *The Texas Chainsaw Massacre*, *Evil Dead 1* and *2*, *Night of the Living Dead*, *The Sixth Sense*, *Suspiria*, *The Babadook*, *The Witch*, and practically every other horror movie that you might find on a list of essential horror movies. I've binged slasher movies from the 1980s and '90s. In the early 2000s, I dabbled in *House*, *Ringu*, *Audition*, and other classics of Japanese horror. I saw *The Blair Witch Project* in the theater the day it came out. I've been scared by all of these movies, but it's the kind of scary that one seeks out for a controlled thrill. It's roller coaster-scary more than existentially scary. I know what it's like to feel bone-chilling, blood-curdling fear in a movie theater. To this day, though, no movie has ever scared me as much as *Willy Wonka and the Chocolate Factory* and *Midnight Cowboy*.

Horror exists between the ears as much as it exists on the screen. I have walked home from restaurants after rich meals, and as I committed to the second uphill mile, I have felt rumblings in my gut. By the time I get home, I am racing to the toilet for various levels of gastrically intense elimination practices. I have never shit myself in public, but the fear exists within me. I was the oldest person at a summer party at a writing conference. After too much espresso and beer, I pissed myself. My mind thought my body was ready to party the way it used to thirty years ago. I wet myself in a noticeable way. I watched myself shift in the visions of onlookers from the interesting old guy to the sad sack with the weak bladder. Fear on the screen gives me relief from fears cultivated daily by the state of my body.

Perhaps *Jaws* is my favorite movie because its horror emanates from fear of how the natural world might ravage the human animal. When I was in seventh grade, the movie hadn't come out yet, but the book was a phenomenon. Cool boys passed around copies of the paperback in English class during junior high. There were sexual passages that never found their way into the film. The movie was wildly anticipated, and when it opened, it changed cinema by introducing the concept of the summer blockbuster. Admittedly, this is not a 100% great thing. Such film history is part of the history of my childhood.

Horror is not my favorite film genre. I probably like noir and crime stories better. I love Westerns too even though I know that's a genre based on genocidal, colonial notions. I like whatever genre *The Apartment* falls into. Horror speaks to the part of me that knows some man somewhere is keeping Oompa Loompas in his basement. Someone is killing someone and burning someone's property. Horror movies keep me aware of the existence of devils. If I can fear those devils on screen, I don't have to face them in everyday life. This is what I tell myself whenever a really scary movie threatens to trigger another panic attack.

I'm more likely to panic in church than in a movie theater. In situations of public worship, it's more difficult to disappear in the dark. I appreciate the silence cultivated in Quaker services. I've only been to one of those in my life. In 1991, I attended a teaching conference in Pennsylvania at a Quaker Friends school. When the Sunday session began with a Quaker meeting, I found myself breaking the silence by standing up to give testimony about my father's influence on my movie-watching life.

Growing up, my siblings and I were not allowed to watch TV on weeknights. After dinner we'd do our homework, then read our books in the living room while easy listening music played from large speakers. I missed the blockbuster television miniseries that my algebra teacher, Mr. Bordeaux, raved about as he smoothed answer guide transparencies onto the glass surface of the overhead projector. No *Roots*. No *Winds of War*. No *American Family*. I missed them all. So strictly enforced was the weeknight TV prohibition, that when it was occasionally lifted, I remember the circumstance as much as I remember federal holidays. My father broke the rule for *The Godfather*.

In 1973, a year after *The Godfather Part II* dominated the Oscars, NBC broadcast both Coppola films in a recut edition and presented them on television as *The Godfather Saga*. This version was presented as a miniseries, one hour a night. The editors at NBC rearranged the footage from the first two movies into chronological order, so that scenes from the second film aired before scenes from the first. Dad let us watch this show four school nights in a row, then three again the next week. I saw my very first viewing of *The Godfather* and *The Godfather Part II* at age ten, out of order.

My best dad memories are movie memories. *Shane* was his favorite. He liked Alan Ladd, George Raft, Humphrey Bogart, and to a lesser extent, James Cagney. On the couch next to my father, I watched men be men in flannel suits. Dad pointed out to me that Shane wore a white hat. When my father drove me home from seeing *Network* at Central City Mall, he asked if I noticed that Faye Dunaway squatted on top of William Holden during the sex scenes. I assumed it was because they could show more of the actress naked that way. He said it was symbolic. He said it showed the director of entertainment was topping the director of news. My dad used movies to talk to me about all his big ideas. Movies didn't give us an opportunity to have dialogue as much as they gave him ways to make points during his monologue.

It took me years to realize that gaps in my awareness of Hollywood actresses grew from my father's biases. I never watched movies with Bette Davis or Katharine Hepburn. Mae West and Barbara Stanwyck were Dad's favorites. He didn't dismiss strong women on film as much as he dismissed strong women who upended his notions of traditional gender roles. He wasn't interested in any blending of the feminine and the masculine. That's pretty much all I was interested in. On Friday nights as a teenager, I usually didn't have anywhere to go, so I'd watch TV with my parents. Dad loved watching James Garner as Jim Rockford, a detective who drove a cool car to jangly theme music. While Rockford was smooth, I preferred Angie Dickinson in *Police Woman*. She played an undercover cop named Sgt. Pepper Anderson who more often than not wore go-go boots and handcuffed assholes.

If comfortable father memories foreground Humphrey Bogart, then the mental map of our relationship's decay centers around Barbra Streisand. We were watching the Oscars as a family. I sprawled across a beanbag chair in yellow flannel in front of the couch. I cried when Barbra Streisand sang *The Way We Were*. I clapped and giggled as the song ended. I don't know if it was the way I flapped my hands around, the squealing, or my wriggling expression of unbridled enthusiasm, but something set my father off. A switch flipped. He was yelling. He didn't like Barbra. He didn't like watching me like Barbra. It's not an exaggeration to say that our relationship changed forever that Oscar night.

My connection with my dad couldn't survive the shift from Old Hollywood to New Hollywood. He wasn't interested in *Taxi Driver* or *Harold and Maud*. I wasn't interested in watching his old VHS recording of *Going My Way*. He and I never could negotiate that divide between John Wayne and Jane Fonda, between *Sister Barbara* and Barbra Streisand. I said as much in that Quaker meeting at the teaching conference in 1991, the year before I moved to Hawai'i. It was Father's Day. I was sitting in silence until I was standing.

I can't recall everything I said. I talked about my father. I know I talked about the way my dad looked at me when I blew kisses in my pajamas to that goddess in a Bob Mackie gown. I know I told parables about my love of movies. On Sunday morning in someone else's house of worship, I testified about the little boy who shouts, "Come back, Shane. Come back!" at the man in the white hat. Everyone was looking at me as I punctured the silence of the only Quaker meeting I've ever attended. I told stories about how my feelings for my father have always been grounded in love and fear. I testified to the power of watching stories unfold in dark rooms. On a Sunday in someone else's temple, I preached the gospel of the Oompa Loompa: movies provide fantasies that reveal truths about life.

SEVEN

WE ALL HAVE STORIES WE COULD TELL FIVE HUNDRED times and never get right. When we live through all that we experience, time doesn't move as it does in a narrative. As events occur, action doesn't rise and fall with a discernible beginning, middle and end. Sometimes I've told this one story as a joke. Other times I've told it as a ghost story. For the first few years after it happened, I told the story about the twelve-dollar mango straight, episode by episode, but I never was able to convince anyone that what I was telling was true. I haven't wanted to show anyone the physical evidence. I feel like that could lead to irreversible negative consequences.

I'm not sure how many Whole Foods Markets there are in Hawai'i now, but when the very first one opened at Kahala Mall in the late '00s, several of my friends were really excited. Especially my haole friends. *Haole* technically means "foreigner," but in Hawai'i today it refers to white folks. I'm haole. Obviously. Jacqueline had a Whole Foods app on her phone. This was back in the day when apps and iPhones were novel. If Jacqueline typed the name of a vegetable into her device, all of these recipes would pop up. She told me she wanted to make barley stew in her new apartment in Palolo. I told her I had no problem with barley stew.

We made a plan to meet up at Kahala. By the time I got there, she'd made a shopping list. The app had separated the items into two equally priced sub-lists. I've only had an iPhone for the past ten years. I'm not the world's slowest technology adopter, but I'm close, so back then Jacqueline had to hand me a physical piece of printed paper. I accepted my mission. I would purchase these items. According to the app, it would take me twenty-five minutes to procure everything on the list and five minutes to check out. We synchronized our watches. I gripped my shopping cart with two hands and told Jacqueline I'd see her in half an hour.

I saw her ten minutes later. I was moving from the vinegar aisle to the fresh herb area when Jacqueline cut me off with her wagon. "Check out these mangoes," she said. She stood in front of her shopping cart with a mango in each hand.

"Was mango on our list?" I asked. I shuffled the piece of paper.

"No. Look at these, though. They are so big and perfect looking."

"Those are definitely nice."

She put one in my cart. "You should have one," she said. "For later. They're like the Platonic ideal of a pair of mangoes." I grunted something affirming and grabbed what Jacqueline was offering. She U-turned her wagon and headed toward the nondairy milk area.

From the checkout line, I could see Jacqueline through the front window. She had finished her shopping and stood outside by a post with four plastic grocery bags at her feet. Jacqueline seemed like the kind of person who would have carried her own bags, probably macrame or canvas. I looked back to the groceries on the conveyor belt just as the cashier picked up the mango. The scanner said this one piece of fruit cost $12.

"Holy crap. Is that right?"

"Sorry?" the cashier said. "What's that again?"

"How much is that mango?"

The cashier pointed to the register, then flipped through a plastic notebook. "Those are twelve-dollar mangoes," she said. "They're from Maui." She told me the name of the farm. "They've got something going on over there. Their mangoes are something special. No GMO. Just good juju."

"What do you mean 'juju'?" I asked. "You mean like *mana*?"

The cashier shrugged. She touched her glasses with her middle finger, then spoke deliberately. "I'm half Filipino, with some Irish, Jamaican and Slovenian in me," she said. "I don't feel qualified to talk about *mana*."

I think I actually said, "Um."

"I feel like it's a Native Hawaiian term," the cashier said. "I don't want to be disrespectful."

I couldn't help myself. "Is that what you mean, though? What did you mean when you said the farm had good juju?"

I saw the cashier look at the customer behind me in line. She lifted the barrier that separated my items on the conveyor belt from the next person's and sent the rubber item flying through its little chute. "Look, sir. I just work at Whole Foods. Do you want the twelve-dollar mango or not?"

I looked toward Jacqueline outside. She was staring at her phone. I sighed. It seemed like a hassle to have the cashier negate the purchase. I didn't want to infuriate her or anything. "Okay," I said. I thought something rude to myself like, "For twelve dollars that mango should give me a blow job." I don't know why I thought this. I've already declared myself as asexual. My discovery of asexual identity is another of the narratives I've never figured out how to tell well. That's another true story that people don't always believe. I digress. When I got outside, I asked Jacqueline if she knew those mangoes cost twelve dollars. She said she had no idea until she got to the checkout. She said she ended up returning hers. I stifled some negative feelings.

The barley stew was fine. When I got home after dinner, I put the mango on a plate on top of a paper towel. My mother taught me that fruit ripens best in cool, dark places. As I live without air conditioning in a cinder block apartment in the most population dense district in Honolulu, I don't really have a cool place for ripening, so I put the plate and the mango on the second shelf of the cupboard over my sink. When I opened that same cupboard the next morning to see if the mango was ready to slice, I was confused. Perplexed, even. The plate and the paper towel were on the top shelf, but the mango was sitting on the bottom shelf next to my *Godfather, Part II* coffee mug. I knew I hadn't put it there.

I don't really know how to describe my train of thought. The mango couldn't have rolled from shelf one to shelf two. That explanation violated several established scientific principles. Had I sleepwalked? I won't even try to describe the inner voices that spoke to me as I attempted to comprehend how this twelve-dollar mango could have moved. I picked it up and put it on the cutting board. It felt ripe enough to have for breakfast before I went off to work.

I have told this story to students before. I've regretted each attempt. I used to tell it on days when we'd talk about that Emily Dickinson poem, "Tell All the Truth, But Tell It Slant." My intention was to ask students how they would tell a story like this if something like my twelve-dollar mango experience had happened to them. I tried to get them to think about how the truth must dazzle gradually. The lesson plan never really worked. Each student was sure that nothing like this could ever happen. As soon as I brought the blade down toward the fruit on the cutting board, I felt a pain shoot through my slicing hand. I dropped the knife. Bewildered, I picked the knife up and tried again. I felt the pain a second time. I swore I heard the mango squeal, "Don't kill me."

I have a complicated relationship with the supernatural. Is it possible to be a spiritual atheist? I believe in God stories as stories. Stories are close to religion to me. Religion is a story folks tell to reinforce their world views. I've told the tale about the stuffed rat toy and the mysterious packs of Marlboros. I've said already I struggle to understand how a world view without God can make room for ghosts. I'm not a séance person. Ouija boards have to do with psychology more than spirituality.

No law of science explained the phenomenon I wrote about earlier with the Ratatouille doll and the cigarettes. No principal of botany or physics justifies the belief in a talking mango. I do believe, though, that I'm telling the truth. I know what I went through.

For the next three days I avoided my apartment. I worked late grading papers at school. I live alone, and I don't really sleep over with anyone, so I had no choice but to confront the quiet of my Makiki condo unit at night. I stayed out of the kitchen. I didn't open the cupboard until finally, on a Friday night, I braced myself and pulled the door open. The mango was on the paper towel on the plate on the top shelf of the cutting board. It was as if nothing strange had ever happened. I stared right at the expensive fruit. It was ripe. Tomorrow, I would slice it for sure.

I invited a guest over the next night for oven-fried chicken with mango salsa. I would slice the fruit in front of another person. Most likely the mango wouldn't act up with someone else around, but if it did, at least I would have a witness. At least I would know this was not all in my head. The guest's name was Ben. I'd known him for about a year. We would be each other's plus one if we had symphony tickets or if we wanted to eat something expensive at Roy's Hawaii Kai. We picnicked. We had never fooled around or anything close to it. I couldn't tell if he didn't want to have sex with me, or if he didn't think I wanted to have sex with him. For whichever reason, he wasn't sending the vibes. I didn't want him to.

I had decided to tell my friend Ben that I was asexual. Ben's a family therapist. I knew he was going to want me to name some traumas. I had wanted to talk to Ben about this for a while, but as a result of a lot of experiences and discoveries and epiphanies that are hard to describe, I'd figured out that my lack of desire for sex has more to do with identity than with emotional damage, so I didn't really want to talk with Ben about my mother. I put off the conversation. Our friendship drifted along, destined to fade away unless we named a few things. Tonight seemed like a good night for clarification.

I served Ben his Manhattan with a cherry from a Trader Joe's jar my sister sent from Phoenix last Christmas. We don't have Trader Joe's stores in Hawaii. We listened to The Postal Service from a CD player. This would have been a week before Halloween, 2008. For cocktail hour we stayed in the living room area of my 800 sq. foot one-bedroom. Casually, I rose and led him into the galley kitchen. The chicken was smelling good. I put on oven mitts. Everything was going according to plan. Opening the door to the cupboard above the sink, still mitted, I grabbed the mango. I placed it on the cutting board and picked up the knife.

"Are you going to take those off?"

"What?"

Ben was talking. "Are you going to cut the mango with oven mitts?"

I forced a laugh. Silly me. I slid the left glove off while staring at Ben. I slid the right glove off while staring at the mango. It rolled over on the cutting board. I looked at Ben to see if he'd seen the fruit move. He didn't seem alarmed at all. I decided to go to the bathroom. I needed to splash water on my face and give myself a quick pep talk before I sliced the twelve-dollar mango. Excusing myself, I went into the half bath on the other side of my bedroom. I closed the door behind me, and then ran a wet washcloth over my face. I looked in the mirror and whispered, "Control yourself." I heard a door slam. When I came out of the bedroom, the rest of my condo unit was empty. Ben had bolted. What had the mango done? I walked into the kitchen. The chicken cooked. The mango was back on the paper towel on the plate. The plate sat next to the Fredo mug on the bottom shelf of the cupboard.

The next morning was a Sunday. I called the farm on Maui anyway. I needed to ask questions about the juju. It took a long time to reach a human voice. When I did, no one wanted to talk to me about spiritual issues. Finally, a customer service representative took pity on me. She told me she wasn't able to give me the information I requested, but that if I wanted to talk to someone who knew what was up, she could give me a friend of a friend's cell number. I thanked her and pulled a pencil and paper off of the phone table. She gave me an 808 number and told me to ask for a guy named Tholemew.

"Tholemew?" I asked.

"Yeah," she said. "That's his name. He knows what's up about the mangoes."

"As in Bartholemew?"

"That's what he used to go by," the customer service representative said, "but he's in AA now. Been sober almost seven years. He calls himself Tholemew. He says he doesn't want to have anything to do with the bar part anymore."

I couldn't tell if she was messing with me or not. I took the number. I knew that if I didn't call right away, I'd lose my nerve, so I dialed on the old land line and let it ring seven times. When a man answered, I asked if he was Tholelmew.

"Yeah," he said. "Speaking. What's up?"

I explained the situation. We kind of went back and forth with each other for a while, and then Tholemew told me to hang up, send him fifty bucks on PayPal, then call him back in fifteen minutes. I did as I was told.

Quick digression: You know the story of the Garden of Eden? So, there's a lot more to it than this, but basically Adam and Eve are naked and innocent. A serpent gets involved and Eve tempts Adam to eat an apple from the Tree of Knowledge of Good and Evil. When God finds out the apple is gone, Adam and Eve are banished to a life of pain and sorrow. Pregnancy hurts, and Adam has to work for a living. From then on, everyone is born with Original Sin. There has been some historical speculation that the Forbidden Fruit was no apple. Apples don't really grow naturally in the Middle East. Some people say the actual fruit would have been something like a pomegranate. Tholemew said it may have been a mango. He spoke softly but forcefully. He told me not to bother to google as some truths are too heavy for the Internet to handle. He said it sounded like I may have picked up a fruit that was spawned by the Serpent. If anyone thinks I'm gullible for believing Tholemew, I'd say that such a person has no idea what it's like to live in fear of a twelve-dollar mango. I asked Tholemew what I could do. He told me to PayPal him 50 more bucks, and he'd tell me how to get rid of my problem. I did as I was told.

According to Tholemew, I was going to have to exterminate the mango ritualistically. He said I needed to slice the mango on the altar of a church with a pink knife on Halloween at midnight. I happened to own a pink knife. I bought it on sale at The Complete Kitchen at Kahala Mall. I also had a key to the chapel at the school where I teach. It's a private school, founded by missionaries, and for over a hundred years, the school has required students to attend weekly religious services. At the turn of the Millennium, a new principal expressed interest in expanding the spiritual scope, and as these things go in the field of education, committees were formed. A pilot program brought me into the chapel program. I'm an asexual, queer atheist. At the end of every religious service, I'd lead the congregation in a Godless Sacred Moment. Typically, I'd read that Mary Oliver poem about the grasshopper on a summer's day and ask students to think about what they each were going to do with their one wild and precious life. I can't say I was great at the job. I can say I carried a key to the chapel on my keychain.

Halloween arrived on a Saturday. When the time came, I acted decisively and forcefully. About a half-hour before midnight, I put a small cutting board, the twelve-dollar mango and the pink knife in my backpack. I put the mango and the knife in two separate compartments because I didn't want the fruit to stab me in the back. I walked to school. Carefully avoiding security, I made my way to the chapel. I entered the temple in darkness, flicking a lighter on and off to guide my way to the altar where I lit a candle. I spread a towel and lay down the cutting board. I placed the mango in position. I raised the knife. As the pink blade made its way toward fruit-flesh, I heard a horrific and unnatural squeal. Momentum for vengeance whooshed out of me. I heard the mango say, "Don't kill me." It was the saddest sound I've ever heard in my life.

I couldn't do it. I couldn't kill the mango. I put the knife in one backpack pouch and the cutting board and mango in the other. I made the walk of shame back to my apartment in Makiki. The next day I called Tholemew. He told me that as the mango rotted, it was going to become a lot surlier. I asked him if there was anything I could do to live with the mango. He told me to PayPal him fifty more bucks and he'd tell me. Again, I did what I was told.

I have been living with the twelve-dollar mango for almost two decades now. Every morning when I wake up, I anoint the fruit skin in coconut oil and profess my eternal loyalty. I tell the mango that I will always take care of them. The mango prefers they/them pronouns. They mostly leave me alone. They have free reign of the kitchen. They can rest on whatever shelf they want. I still live without a human partner. For the most part, everything is fine. I will say that things got kind of difficult during the Covid pandemic. I seldom left the confines of my home, my expensive cinder block box, and I lived in constant panic that the twelve-dollar mango would show up on Zoom calls or in my Webex room when I taught online classes. So far that hasn't happened. I'm glad. I mean, on one hand, maybe it would be good to verify the truth of this story by showing the twelve-dollar mango to others. On the other hand, it seems like too big a risk. I can only imagine all the trouble I could cause if I let the mango go viral.

EIGHT

THE BREW SPOT CAFÉ CLOSED ITS DOORS ON MARCH 16, 2020. For a couple of months, the owner posted a sad note on her shuttered storefront: the shop would remain closed until there was a vaccine. We've had vaccines for more than four years now, but the Brew Spot doesn't look like it's ever going back to in-shop dining. They eventually opened for takeout. There's a rumor going around our neighborhood that in the next year, the Brew Spot will close for good. Over the past twenty years, I've spent thousands of dollars at this Makiki institution, one cup of coffee at a time.

On Saturdays the Brew Spot would serve waffles. I'd sit at one of their battered black and white tables and stare at the art on the wall. The owner allowed her walls to function as a community space. She mostly featured drawings by residents of the nearby YWCA or from patients of the local Shriners Hospital. If I spent an hour there on a Sunday, I'd see five or six people I knew. I'd wave. Occasionally I'd engage in conversation. Mostly I liked to eat my waffle in pieces, dunking scraps of crinkled dough into my iced coffee. Maybe I'd read a book or think about some ethical question related to what I was writing. This question would be some version of what I am always thinking about: what does it mean to write truthfully, and how bad is it to tell stories about folks who are friends of mine?

If I am going to tell stories about my bad yoga teacher, I should consider the consequences. If I call out the behavior of people I know, will people I know call out my behavior? If I am going to tell stories about being treated inappropriately by a teacher, I need to do my own mental inventory. Have I ever blurred any lines in the classroom or workplace? I've tried to be the cool teacher before. The psychodynamics of adolescent coolness—the psychodynamics of both adolescence and coolness in and of themselves—are treacherous. Indeed. I have said things in teaching situations in the past that I wouldn't say now. I have not sexually harassed or assaulted anyone. I used to teach certain Denis Johnson or Mary Gaitskill stories that I wouldn't teach today. A future university art student told me reading was boring, so I handed him *Sabbath's Theater* by Philip Roth. I had just finished it. The kid was 18. I didn't think he would think it was boring. In a similar situation, I gave a paperback copy of *Geek Love* by Katherine Dunn to a sophomore. I'd never hand those books to teenagers in English class today. I don't even really teach Flannery O'Connor all that much anymore, though I do teach her some. I find it hard to resist "Good Country People."

Gaslighting is a real thing. I could write about bad things people have said I have done. If I write about how I reject those rumors, people will think I am gaslighting when actually I would be trying to write about how I was gaslighted. I'm not going to write about gaslighting. The word is overused. I just overused it. I was a fan of *Gaslight* with Ingrid Bergman and Joseph Cotton before I ever heard the word used in a contemporary context. There's a riff on *Gaslight* in an old *I Love Lucy* episode. Lucille Ball was seriously ahead of her time. I aim to write truthfully. I won't write about everything I have ever said or done. I won't write about everything others have said about me. Writers get to choose what they keep private. As soon as I write that, I wonder if that's fair. Should writers get to guard their own privacy while exposing the privacy of others? What does *should* even mean?

The Brew Spot Café never provided internet access. I could sit there with my computer and take my chances with free, stray internet from the neighboring buildings if I wanted to risk getting my identity stolen. The

Brew Spot didn't offer a restroom to its customers. Everything unfancy is unfancy for its own reasons. Someone told me he heard in an AA meeting that the owner closed the Brew Spot bathroom because a man died in there of a heroin overdose. This rumor could be true. Imagine opening a coffee shop with the hopes of making a living selling scones and espresso and then confronting the realities of dead addicts behind locked doors, followed by a global pandemic. That gossip about the dead guy in the Brew Spot bathroom plays on some Makiki stereotypes. I went there to pick up an iced coffee from the takeout window on my way to work. One minute before they opened, I stepped around a shirtless, barefoot man sleeping nearby on concrete using his own hands as a pillow.

My best friend from youth died when we were each in our forties. He was facing jail time for his third DUI. He'd lost his job and his wife. His last name was Vanderwolff. I called him "Wolfman." His eight-year-old kid still thought he was a superhero. Wolfman, my best friend, died by suicide or overdose. The wolfman—as classic monster figure—comes in and out of vogue. Though they make good lycanthropy movies every now and then, I don't seek them out like I used to. I still think of the wolfman when I see a full moon.

I met my friend Wolfman at summer camp in Tennessee when we were seventeen. It took a while for us to develop complete trust. When we did, he became my guide into the world of recreational debauchery. For the first ten years of our association, Wolfman convinced me that his thirst for whiskey, his lust for weed, and his propensity to experiment with every kind of drug he could get his hands on served his greater mission of seeking transcendence and enlightenment. In hindsight I understand it was all addiction. His transformations had nothing to do with full moons.

The first edgy movie I saw without my parents was *American Grafiti*. I remember being shocked at the mooning scene. I thought I was watching something super illicit when that young man stuck his bare butt out a car window. I had never seen adult male asses outside my own family before. George Lucas made that film right before he made *Star Wars*. *American Graffiti* introduced me to celebrity disc jockey, Wolfman Jack.

Wolfman's father died by the bottle when my friend was fourteen. Wolfman would eventually die under similarly tragic and premature circumstances when his son was eight. While we were in our twenties, we convinced ourselves our abuse of mind-altering chemicals served a higher purpose. I suppose that's a pun. LSD became sacrament. Magic Mushrooms became a way to find God. I learned to roll a perfect joint. I thought I was opening my mind and broadening my horizons. I thought I was reaching harmony with lunar cycles.

The *American Werewolf in London* came out when I graduated from high school. I watched this movie about a decaying teenager while sitting next to an eleventh-grade classmate who wore a lightning bolt earing, an Ocean Pacific tank top, and tiny, bulging, corduroy shorts. Flip-flops and perfect toes. Though I didn't recognize any connection to a queer textual analysis as I watched *An American Werewolf in London* as a teenager, I did recognize in the wolfman tale a story of hating the unnatural abomination inside oneself. I recently told my friend, Taylor, this analysis of the wolfman trope. He said I was trying too hard to be deep. Before the pandemic, my friend, Taylor, and I used to meet up at the Brew Spot on Sunday mornings. This Makiki institution was the perfect place to share theories with friends about horror movies. Taylor indulges me. He knows how I can get about my cinema addiction.

The Brew Spot Cafe will probably be gone by the time anyone reads what I'm writing right now. The nonbinary person who operates the order-and-pickup window told me the days of the shop were numbered. I once watched that barista (Is "barista" a gender-neutral term?) walk outside and tell the man sleeping on the sidewalk that he would have to leave. This appeared to be daily routine. They were polite about it. The man moved to the bus stop. I've also seen him at Makiki Park under my favorite monkeypod tree when I've sat on the bench across from the soccer field with Taylor.

Taylor came out to me as trans about six months before the pandemic hit. We've known each other for years and years. During the early part of the pandemic when the shops and parks closed, Taylor and I kept our Saturday meetup routine by switching to Zoom for virtual coffee. Everyone knows that virtual socializing sucks, especially between introverts. After we got vaccinations, we made a point to show up at adjacent benches in Makiki Park. We'd socially distance as we'd pull down our masks to sneak sips of coffee from cups we'd bring from home.

When I was seven years old, my family lived in Manhattan. This may be where I developed my affinity for public parks. When my brother, Caleb and I were children, he was allowed to stay up with my parents on Saturday night to watch "The Creature Feature," a weekly TV showcase for classic black-and-white monster movies. Only occasionally would my parents go out. Only even more occasionally would an irresponsible babysitter permit me to stay up. I distinctly remember the first time I saw *The Wolfman* starring Lon Chaney, Jr. on the Creature Feature.

When I am alone for too long, I start obsessing about all the ways I am inadequate. Here are just a few items from my list: if I don't monitor my ego, I can make everything about me; I expect people to follow my thought-tangents; I am never able to make the most basic things work on my computer or phone; I'm no good at apologies; I talk about communing with nature more than I commune with nature; I have lived with more than one insect infestation. That's not the kind of communing with nature I mean. I can't Zoom. Can't make a decent cup of coffee. I still type two spaces between sentences after every period. I'm crap with GPS. I can't whistle or snap. I've let people down in key situations.

When I sit in Makiki Park with Taylor, we mostly talk about trivial things. He likes F1. I usually describe some new recipe I'm dying to try. He only likes movies made locally by indigenous people, and I try to get him to check out my favorite shows on Netflix and Hulu, neither of which he subscribes to. Taylor described a colonoscopy to me once. I tell him about my eye surgery. We've discussed testosterone. I wouldn't say we make small talk as much as I'd say we make micro-focused talk. We talk about whatever is on our minds or within our bodies.

Last year Taylor had a bad experience at his family's Thanksgiving dinner. I know some of his family as we've all lived on the same island for decades. Thanksgiving was Taylor's family's first big gathering since the pandemic began. It was Taylor's first huge family holiday since transitioning. Apparently, the husband of one of his cousins started to say something rude about queer people. This cousin-in-law felt the need to say he didn't believe transgender folx exist. He thought homosexuality was a sinful lifestyle choice. He said "transgenderism" was a mental disorder. He said that thing bigots say about AIDS and the will of God. Taylor kicked his father under the table more than once. His dad stared at his mashed potatoes and pretended nothing horrible was happening.

I empathize with anyone who tells sad holiday stories. I came out as gay to my mother two days before the last Christmas of the 20th century. I could tell some stories about dinners during that holiday, but I don't want to make anyone in my family look bad. They were all doing the best they could with the information I was giving them. Or if that's not exactly true, then maybe I'd say they were doing the best they could considering the anti-gay brainwashing my closest family members had absorbed from church and from dominant 20th century world culture.

I commiserated with Taylor. We were sitting on adjacent benches in Makiki Park without masks. He told me there was one person who came to his defense at that horrible Thanksgiving dinner. Apparently, Taylor's stepmom told the offensive family member to stop talking and pass the stuffing. Taylor's stepmom changed the subject by telling everyone at the table how much she loved the music of Shawn Mendez. Taylor knows I have had periods of friendship with his father and stepmom. Taylor doesn't know I am writing about his stepmom in a less than flattering way.

Taylor's stepmom is my bad yoga teacher. The one adult at Taylor's Thanksgiving dinner who asserted support for non-binary people is the same person who tried to turn exercise into sex with me in the early 1990s. When I first met Taylor's stepmom, she wasn't Taylor's stepmom. She was my yoga teacher, married to this Navy guy I'd only met a few times. They had me over for potluck when I first moved to town. Nine months after I moved to Hawai'i in 1992, my bad yoga teacher's then-husband, the Navy guy, called me on the phone.

He got my number off his wife's class roster. I distinctly remember holding onto the receiver of a wall phone in my Makiki apartment kitchen in the spring of 1993. My roommate was sitting at the table paying routine bills the old-fashioned way. Checks, pens and envelopes lay strewn across the cheap tablecloth. He looked up when he heard my side of the conversation. I remember how wide my roommate's eyes opened when he heard me say to the bad yoga teacher's husband, "Are you asking me if I slept with your wife?"

I would be crossing a line of writer ethics if I used my memoir to project shame upon a woman from my past. I showed a writer friend, Delorius Tapwot, my chapter about the bad yoga teacher. Delorius told me it made them sad I was reinforcing the faulty notion that sexual harassment is a crime committed equally by men and by women. I'm not saying that. I would like to keep my story as focused on what happened to me as possible. If I am making any kind of universal statements, those statements probably have something to do with asexuality: when you live in a culture that tells you your worth as a man (as a person?) depends upon fucking, it can make you vulnerable when you aren't a fucking type of person. People think they need to sexually save you. I'm pretty sure my bad teacher thought she was doing me a favor each time she propositioned me and lifted my hips with her hands during yoga class.

I know that almost all rapists are men. I know that unreported rapes are much more common than falsely reported ones. Several celebrated male writers have centered their rape-driven narratives on false accusation of innocent dudes. These books about lying women are taught in school more often than stories about sexual assault against women. Think of *If Beale Street Could Talk* and *To Kill a Mockingbird*. It's true that most sexual harassers are men, yet despite this fact (or perhaps because of this truth) male writers in the 1990s wrote stories where suspiciously ambitious women were the enemies in the sexual harassment narrative.

In Michael Crichton's book, *Disclosure*, a woman, played in the movie by Demi Moore at her iciest level of smoldering, uses her professional underling, played by Michael Douglas in his best haircut, as a sexual plaything. In David Mamet's play *Oleana*, a female university undergrad manipulates institutional systems to get an innocent college professor fired for sexual misconduct he never committed. Both stories annoyed me when I read them. They felt petty. When Delorius read the first part of my memoir (with lies in it), they told me they were disappointed. Why was I writing about a sexual harassment story with a woman as the villain? Maybe they thought I was being petty. Maybe they thought that what happened to me was not that big a deal in the grand scheme of things.

I don't see my story about the bad yoga teacher as metonymic. My story doesn't act as microcosm. I'm not using my story to paint a broader picture of societal trends. My story is a tiny, focused snapshot. It's a picture I have found myself looking at, thirty years after it was taken. I'm trying to describe what happened to me without shame and without shaming. I hadn't slept with the Navy guy's wife. I am asexual, and I don't sleep with anyone. Some asexual folks are sexually active, but I prefer not to be. At the time, I didn't think to identify myself this deliberate way. Into the phone, I said more than once, "Are you asking me if I am sleeping with your wife?" A year after that call, this yoga teaching friend of mine divorced her Naval husband. Three-and-a-half years after that, she married Taylor's father. A decade later, I started to run into Taylor at The Brew Spot.

The Brew Spot was a place where I could be alone around other people. It's not the same place now that it has been reduced to a walk-up window. I miss that spot where I could dip a plain bagel into an iced blackeye on a weekend morning and hear "Love Song" by the Cure again. Eventually the stories I tell based on my memory of the Brew Spot will take the place of the shop itself. The concrete will turn abstract. The shop will be converted into a payday loan place or a yogurt shack.

Time to wax poetic. Imagine a lake where your memory and your imagination meet at the shore. Imagine how far you'd have to wade into the imagination side of things before you'd start worrying about drowning. Imagine a memory you've held tight to your chest. Imagine writing that memory down, showing it to others to read. Imagine how far you'd go in your memoir before you'd start worrying about wading into your own anxieties over concepts of truth. A good café allows me to ruminate and daydream. If I have too much coffee I get the runs, but if I have just one cup of strong espresso, I feel pretty good all day.

NINE

TONY CAME OVER TO PICK UP A PACK OF THC GUMMIES. I had a few bags. I told him he could have one for thirty bucks. He wasn't sure where I lived. We are coworkers, teacher friends. I didn't want to bring a bag of drugs to the high school where we work. I live in a state where recreational marijuana is both illegal and ubiquitous. I'm not actually a drug pusher, but I'm friends with a lot of cannabis users, and we tend to buy wholesale, then share amongst ourselves. Tony and I agreed to meet up in my condo parking lot. He knew to turn right at the Scottish Rites Cathedral. I'm not sure what the Scottish Rites Cathedral is, but it provides a stately landmark for my drug deals amongst friends.

Some of my ancestry traces to Scotland through Ireland, then Appalachia. What matters more, the places where we've landed or the places we come from? What matters more, the ocean the river feeds or the river the ocean consumes? What matters more, the fact that I've lived for over thirty years in Hawai'i, or the fact that I'm not from Hawai'i? Maybe in the case of Hawaiian history, those two positionings of settling into the place and not being of the place are indistinct; maybe the one implies the other. Tony edits an online journal, *Precarious Rooster Quarterly*. He told me on the day before we made the THC transaction that his magazine wasn't going to be publishing my story about the twelve-dollar mango. No one likes rejection, but for the most part, I understand how to weather disappointment. Tony pulled his car into the alley next to the fire hydrant.

With the funny gummies in hand, I leaned in through the window. Tony didn't have the full thirty dollars, but he was close. He handed me twenty-nine dollars and seventy-five cents. There are surveillance cameras everywhere in Makiki. Tony suggested that if anyone grew suspicious of our activity, we could say we were making a Craig's List transaction. I didn't ask Tony what he thought I might sell him in an alley in Makiki via Craigslist. I imagine some possibilities. Maybe I have a snow globe collection. Maybe he's willing to pay top dollar for the snow globe of the church at Christmas in Pittsburgh. Maybe he's buying a set of steak knives I bought off TV when infomercials were a big thing. Social media and the shrinking of cable television markets have contributed to the demise of that kind of faux talk show that appeared on off-channels late at night, the kind of hour-long infomercial that pitched expensive towels and knives rendering paper-thin slices of tomatoes. A select group of people made themselves famous by selling exercise equipment, sugary nuts, vegetable choppers, Jim Reeves collections, and other non-essential but quasi-desirable products through the performance art medium of infomercials.

Ron Popeil died a few years ago. He was the King of the Info-mercials. Perfecting the form as he established the form, Ron Popeil invented veggie choppers, gimmicky cleaning products, and numerous curios made from plastic. My favorite Ron Popeil contraption was the square egg maker, a gadget that first ignited my interest in food styling when I was eleven. All one had to do was place a peeled, boiled egg into the boxy housing and turn some screws. Stick the thing in the fridge, and a day later, the egg would be cube shaped. I desperately wanted one of those square egg makers. Ron Popeil named his company Ronco, as in "Ron's Company." Maybe this is what I was selling Tony in the alley by the fire hydrant near Makiki Stream, across from the Scottish Rites Cathedral. This could serve as our cover story if anyone suspected us of selling and buying edible THC gummies.

My cannabis use seems rather routine to me now. Ever since the pandemic, I've preferred edibles to products I'd inhale. Once I became aware of what Covid was, I became interested in protecting my lungs. Perhaps the healthiest course of action would have been to stop my marijuana consumption altogether, but I possess enough self-awareness to know that's not going to happen. I drink a cup of coffee in the morning. I get high on THC before I go to bed.

I was raised to fear any kind of illegal recreational drug use. Alcohol was romanticized in my family. Cannabis was vilified. My maternal grandparents lived with my family during my college years. My grandmother drank two cans of Budweiser every evening before dinner. She'd watch Tom Brokaw with a bowl of Cheez-Its balanced atop the blanket covering her lap. I don't remember my grandfather's signature drink, but I know he wasn't a teetotaler. From an early age, I became familiar with the idea of a cocktail hour. Cocktail hour was almost like a meal in and of itself, something akin to pre-dinner. That blanket on my grandmother's lap with the Cheez-Its is something she made with her own hands from wool. Cocktail hour speaks of hominess to me.

My father fancied himself a social drinker. In Dad's conception of his role in our family, he would walk through the front door after a hard day of work. My mother would greet him in the foyer, take his hat, and kiss him on the cheek. This wasn't exactly what their relationship was, but it's how my dad wanted it to be. My father wore Rex Harrington-ish tweed Brooks Brothers hats. When he got home from his hospital job, he would take off his jacket, but not his tie, and make his way to his favorite chair in the den. This would have been Redlands, California in the early 1980s when the town still had an evening paper, the *Daily Facts*. His shirt stayed tucked in until he took it off to go to bed after Johnny Carson's monologue. My father wanted my mother to hand him a gin and tonic in the summer or a bourbon, neat, in the winter. He'd say, "I wonder what the market did today," then turn to the Dow Jones listings in the tiny, two-section newspaper. Alcohol was a way of winding down. Alcohol was culture and status.

Marijuana was sin. My dad smoked a cigar and a pipe full of tobacco all through my childhood, but he eschewed cigarettes. To him, they were low-class. I didn't really know what he meant, but by the time I was in high school, I understood that my dad drank and smoked, at least in part, to build his persona. He was like a character in a John Cheever story or a William Powell movie from the 1930s. The man in the grey flannel suit, except my dad preferred tweed and bowties. He ordered corduroy ski knickers and wore them with argyle socks and Bass Weejuns in Southern California in the 1970s. He stayed committed to the bit, which I admire. Alcohol fit his vision of success. All other forms of recreational drugs fit his vision of criminality. My father romanticized drinkers and vilified pot smokers. He was neutral about caffeine.

My father's *Mad Men* fantasy didn't last forever. He and my mother divorced in their fifties after thirty years of marriage. Mom was a trained doctor who had given up her pediatrics practice to raise four children. She wasn't going to spend the rest of her life making my dad cocktails and kissing him on the cheek when he walked through the front door after work. Not when he treated her with enmity much of the time. After the divorce, after all their children had moved out of the Redlands house, Dad's use of alcohol and tobacco crept past cocktail hour, and while I wouldn't call my father an alcoholic, I would say that he was a social drinker for whom the drinking part lasted longer than the social part. My older brother, Caleb, picked up the social drinking mandate. Caleb was the president of his fraternity at Tufts, and through my brother's example, I entered college thinking that keggers and beer bongs were rites of passage. Caleb was an accomplished basketball player. Alcohol was part of how he enjoyed sports. Drinking was for winners. Smoking weed was for losers.

The first time I ever got drunk was at boarding school when I was fifteen. That's also the first year I smoked from a bong. Alcohol and drug use introduced me to new ways of being socially awkward. At boarding school, I vomited in Scotty White's dorm room and a couple of other places where I never should have vomited. I said some ridiculous things while high. A memory comes to mind of something I said to Hamilton Abernathy the night he showed me what hashish was, but I'm still too embarrassed by that story to write it down. By the time I got to Wesleyan for college, I think I'd decided that drinking and drugs weren't for me. I wasn't opposed to the idea of altering my consciousness, but I had yet to find a way to look dignified while getting shitfaced or baked.

In my twenties, I became attracted to the counter-cultural aspects of illicit substances in ways that were not so different from how my father and brother were attracted to the dominant-cultural aspects of social drinking. Perhaps because of the illegal status of weed and psychedelics, I never completely lost my feelings of guilt around "partying." As I entered the teaching profession, smoking marijuana seemed like an ethical issue. I told one of my peers, a history teacher my same age named Mick Watson, that if I was telling students not to smoke, it would be hypocritical for me to smoke after school. Mick scoffed. "Teaching is just a job," he said. "You can't let it become your entire life." I thought of Mick's assertion after I moved to Hawai'i.

On my third night in Honolulu in 1992, before the school year had officially started, a married couple named Tina and Carl Ventinelli, soon-to-be colleagues of mine in the English department, invited me over for dinner and a movie. After eating salmon pasta and watercress salad, we settled into a sofa to watch *The Prince of Tides*. Carl asked me if I was comfortable. Tina passed me a glass pipe and a lighter and smiled.

That gesture marked a clear turning point. I understood that if I said, "No thank you" and passed the pipe along, the Ventinellis would have shrugged. We would have started the movie. I grabbed the pipe and the lighter. I said thank you and lit the bowl. I have continued to get high most every evening since then for the next thirty years.

Wolfman died on his bathroom floor with alcohol, cocaine, lithium, Adderall, and Vicodin in his system. Tina Ventinelli, the hostess at the *Prince of Tides* dinner, died from stomach cancer. While I've lost touch with Carl, he told me the last time I saw him that he was clean and sober. I don't associate drug use with enlightenment. I also don't associate it with sin. I think I have used marijuana as self-medication. My mind races too fast sometimes. I can let anxiety overrun my thoughts. I'm not saying that THC is the perfect medicine. It's the imperfect medicine I settled upon. I try not to romanticize my drug use. I try not to hate myself for my drug use. I have a fondness for a gin martini with two olives at daily cocktail hour. I have a habit of chewing a weed gummy before I go to bed. Hawai'i hasn't legalized recreational cannabis yet, but it's certainly not hard to find. I buy my edibles from the same guy I've been buying cannabis from since 1998. Sometimes I sell a bag or two to friends at cost in the parking lot across from the Scottish Rites Cathedral.

Nothing that happens in Makiki stays in Makiki. Security equipment points outward from every telephone pole. A visit from a friend to buy gummies becomes a way to think about surveillance. The story I tell is less about the way cameras watch me and more about how I view the events in my life when I surveil my memories. Makiki travels with me, even as I move outside of its environs. Makiki is defined by its density. Everything happens in Makiki all the time. No one ever said anything to Tony or me about our parking lot drug deal. If they had, I was ready with my story about selling a Ronco product on the street. I imagine the Craigslist ad: *One Ronco Square Egg Maker: less-than-mint condition, used often, not pristine.*

TEN

FOR THE FIRST SIX MONTHS OF THE PANDEMIC WHEN everyone struggled to learn how to do everything from home, my only excursion outside was onto the balcony of my Makiki apartment. From my vantage point, I'd see other people on other balconies, but as far as I know, no one communicated with anyone. I heard no singing. I drove to Safeway once a week, masked.

I live on an island in the middle of the Pacific. Disease spreads fast here. Hawai'i state lawmakers implemented rules restricting airline travel. City and county government closed the parks and beaches. I didn't disagree with the need for isolation and social distancing. Even now, memories are fading when it comes to how we lived between the emergence of pandemic conditions and the successful distribution of viable vaccines.

After a week of cinderblock confinement, I allowed myself to stroll a daily lap around my block. When I walked outside, I felt furtive, like a rabbit in a suburb: I'd better get where I'm going without calling attention to myself; threat is everywhere. I would wake up, eat breakfast on my balcony, teach school from my desk, read on my balcony, drink a cocktail on my balcony, go to bed and repeat the same sequence the next day. Makiki Park provided refuge until it didn't. I escaped from reality by reading fat books about long-ago times in places far away. I went crazy for classic literature, mostly—but not exclusively—by dead white men. For the first time I read Tolstoy, Dostoyevsky, Hardy, Dickens, *A Tree Grows in Brooklyn*, and *Beloved*. I also started drinking dairy again after forty years. I was looking for comfort and escape, classic books and milk from the bottle. My own attempt at time travel. Regression to the past.

During Covid, all I had was my balcony, a patch of elevated cement six stories above a parking lot. Eventually, my Makiki wilderness expanded. After the park closed, I'd walk past it and stay on the sidewalk side of the gate. Birds fluttered in the field, freed from the trespass of youth soccer and the Hula-Hoop woman. From the edge through chained link, I'd watch little finches flit and frolic. I admit to envy. The birds had the city to themselves while I was confined to the cage of my apartment where I'd attend Zoom cocktail parties that never went well. No one needs to hear my specific stories about early pandemic quarantine loneliness. Everyone has their own stories about that. Before March 13, 2020, I would attend some poetry readings and bookstore events around town. It was a good way to keep up with friends I don't see enough. A year later I hadn't attended any live events of any kind. Again, everyone has their own stories.

By Easter 2021, right as the vaccines were being rolled out, people were searching for some kind of resurrection. I got a Facebook message from a writer in town. She wanted me to know she gave my name to some folks who were organizing an event at the Hawai'i Theater. The Hawai'i Theater was built in Chinatown during the Golden Age of Cinema as a movie palace, the kind of place with a calliope and a proscenium stage. Painted cherubs played bugles from the ceiling mural. After years of decay, the Hawai'i Theater was restored and now hosts concerts and special performances. The symphony plays at the Hawai'i Theater. For more than two years, the marquee of this majestic building was dark, and its stage empty. My Facebook friend seemed to be inviting me to perform there.

I didn't really get what she was saying. One thing led to another, and on Easter Sunday, 2021, I walked from Makiki to Chinatown to show up at the stage door of the still-shuttered venue at 9 AM wearing a mask. To be honest I'm still not sure what the event was. The effort was professional. The people who ran the proceedings seemed to be involved with an online local fashion magazine that I had never heard of. I was told to come with an original poem to read. I would perform from a podium to a camera and an empty house. There would be local children singing, a couple of fashion shows and some Hawaiian music. I didn't have to stay for any of that. It would all be edited together and presented online on Mother's Day. That sounded fine to me. I showed up and read the poem I wrote for the occasion.

The organizer told me via text that my poem could be about anything as long as it fit the basic theme of community. I looked through stuff I'd previously written and nothing seemed fitting. Eventually I decided to write a poem about the park I'd been walking past every day for the past thirty years. I texted the woman and said I was going to read an ode to Makiki Park. She texted back the confused-look emoji.

She told me where to stand and when to pull my mask down. I read my poem. She told me she liked it. She said that when she first heard that I was going to write about Makiki Park, she wasn't sure what to think. She asked me to read it a second time. Two months later, I clicked a link and watched the fashion show. At some point, my filtered face floated onto the screen and delivered a poem. Then the fashionable models reappeared. Somehow the whole thing made me feel good. It was one of those singular pandemic experiences that was too weird to ever happen again. I thought maybe I would share the poem here as a couple of prose paragraphs:

Ode to Makiki Park. You got your pool, your basketball courts, tennis. You got one soccer field and community gardens. Those piss-colored buildings house yoga or aerobics explorations or something. Someone told me they'd get coffee on weekends at the library there, but that library shut down before I ever had a chance to check it out. Funds ran out years ago. Makiki District Park, you will never see yourself on a postcard. The beach is miles away. Graffiti attracts and repels the eye. Your park benches are super uncomfortable, probably so folks without beds won't sleep there. During early quarantine, after the Brew Spot closed, I was still teaching from home. Needing sun, relief from cinderblock squalor, I'd sit and read there. At Makiki Park I mean. I meant no harm that one Sunday when a policeman told me to stop reading. I had left most of my books in my classroom before I understood I would not see my classroom for six months. For forgotten reasons, I had an old paperback of *The Rainbow* by D.H. Lawrence at home. Picked it up.

I thought the policeman was objecting to reading D.H. Lawrence, but it turns out the whole park was closed. Little birds picked bugs from grass in peace for months as humans stayed away. Makiki Park, you are a calendar. I clock pandemic time by walking past you, walking through you, turning pages as clouds drift by. Yesterday I met Heather and her kid at Makiki Park. The place has gone full-on, mid-pandemic dog park. Heather carried her puppy's leavings in a Long's bag. Kid surfed concrete at the Rat Cage under the highway. One day I'm going to start running laps again. For now, I'll sit on this park bench and stare at pages of a horror novel about desperate South Dakotans. When I need to pee, I'll walk home. I only live about a half-block away. They have public bathrooms at Makiki Park, but the less said about those, the better. Speaking of better, Makiki Park, you probably deserve a better ode. This is the one you get, though. It's nothing fancy, but neither am I. Neither are you.

ELEVEN

I DECIDED TO WATCH AN EPISODE OF *THE UMBRELLA Academy* on Netflix before I sat down to write this. A character played by Elliot Page sat in their writing room. They typed at the keys and spoke out loud. They said, "My name is Vanya Hargraves, and this is my story." The scene motivates me to begin. My name is Tim Dyke, and this is my story.

I could say this is only one of my stories. Not too long ago, I read something somewhere about how when we remember something, we don't remember the experience, but we remember the memory. The memory is the way we told ourselves the story. We remember recalling more than we remember doing. I remember 1999 as the year I came out of the closet as gay. I was 36 years old. I could tell that story in so many ways. I find myself telling it this way.

At the end of the 20th century, I took a sabbatical from my teaching job and moved from Honolulu, HI to Martha's Vineyard, MA to work on a novel. For the winter, I stayed rent-free in a vacated summer home owned by my sister and her husband. I read books and wrote stories alone. After a few weeks in this cold house on this island off the coast of Cape Cod, I began to crave company, so I signed up for a writing workshop. The class met every Monday night for six weeks in a heated barn. I enjoyed it and made some friends.

After the final class, a woman I appreciated asked me if I was interested in a one-day poetry class. I said I might be. She told me it met next Saturday in the home of the best poet on the island. I didn't have anything else to do. I called the number and talked my way in. When the morning came, I arrived a few minutes early with my pen and pad.

I looked around. I saw white women dressed in beautiful sweaters and corduroy. Was I the only man in the room? Fair enough. I took a seat in a comfy chair and looked at the handouts on the coffee table.

I picked up a flier. I hadn't realized this poetry class had a title. I looked at the piece of yellow paper in my hand. No one had informed me that this class was called "Finding the Goddess Within." No one had mentioned that this class would involve goddess finding. To me, this seems like an important detail to omit. For an instant I was embarrassed. Then I decided to go with the flow. I was leaving the island soon. I would never see any of these women again after this month. I settled into the comfy chair and made an effort to relax. I didn't know if I had a goddess within, but I figured that if I did, it wouldn't hurt to find her.

Eight hours after I arrived, I left with a notebook full of half-baked poetry. A week later there was an open mic at the bottom of a Unitarian Church in Oak Bluffs. I showed up and recognized a few folks from the goddess workshop. I sat by myself at a round table. I noticed two tables over that a motorcycle helmet had been positioned where the candle should have been. Looking to see who sat there, I saw a young woman with a shaved head. She looked to be about 19, maybe 20. She wore blue jeans and a leather bomber jacket.

The open mic got off to a good start. A woman played a song on a zither. These two brothers performed an original, three-minute choreopoem about their mother, a scalloper. When it was my turn, I read five poems when I should have read two. After I presented, a guy read a personal essay about his connection to a Cape Cod clam shack I'd never heard of. Then it was the motorcycle woman's turn to read. Her name was Angela. She said she was feeling vulnerable. She read a poem about being assaulted by her pediatrician when she was fourteen. It was intense. The same thing had happened to me. I felt a connection. I wondered what other secrets she and I might share.

When the open mic ended, I stayed behind to help put up chairs. By the time I left the church basement, the parking lot was nearly empty. I put my key in the car door. I heard someone scream "Hey!" over and over. I squinted into darkness. Angela appeared. She introduced herself and told me she liked my work. I told her I liked hers. Before I knew it, we had made plans to have breakfast two days later at her apartment. I remember thinking that because we had each outed ourselves in our writing—I as a gay man and she as a lesbian woman—there was no sexual tension. I looked forward to seeing her again.

Breakfast was fun. She lived above a hair salon owned by her parents near the center of Edgartown. We listened to Prince and ate scrambled curry tofu. We talked about writing. We talked about coming out of the closet to our mothers. We didn't talk about age, but I was probably twenty years older than she was. It didn't seem to matter. We shared some common experiences. It seemed like we could be friends. There were no iPhones and no social media accounts at the time, or if there were, I knew nothing about them. At the end of the breakfast, we exchanged email and snail mail addresses. I left Martha's Vineyard a week later. I never saw Angela again.

After the sabbatical, I returned to my Honolulu home. The new millennium had just begun. The Defense of Marriage Act was on the verge of being passed with both Democratic and Republican votes. "Don't Ask, Don't Tell" was the law of the land. I had no blueprint or role model for coming out as a gay employee at the school where I worked. Every now and again, I would think about Angela. It would have been nice to touch base. I sent emails, but they bounced back. She must have changed accounts. I sent her two paper letters that were returned to sender. One day when I'd nearly stopped thinking about her, I noticed an email from Angela in my inbox. I clicked quickly. The email was four words long. It said, "Think about butterflies often." This seemed to be decent advice. Think about butterflies often. I zeroed in on the obvious metaphors of transformation and metamorphosis.

My attempts to respond were unsuccessful. I wrote back. Emails returned with notices of non-existent, "Daemon Mailer" addresses. I went so far as to call the teacher from the goddess class. I had kept the flier as a souvenir. She was friendly. I think she remembered me. I asked her if she knew how to get in touch with Angela. She didn't know who I was talking about. I reminded her of the open mic. I told my former teacher she must remember the young woman with a shaved head in leather. My teacher insisted she didn't know anyone like that. "The poet with the motorcycle helmet on her table," I said. "You must remember her." She became dismissive. I think she assumed I'd been drinking.

I never was able to get in touch with Angela. I have come to believe that maybe Angela didn't exist. I don't think I made her up. I think maybe I was the only one who ever saw her. I think of her every time I see butterflies. I think I must have met her for a reason. I think about transformation. I think of metamorphosis. Even though she may not have existed, meeting this woman with the motorcycle helmet turned out to be a blessing in my life. I've come to believe that Angela was my goddess within. My name is Timothy Dyke, and this is my story.

TWELVE

I AM GOING TO STOP TALKING ABOUT MY SUPERNATURAL self-mythology for a while so that I can tell this story about a childhood friend of mine who grew up to fake a cancer diagnosis. His name was Gordon Tyler. He wore this bucket hat with the logo for Pabst Blue Ribbon all over it. Pab. That's what everyone called him. I don't know why we didn't call him Pabst—or Gordon, for that matter. We just didn't. For as long as I knew him, his name was Pab. We met at summer camp in 1976. I was from Redlands, California. He was from Metairie, Louisiana, a suburb of New Orleans. We literally had our first conversation wearing Uncle Sam beards. Two white boys on the backs of white ponies at a 4th of July, American Bicentennial parade on a mountain in Tennessee. We stayed friends for decades. I have tried to write about Pab before, but every time I started to tell his story, I became aware that maybe his story wasn't my story to tell.

If my students ever were to read this thing I'm writing, some of them would ask me if they were allowed to go on tangents like I do when they write assignments for class. I have had these conversations with students many times. We often end up talking about the differences between stories, journal entries, and collections of random sentences.

In this kind of discussion, I might first assert that what I'm writing is not random because I am thinking about which sentences belong next to each other. Second, I might say that in anyone's life, a bunch of storylines are happening all at once, so wouldn't it make sense to make a story out of a bunch of sentences crashing together? Sometimes students are compelled to conduct their own creative writing explorations, and other times they are not. When Pab and I returned to Tennessee summer camp the year after the Bicentennial, we bunked in the same cabin called Beaver Lodge. Many students might tell me they want to hear more of these kinds of details in my stories and less of my philosophical rambling. Each of the cabins at that summer camp was named after small, fur-bearing mammals.

When Pab and I were in Beaver together, there was a television show that was vaguely popular about a crime-fighting lawyer named Petrocelli. For some reason, Pab thought it was funny to call me "Dykeocelli." Because my name is Timothy Dyke, as I have already said, and because I don't live in the Netherlands, my name inspires snickers and jokes. By the time I graduated high school, I'd heard all kinds of cruel comments about my last name. "Dykeocelli" didn't seem that bad.

I am writing a story about Pab and his fake cancer. I am also not writing a story about Pab and his fake cancer. I am writing about how, as we get older, we carry all these memories around with us. If my students wanted to use a creative writing assignment to swirl or crash some sentences together, I would be willing to read what they came up with. Today in 10th grade English, we got into a conversation about what "theme" means and whether or not writers put hidden messages in their work. I told my students about the conversation I had with my mother after I first saw *Saturday Night Fever* in the late 1970s. I guess I am still telling a self-mythologizing story, after all. This one is not so supernatural, though.

None of the 10th graders had heard of *Saturday Night Fever*. When I described it, a girl said it sounded like *High School Musical*. I told her I have never seen *High School Musical*, but that seems about right. We speculated about ways *Saturday Night Fever* may be more problematic than *High School Musical* when it comes to questions of sex and gender. Someone asserted that *High School Musical* is problematic in its own way. Then we read

"Hills Like White Elephants." A student wanted to know how I could be sure the couple in the story was talking about an abortion. When I pointed to some text and asked what else they could be talking about, a student wanted to interpret the couple's relationship through a lens of transgender identity. I would like to read that student's re-write of "Hills Like White Elephants."

On my walk off campus at the end of the day, two students from that English class were playing catch on the quad. One motioned for me to receive her throw. I was about a quarter of a football field away from her. I could make the catch, right? I forgot to consider that I walk around with only one working eye. The tennis ball hit me on the head. The two kids looked at the ground, avoiding eye contact as I giggled awkwardly and retrieved the projectile. One of the school psychologists, Dr. Espania, was sitting at a picnic table, watching the scene like it was bad sport. Which I guess it was. I wondered, not for the first or last time, what the school psychologist thought of me. On my way home, I stopped for a baguette at the Japanese bakery. They were sold out, perhaps because it was 4/20, the date of the annual stoner holiday.

As I walked into my apartment in Makiki, I said out loud to my parrots, "It hasn't been a bad Wednesday, but it's definitely been a Wednesday." Wednesdays are liminal days, hovering between the beginning of the week and the end of the week. I am trying to tell a story. I am trying to throw a bunch of sentences together about a variety of topics. Maybe this is a Wednesday type of writing. I am writing it on a Thursday, though. I am revising it on a Friday. I've worked on it every day of the week for a month. That month turns into five years.

After Pab and I grew past our summer camp days, we kept in touch through occasional letters and phone calls. When I moved to Hawai'i in 1992, I had to decide what to do with my pet dog. I don't really like to tell this story because it triggers my self-hatred. The short version of the dog story: I had been living in Houston with a dog I didn't train well. After getting a job offer to teach in a school in Honolulu, I decided not to move my pet to Hawai'i. I tried to find him a good home. My friend, Pab, knew my dog and told me he was eager to adopt him.

I should have seen the red flags. He came to visit me from New Orleans when I first moved into that Houston apartment with the dog, Pepper. A half an hour after Pab got off the plane, he announced that he couldn't find his wallet. He called the airlines. I told him that I'd float him whatever cash he needed, and he could pay me back. At the time, it never occurred to me that he could be broke and full of shit. During his visit, we got along well enough. Eventually, he agreed to adopt my dog if I accepted this job offer in Hawai'i.

Pab and I made arrangements. Two weeks after I left Texas and flew to O'ahu, he had ghosted me. We didn't use the term "ghosted" at the time. In those pre-internet days, it was not that hard to stop communicating with someone. During my third week in Honolulu, I heard from another friend that Pab had my dog put to sleep. This is a story about my dead dog. It is a story about regret. Maybe I should write a few sentences about how regret changes the way we remember things. Regret changes the way we remember things.

That's really all I have to say about that. I stopped talking to Pab and refused to acknowledge any of his attempts at reconnection. Ten years after our last communication, I heard he had cancer. Pivot. Quick tangent: whenever I write anything in the first person, I end up saying something about being queer. Pab made it clear to me ever since we were kids that he hated queers, so I never came out to him. I let him use the anti-gay "F-word" around me. I probably used it back a few times. I think I wanted, ever since I first met him, to be liked by him. During my closeted years, and for a few years after I came out, I found myself drawn to my bullies. If someone treated me like shit, I reasoned that they might like me if only I could be nicer to them. I rewarded my bullies with fawning attention. I'm not saying I was exactly like this in my relationship with Pab. I'm saying this dynamic was a factor. After my dog died, I kind of came to this epiphany: I didn't want to be nice to Pab anymore.

By the time I came out as gay in 1999, Pab and I were no longer communicating. A few years later, in the middle of the first decade of the new millennium, another acquaintance from Tennessee summer camp told me that due to the spread of his pancreatic cancer, Pab had moved in with Tucker Von Meeses, yet one more summer camp alumnus who also had a fatal diagnosis. My one friend called Pab and Tucker "cancer buddies."

I made no effort to reach out to Pab, even when I heard he was dying because I still held a guilt-ridden grudge about the animal we mutually killed. Whenever I write an autobiographical story and read it to my students, I worry that maybe I am giving them TMI, too much information, that I am not being professional because I am talking about my personal self, my TIM self in school. I don't want to cross the boundary that separates professional comportment from personal behavior, but I also think that if I am thoughtful, I can teach them something about how to use memory for solving writing problems or how to use writing for solving memory problems. A swimming coach should be able to swim, and a story-writing teacher should be able to write a story. On the other hand, this may not actually be a story. How many hands do I have anyway? I can see how that swimming coach analogy could go awry.

In early 2010, I received Facebook friend requests from Pab. After ignoring Pab's efforts to communicate on social media, I started to get phone calls from other people who knew us both. This guy named Sam McCord told me that Pab was on the verge of death and that he wanted to speak with me before his cancer destroyed him. Maybe it sounds terrible, but even though I thought Pab was dying, I didn't want to reconnect with him. Do we have to be nice to people who have hurt us just because they are sick?

Maybe? I'm not sure I know the answer to that question. Even though the Japanese bakery was out of baguettes on 4/20, I still managed to find a loaf of garlic bread to have with my dinner. French-influenced Japanese boulangeries and patisseries are popular in Honolulu. Each shop is filled with baguettes, eclairs, squares of layered doughs, mini-custards, and donuts filled with azuki bean paste. I prefer the baguettes at the Japanese bakery in Makiki over any other bread I could buy in Honolulu. I keep making these tangential pivots. There's something about this Pab story that is hard to tell. One day I woke up and there was an email in my inbox. Someone was sending me some information. The subject line of the email read: Cancer Hoax Never Mind Calling Pab.

Pab's cancer buddy, Tucker Von Meeses, really did have cancer. He passed away in 2012. Pab had been staying rent-free in a house Tucker owned. After Tucker died, his brother, Carl, inherited the property. When I was in creative writing school, one of my teachers told me I always had too many names of people in my stories. At least I haven't referred to myself as Dykeocelli again. Carl Von Meeses told Pab he could stay in Tucker's house for free until he died. Carl thought Pab would leave this world before spring turned to summer.

Pab lived in the Von Meeses' house in the Garden District for another fifteen months. In July of 2013, Carl took him to MD Anderson, the Houston cancer hospital, to discuss possibilities for hospice care. That's when the doctor told Carl that Pab didn't have cancer. Pab had these welts all over his face. They had grown steadily worse, so no one had questioned that he was sick. The doctor told Carl that Pab had confessed to searing his skin with the end of a glass bottle-stopper and a Bic lighter.

On the day Carl arrived at his house with police to throw Pab out, Pab locked himself in the bathroom and stabbed himself in the throat with a pair of scissors. His self-inflicted wounds were deep but not fatal. My reaction was so self-serving when I heard about Pab's struggles. I wasn't glad that Pab was in trouble. I was glad that I wasn't going to have to listen anymore to mutual friends telling me I should communicate with him. I felt vindicated because everyone thought I was bitterly shunning Pab as he approached death. Maybe I am a little bitter. I knew deep down in my bones that he could never be trusted. Liars recognize liars.

I spent my time in the 20th Century pretending I was attracted to women, so I know what it's like to convince yourself that the lie you are living is not a lie. As years pass, I still haven't talked to Pab, but I've started to forgive him a little bit. I've heard from others that he is still alive. Pab is obviously a troubled person, so what good does it do for me to hate him?

Tucker's brother, Carl, thinks Pab played a terrible trick on everyone. On Facebook, Carl wrote that Pab took advantage of their family's kindness by moving in with Tucker without paying his share. Carl says Tucker was duped, but I'm almost positive Tucker knew what was up. Tucker and Pab were Baptist Republican white men in the South at the turn of the millennium. Neither married or ever had a girlfriend, as far as I know. Maybe they were attracted to one another. Perhaps they were in love. Maybe the Cancer Buddy story provided cover. Perhaps faking cancer was the easiest way for Pab to live as Tucker's residential companion indefinitely without social stigma. Maybe the welts that Pab burnt into his face were manifestations of mourning and intense grief, mixed in with some of his own self-loathing.

In the end I decide not to show any of this writing to students. I had persuaded myself that I was writing this story for teacher demonstration purposes. I was telling myself this to create a little distance. I wanted to approach the story of Pab with a kind of neutrality. I realize that's not really possible. If memories stay with us long enough, they seep through our skins. You can't distance yourself from everything you remember. I remember that Pab and I were once good friends who bunked together in Beaver Lodge. He called me Dykeocelli, and I watched him mount a white horse in his Pabst Blue Ribbon hat. That was a long time ago.

THIRTEEN

MY COWORKER WHO TEACHES CHINESE TELLS ME TRAFFIC will be bad for another hour. I am not sure why I don't tell her I live in Makiki, less than half a mile away. I walk back and forth to work. I wear a mask. She wears a mask. You have lived through these years in the 2020s, so you know I am not being metaphorical. Our expressions are blunted by cloth. I thank my colleague for the traffic report and retreat to my cubicle to pack up my backpack: both computers, both chargers, Tupperware (empty, except for one dirty, bamboo fork), and a paperback copy of Neruda's *Book of Questions*.

It's not actually Tupperware but some similar type of molded plastic container. When I walk to work, I usually climb Kewalo to Nehoa. When I walk home, I exit campus from the lower gate, follow Wilder to the parking lot of the Scottish Rites Cathedral, bear right, *mauka*, toward the mountain: Tantalus. I ran up that mountain in my marathon training days more than twenty years ago. I should know its rightful Hawaiʻi name, but I don't. I walked it as recently as five (maybe six?) years ago, seven and a half miles up, switchbacks and potholes, past mansions I might describe as Makiki Postmodern Gothic. Some mix of old and new, beautiful and scary. Some mix of growth and decay. In a bamboo forest at the highest point of the climb, I'd smoke the joint in my pocket, then walk down: carnival of descent, knee teasing, tendons jolted.

I huff when I walk up my street now. In my head, as I ascend the hill at the end of Kewalo, I recite this specific Langston Hughes poem, "Mother to Son", about, on its most literal level, climbing stairs. Today on my walk home, a man jogged past me shirtless. The one soccer field at Makiki Park seemed particularly green this afternoon. Sometimes I remember events as stories. Sometimes I remember images as poetic moments. When I am most magical, I can hear hibiscus blossoms sing. When I am least magical, I accept that in my advancing age, I have developed an unceasing ringing in my ears.

Today I am magical enough to understand that all flowers know songs of promise and loss. I'm on a Saturday afternoon cannabis high. I'm walking again through Makiki. I think about stopping in the park to read, but I decide to keep moving, stay on the sidewalk. I'm magical enough but not very magical. How magical would I have to be to think I had anything to say about school shootings? At work I had to take an online course about dealing with violent campus intruders. I learned I am supposed to keep books in my classroom so students can throw them to distract a shooter. That's not why I keep books in my classroom. A tenth-grade student asked me if I would throw my body at a hostile gunman in order to protect my students. I said, "I'd like to think I would." They didn't think that was a very good answer.

The day after the massacre in Texas where fourth graders were murdered in their classroom—Wait, let me start again:

The day after the massacre in Texas where fourth graders and their teachers were murdered in their classroom, I showed up in the library at the school where I work—Wait, let me start again:

The day after the massacre in Texas where fourth graders and their teachers were murdered in their classroom, my students showed up in the library at the school where I work to perform at this previously scheduled poetry reading event—Wait, let me start again:

The day after the massacre in Texas where fourth graders and their teachers were murdered in their classroom, my students showed up in the library at the school where I work to share space inside a glass room to read poems and stories to—Wait, let me start again:

The day after the massacre in Texas where fourth graders and their teachers were murdered in their classroom, my students showed up in the library at the school where I teach to share space inside a crowded glass room to read poems, stories, a screenplay, and a reflection on a grandmother's house. Wait, let me start again:

The day after the massacre in Texas where fourth graders and their teachers were murdered in their classroom, my tenth-grade students met to read original compositions to each other at an event I helped organize with my English teacher colleagues and the library faculty. One girl read a reflective passage about the smell of pine-scented candles in her grandmother's house. A boy's poem about his demanding father evoked some anger in me while a girl's poem about her father's passing provoked tears. Wait, let me start again:

The day after the massacre in Texas where fourth graders and their teachers were murdered in their classroom, my tenth-grade students met to read original work to each other at an event I helped put together. One girl read a reflective piece about the ways memory can be triggered by smell. One boy wrote about freezing. The girl who sometimes plucks her guitar before class wrote a poem about her father's memorial service at the beach. She threw flowers into the ocean and whispered a recollection into the wind. She teared up as she read. I teared up as she read. We all teared up as she read. Wait, let me start again:

The day after the massacre in Texas, we met in the library and cried about loss.

I mean for this thing I write to be a tribute, a thoughtful reflection in memoriam, but I can see how in some sense, I am centering myself in someone else's trauma narrative. In ways similar to how I don't believe confession leads to absolution, I also don't believe that admitting to coopting someone else's story grants me permission to continue. I'm working on this in the immediate aftermath of the fires on Maui.

I choose to acknowledge the loss of life. I choose to acknowledge the loss of history and culture. I recognize how colonialism and extractive tourism attack the health of Hawai'i and Hawaiians. I choose to give a charitable donation rather than insert myself into the story more than I am in this paragraph.

The phone pings while I'm watching *Castle in the Sky* in bed after the last day of the '21/'22 school year. An acquaintance named Terry Fujioka is texting. He is the president of the condo board at Mountain Shadow, the condominium building in Makiki where I've lived for almost twenty years. Anyone who knows me knows how much of a joke it is that I'm on our condo board. I'm a high school English teacher, a poetry enthusiast. I know nothing about money management or building maintenance. For ten years our Condo Association paid a particular management company to oversee our finances and then six days ago they went bankrupt and shut down their business. Terry wants to convene an emergency meeting.

Here are some of the ways I am a terrible resident of Mountain Shadow: I have pet birds when pets are not allowed on the premises; I blow weedsmoke out my window; I have a cleaning avoidance problem and may or may not have contributed to the cockroach infestation everyone complains about; I park my Subaru too close to the bougainvillea and piss off the gardeners who trim the hedge twice a month. Here is one way I am an excellent resident of Mountain Shadow: I get along with everyone else on the board and with everyone I run into in the parking lot. Mostly I smile, nod, and then leave people alone.

It's probably illegal for me to describe specific condo association business even if I am going to assert once again that I'm telling tales with elements of fiction. This is a memoir with lies in it, after all. Please assume that this particular chapter is extra lie-filled. Being super-general and making no specific allegations, I would say that if someone asked me if any board member ever swung a bike lock at any other board member, and if someone asked me if that same board member ever referred to the family in 204 not by name but only as the Micronesians, and if someone asked me if that same board member frequently made wanking gestures behind another board member's back while calling her a name that would get him fired in any modern workplace, I would look down at the floor and say, "You shouldn't really be asking me those kinds of questions."

I have come to like this board member who I will refer to as my problematic neighbor. When I first moved into this six-story low-rise in the heart of Makiki, George W. Bush was President. The United States hadn't invaded Iraq yet. Barack Obama grew up in this neighborhood and attended the school where I now teach, though I would have no idea who Barack Obama was when I first moved into this neighborhood. My problematic neighbor helped me carry an oversized recliner up six flights of stairs. He leant me his cellphone when I locked myself out of my apartment. I am trying to establish that this man has assisted me in tangible, measurable ways. He also drove a truck in the early 2010s with racist graffiti painted on the tailgate. "Obamacare Will Make US Slaves To KENYA." "Democrat Demon Rats Are the New KKK."

I have always considered it a virtue to be able to find common ground with most everyone I meet. This definition of kindness is self-serving. My problematic neighbor makes a better friend than adversary. This definition of kindness relies on privilege. We are each of us middle-aged white men who moved to these islands from the center of the North American continent. We each, independently, bought condo apartments on land we have no claim to. I can enjoy his company. We talk about sports. He likes the Green Bay Packers. I like the Minnesota Vikings. We maintain a rapport of friendly opposition.

During the early part of the pandemic, I could go more than a week without seeing the mouth of any other human being. Everyone kept to themselves and wore masks outside. Twice my problematic neighbor and I took walks together to Makiki Park. I wore a mask, and he did not. When he talks to me, he tries to shock me. He told me gruesome and morally repugnant stories from his Vietnam War Days. I figured out that the best reaction to hearing these stories is to have no reaction. I am not sure whether he and I have conversational boundaries. Once I told him about my visit to the urologist. Mostly these days we are back to talking about sports again.

My neighbor reminds me of my father. Of course, he does. Each is gregarious in their performance of generosity to waitstaff in restaurants. Each has put me through tests before they give me their appreciation. My dad lives in an assisted living village in North Dakota near my older brother, Caleb. When I visited him in the summer of 2021, my father proudly showed me racist flyers he had been anonymously posting on the walls of common elevators. I don't want to detail the racism of my relatives. I understand that when we white people get specific in our storytelling with details of our racism, we do not grant ourselves absolution. We make the problem worse. We focus on the wrong protagonist. We insist, as we always do, that every story is about us.

My problematic neighbor once called me a pantywaist as I walked by him in the corridor. My dad called me the exact same thing more than once when I was a teenager. I told my problematic neighbor that I was indeed kind of a pantywaist. "Do you not get along with pantywaists?" I asked. Ever since that awkward interaction, he's treated me with respect. Perhaps I have learned not to reward bullies with unquestioned civility. To spin this anecdote in a less favorable direction, I would say that our bond as white men transcends our differences. We each help the other feel open minded and capable of empathy. He gets to say he's open-minded enough to have a pantywaist for a friend, and I get to say

I'm open-minded enough to have a friend who's a MAGA fascist. We genuinely appreciate each other for this.

My problematic neighbor tells me a lot that he loves me. When we run into one another in the parking lot, he tells me I have a good heart. I tell him I feel the same way about him. Again, this reminds me of my relationship with my father. I don't ever remember my father telling me he loved me when I was a boy. He says "I love you" more often now. From his bed in the nursing home, he tells me he's proud of me. I don't want to make too much of this connection between my dad and my problematic neighbor. I'm not trying to make this parking lot nuisance into a father figure. He is not that for me.

My experiences with my father teach me how a person can have a repugnant world view while also being capable of individual acts of kindness. Individual acts of occasional kindness should not be enough. When I moved twenty years ago from one part of Makiki to Mountain Shadow in this other part of Makiki, I understood that pets were not allowed in the building except by permission. The woman who lived in my unit before me had a cat. I didn't really understand how condo boards worked at the time. A couple of board members told me informally that it wouldn't be a problem if I lived with a caged bird. I mistook this elevator talk for official permission. I've lived with three parrots for twenty years. My largest and greenest bird died last night. Luna, touched with the white spot of a full moon on her head. The sweetest animal. When I found her dead in the cage, I felt an irrational sense of confusion. Wasn't she supposed to live forever?

Terry Fujioka is texting in his capacity as president of the board of our condo association. His recent meeting with an executive from a prospective management company has gone well. My eyes glaze over as I scroll through his message. I'll text him back tomorrow. The problematic neighbor and his wife are also on the text thread. I'm sure that one reason

I have befriended this couple is because I know it's good to have allies on the condo board. Because I am not exactly living according to the letter of the law when it comes to House Rules, I feel vulnerable. I feel like it's in my best interest to cultivate good will. I am not saying that my kindnesses are false and Machiavellian; I am saying that intentions behind my interactions are complicated. I am aware that it serves my advantage to be perceived by my neighbors as good. That's the essential problem with altruism as a virtue; do I serve others because that's the best way to serve myself? It's an age-old question. It's a question Phoebe asks herself in the TV show, *Friends*. I'm not saying that *Friends* is a show worth watching. Queer folx and large-bodied people are ridiculed on that show. I never watched a single episode of that situation comedy when it aired originally in the 1990s. I binged its ten seasons during the pandemic. The characters kept me company.

About to go off on a *Friends* tangent about Phoebe and ethical philosophy, I resist and refocus on picking up the dominant plot thread. I am a writer who is distracted by the shiny object. The year after my father moved into the assisted living village in Fargo, I visited for a week in July. I stayed with my brother and his wife. I borrowed their car to drive across town to visit Dad. We had all agreed that I'd take my father on a daytrip while my brother and sister-in-law went to work. On the first Thursday after Independence Day, I picked him up in a borrowed Honda and drove him a hundred-and-fifty miles West on flat interstate to the American Bison Museum. I was not uninterested in bison. My dad seemed excited to get out and see sky.

After Luna died, I needed to decide what to do with her avian corpse. I am not sentimental about corpses. I have told my friends that when I die, I don't want anyone spending a lot of money disposing of my human remains. I honestly wouldn't mind having my cremated ashes put into a paper sack and tossed into the dumpster at Mountain Shadow.

I held the deceased bird's body as I'd hold a bouquet of dried flowers. I looked for something to put her in. I had to be at work in half an hour. I thought about putting her body in the freezer until I had time to figure out a respectful plan. Was it respectful, though, to wrap her in plastic and stuff her in the icebox next to frozen hamburger and leftover leek stalks? I found an attractive paper gift bag and placed her inside.

The outside of the American Bison Museum was about as hokey as you could imagine. A mile off the interstate, behind a Dairy Queen and a Dollar Store, a gravel road led to a row of small houses set beneath three billboards advertising great deals for patriotic gifts. Behind the houses, a herd of bison grazed in a fenced meadow. We parked as close to the main museum building as possible. Dad used a walker as he navigated the gravel. He wanted to see the live animals before we went inside to look at taxidermy. On our way to the bison field, we pass a tree with a tire swing where three Retrievers lie in shade. I arc to the left to keep some distance, but my father and his walker inch slowly past the sleeping canines. The dogs don't even seem to notice us. Two are white and one is black. My father makes a joke about affirmative action. We smile for a selfie in a pastoral setting. I post on Facebook an image of an idyllic intergenerational family relationship. I receive many likes. This is how it goes when I am with my father. When he says something racist, I say nothing and fret about all the ways I am complicit in perpetuating white supremacy.

As I prepared to throw Luna's green corpse into the Mountain Shadow dumpster, I scanned my psyche for reaction. I teach *Antigone* every semester. I support the plight of this daughter of Oedipus as she fights to assure a decent burial for her brother. When I talk about the play with tenth graders, I ask them why it would be so bad to leave the corpse on the street. After all, Polynices is dead, so isn't Antigone's fight for a ceremonial funeral less about what would help her brother and more about what would make her feel good? As I ask that question, I'm not trying to lead my students to any particular answer. I'm trying to get them to think about issues of altruism and egoism, of morality and ethics.

What are my options when it comes to disposing of my green parrot's body? I could pay for cremation. I could drive up Tantalus to one of the trailheads and find a spot for burial under a tree. I'm not really familiar with those hiking spots. I don't know if I own a trowel or a small shovel. Is it legal to bury pets on public land? Are the Tantalus trails all on public land? My friend Stacia would know the answers to these questions. I imagine texting her, but then I would have to tell her about my parrot's death and receive her condolences. I don't know if I'm emotionally ready for this right now. I have to be at work in fifteen minutes. I could figure something out. I have this weird flash of storyline where I text Stacia for an answer to my question without telling her my bird has died. Are all those trails in Makiki on public land? I see myself asking Stacia this, but because I am not fluent in text speak, I not only write something convoluted like, "R Tantalus trailheads Public Makiki?" In my fleeting daydream, I see myself accidentally typing "Pubic Makiki."

At the American Bison Museum, I sit next to my dad in a small theater and watch a movie about Ted Turner's contribution to the reinvigoration of buffalo ranching in America. I can't remember what my dad thinks about Ted Turner. I know the mogul used to be married to Jane Fonda. I know my dad can't stand Jane Fonda. That's another thing my father has in common with my problematic neighbor. I'm not sure whether or not my problematic neighbor fought in Vietnam. He has told me stories about his war days, but then months later he might tell me the same story and say it happened to a buddy of his. I don't judge him for this. I have done that myself. I do know my problematic neighbor hates Jane Fonda. I have heard him say disparaging things about her climate advocacy. I know he failed out of the police academy in Little Rock. I know he was in the Navy and had been stationed at Pearl Harbor. That's how he ended up settling in Hawai'i and meeting his wives. These are the stories he has told me.

It's impossible to exit the American Bison Museum without passing a gigantic plexiglass display housing a stuffed and preserved White Buffalo. An article describes the spiritual importance of this genetic rarity to indigenous North Dakotans. My dad makes a reference to white genocide. The inappropriate comment prompts me to write something down on a Dairy Queen napkin. I eventually write a short essay about visiting the bison museum with my dad. A small online journal accepts the essay for inclusion in an upcoming issue, but before my article sees the light of day, I ask the editor to cancel plans for publication. This would have been during the last months of the 2016-'20 Trump presidency. I didn't want to be another self-satisfied white person who told a story about his racist parents in order to establish his own anti-racism. The editor understood my concerns. A recent publication in *Poems!* magazine featured the work of a white man who wrote about his racist grandmother. His poems contained racial epithets. The editor resigned a week after the issue hit newsstands and inboxes. My white buffalo essay remains unpublished.

I decided to dispose of Luna's body in the Mountain Shadow dumpster. Though I knew the action was unsentimental, I didn't think of it as disrespectful. I took one last look at the corpse in the paper gift bag. Folding the bag shut, I said something loving and briefly closed my eyes. I put the paper bag inside a kitchen garbage bag and threw the trash in the dumpster on my way to work. The bird still exists in my memory. The bird still exists in hundreds of photos and videos on my phone. I have an image of the bird's tricolored feather tattooed on my lower right arm. The dead body is not my bird's spirit or essence. For about half a day, I felt fine with these rationalizations. By the time my workday was over, I was deep into a wave of troubling second thoughts. It didn't help that during the day I read another essay about *Antigone*.

I texted my friend Stacia and told her Luna died. My Red Belly parrots, Rothko and Fiver, hovered atop Luna's now-empty cage. While it's true that sometimes they had picked on her, I liked to think they realized now that they would miss their flockmate. Stacia's son texted that he would miss Luna. He told me he was sorry for my loss. This fourteen-year-old asked me what I did with my green bird's body. When I heard myself lying and saying I'd buried her under a tree on a hill in the woods, I knew I was going to regret the reality I'd created for myself. I ran home and opened the door to the Mountain Shadow garbage area. This was not a trash pickup day, and I thought I could see my bag of refuse in the back of the dumpster. I looked around. The parking lot seemed quiet. Admittedly, I forgot about the surveillance cameras. I climbed into the dumpster. I stood hip deep in garbage bags. Rancid air filled my lungs. I ripped open one Hefty bag and immediately realized I'd picked the wrong sack of refuse. I touched a soiled diaper and recoiled, falling back against a discarded Amazon box. Righting my footing, I stepped toward another bag. I ripped it open at the exact moment I heard my name. I turned around to see my problematic neighbor outside the Mountain Shadow dumpster looking in.

I had been caught red-handed. We can't control where our thoughts go. I flashed back to the memory of the time my father found me looking at *Playboy* when I was sixteen. I discovered his modest porn stash the summer after 10th grade when I was looking for an application to a summer exchange program that I'd briefly been interested in. Though I'd never been aroused by pictures of naked women, I was aroused by my shirtless friend who was aroused by pictures of naked women. I could look at any number of centerfolds in my father's dirty magazine stash and within five minutes, I'd be fantasizing about the way the J.V. quarterback across the street moaned when I showed him the picture of the naked woman licking the ice cream cone. I wouldn't have said I wanted to have sex with the J.V. quarterback. I never have felt the urge to have sex with anyone, though I wouldn't say I've never experienced sexual desire. It's hard to explain. Asexuality establishes its own spectrum.

When my father caught me with his dirty, heterosexual magazine, he gave me a look that hovered somewhere between surprise, amusement, and disgust. As I stood hip deep in dumpster trash, my problematic neighbor gave me the exact same look. With derisive laughter, he said what my dad had said all those years ago: "Well what have we here?" I told my neighbor that I'd dropped my keys. This sounded plausible enough. He didn't say anything for a couple of seconds, and then he asked me if I wanted him to help me look. I told him I had things under control. He laughed at this. He asked me why I had ripped open a garbage bag. Was my key inside one of the bags? As I struggled to find a plausible answer to his reasonable question, I watched his facial expression soften. He told me I didn't have to answer. He told me that my business was my business. I thought of the last time he told me about his soldier friend who shot an unarmed farmer. As he turned to leave, he said something about how he would never really understand liberals. I told him I tried the best I could to understand conservatives. He told me he loved me. He told me I had a good heart.

I never retrieved the body of my dead pet. It took me three showers to get the smell of garbage off my skin. My problematic neighbor made snide remarks about trash the next three times he saw me. As I said earlier, it wouldn't be right to specifically mention actual business of the Mountain Shadow Condo Association. I will say vaguely that my problematic neighbor stopped teasing me after I stepped forward to vouch for him to the condo board. One of the renters claimed that my problematic neighbor made constant and alienating remarks to him in the parking lot. The renter accused my problematic neighbor of racism. Terry, the board president, asked me if I ever thought my problematic neighbor was racist. I told Terry that I'd heard the man say conservative things, but I never heard the man say specifically racist things. I lied in almost the exact same way when the head of my father's nursing home asked if I thought it was my father who had been posting the racist fliers in the elevator.

I stick up for the racist men who have helped me. I tell my stories from my position of privilege in Pubic Makiki. I think my green parrot would understand that even though his body went in the dumpster, his spirit flew into the clouds above Tantalus. I consider whether or not there is any benefit to taxidermy. I imagine the white buffalo and wonder if the plexiglass in a museum funded by white ranchers keeps her spirit from running free through prairie meadows. In bed at night, I decide I'm not tired, so I pick the iPad off the bedside table and cue up *Castle in the Sky*. I watch a few minutes of this Japanese animated movie. I've seen every Miyazaki movie at least ten times already. The story provides some distraction. I fall asleep. I wake up to news of another school shooting. I close my eyes. On top of the bedcovers, I position myself for a yoga move. I will raise myself into a backbend. I will push back despair.

FOURTEEN

AFTER YOU DIE, YOU WON'T GET ANOTHER CHANCE TO eat candy. After you die, you will have no relationship with Santa Claus. After you die, your philosophies will be neither validated nor invalidated. After you die, no one is going to stash your cremated remains in a brown paper bag and throw you in a Makiki dumpster, the way you half-jokingly requested the other night at the party when you had too much vodka, the way you managed the disposal of your dead pet's corpse. After you die, you will not drink gin martinis with pickle chips. After you die, you won't remember all you've been trying to forget. After you die, you will never again text with Dan about the meaning of John Cheever's "The Swimmer." After you die, you won't find out who wins the Culture War. After you die, you won't understand math, but you will become math as you divide into half-life, as your microbial biodome multiplies, divides. After you die, you will not hear the poems we recite for you. After you die, you will melt no more cheese. After you die, the unreturned voicemails will remain unreturned. After you die, you may become an orphaned address in someone else's phone. After you die, you probably will not reunite with dead pets and human loved ones. After you die, you will become hope for someone who still believes that when you die, you will reunite with pets and human loved ones. After you die, you will not need to work on your pickleball game. After you die, that eight-hour Beatles documentary will be forever relegated to your watch-later folder. After you die, you will not have memory, but you will become memory until you are forgotten.

FIFTEEN

I'M WATCHING *GODZILLA VERSUS KONG* ON MY PHONE on Good Friday from my couch in Makiki. I would prefer to watch epic monster shows on the largest screens possible. As it's the third year of the pandemic, and as I am having internet connectivity issues at home again, I stream the movie through my ATT/HBO account. Corporate overlords bring me this movie about corporate overlords. Titanic monsters fit in my hand. Favorite line so far: "Godzilla left us in peace. You brought us war." Humans are the biggest monsters; this movie tells us nothing new.

My parrot, Rothko, watches from my shoulder. He eats a crouton, sprays graveled bread down my collar. Perhaps it's my imagination, but it seems to me the bird squawks whenever Godzilla appears on the screen. Most Easter weekends turn bad for me. The year of the lapsed safety inspection, I got pulled over on Good Friday. The year of the bed bug infestation, I spent the Saturday night before Easter Sunday in a motel room reading Nanea's hate emails alone. Sounds of sex snuck through the walls from the room next to mine. Other folks found pleasure while I was trying not to hurt myself intentionally. I've never felt so isolated.

The first time I saw the original *Godzilla*, I was with Malcolm and Sandra and Serge in a motel in Hilo. Malcolm and Sandra are two of my dearest friends. Malcolm is gay and not my boyfriend. Sandra divorced her child's father, and then the man died six years later by accidental overdose. Or maybe it was suicide. That distinction is really none of my business. Serge, Sandra's son, was 8 at the time of his dad's death. He said *Godzilla* was his first horror movie. He said he wasn't too scared. Every time I include these particular friends in this story, I give them different names. I tell myself this helps preserve their privacy. Movies don't provide escape as much as they provide places to hang emotions. Or that's not exactly the right metaphor. Movies are more like kaleidoscopes than coat hangers. They turn light into colorful visions. Movies distort realities into new ways of seeing.

Easter is the only holiday I prefer to spend by myself. I don't mind that it is a lonely holiday. Metaphors of resurrection intimidate me. The corporate overlords on my screen want Godzilla and Kong to expire in mutual destruction. I want the monsters to see themselves reflected in the iris of the other, to hug it out, maybe even tongue-kiss. Most Easter weekends, I end up watching *Ben Hur* again. I consider the attractiveness of young Charlton Heston. I wonder if he knew then what he would become: so un-glistening, so gun-loving. I wonder if any of us know what we will become. Godzilla and King Kong center themselves like monster stigmata in the palm of my phone hand. Kong is like Moses. Forced into slavery, he parts seas in order to return to his Promised Lands. Godzilla is like Jesus. He dies for our sins, then rises to remind us of our frail humanity.

SIXTEEN

IN THE PHOTOGRAPH, I AM WEARING A SPEEDO AND cradling a guinea pig. I am nine years old. The animal's name was Harry. I purchased him at a flea market in Crossville, Tennessee. This would have been some time around 1972. Back then at Christian Summer Camp, they let the youngest campers purchase pets for the season. In a clearing between maple trees, our rabbits and guinea pigs, chickens, box turtles and baby ducks lived in pens and cages. They called this place The Nature Center. I never asked anyone what happened to the animals after we left at the end of each session. It was an old-school place where permanent residents lived frugally off the land. I'm sure I don't want to know what happened to our abandoned animals once summer was over.

The photograph hangs over my bed now. This same framed picture had been displayed in the house I grew up in for years. My mother moved into her small apartment in Palm Desert. During her process of downsizing, she gave me the photo. My friend saw the picture and asked who it was. I said the boy in the Speedo was me. My friend refused to believe it. I wondered why my friend thought I would have any picture of a nine-year-old in a Speedo displayed above my bed unless that picture was of me. I didn't ask my friend that awkward question. Instead, I asked why she didn't think the picture looked like me. If I see a picture of myself fifty years ago, I can fill in the dots on the line that took me from that moment at summer camp to this moment now. My friend couldn't fill in those dots. She said the hair didn't look like mine. My hair lay flat until I was about nine or ten, and then for whatever reason, the dry,

Spanish moss-type quality took over—spikes and frizzes everywhere, like I'd stuck my finger in a light socket.

That's the first insult I remember hearing about my hair. At first, I didn't get the joke. I've never stuck my finger in a light socket, so I didn't get how that kind of hair was supposed to look. Eventually I caught on. When I came of age, hair trends for certain white boys mandated smooth and feathered hair. I wanted to look like one of those shirtless singers on the record covers who posed with a coy smile, bronze skin and a small hoop earring in the left lobe. Instead, I was the kid whose hair looked like he'd stuck his finger in a light socket.

Responding to negative comments about my hair became a regular part of the years preceding and surrounding my adolescence. It's taken me a while to realize this, but my father deliberately chose conservative parts of the country as destinations for my family to temporarily settle. We moved a lot. From second grade to twelfth grade, we lived in Birmingham, Alabama; East Grand Rapids, Michigan; Omaha, Nebraska; and Redlands and Orange County, California. In East Grand Rapids, my father was friends with a man who openly made racist jokes in front of me about how my hair made me look Black. My dad and his friend were two white physicians. They thought they were being funny. They were teaching me what racism was.

The easiest way to get a haircut at boarding school was to rely upon the barbers hired by administrators to ply their trade in common rooms once a month. One of these paid technicians cut my hair in a kind of bowl cut, and because my hair is spiky and frizzed, I looked pretty strange. This fear of looking weird was reinforced when I walked into English class. I remember my teacher, Mr. Chompington, laughing as soon as he saw me. "Your hair is ridiculous," he told me. I wanted to tell him his name was ridiculous, but I was too ashamed to speak. Every other boy in that class laughed as Chompington laughed. Of everything

I was told during two semesters of tenth grade English, the fact of my ridiculous hair was the one thing I learned.

I embraced the weirdness in college. I grew my hair out long and taught it to do tricks. I could hide pencils in there. Once I even managed to nest a stapler in my helmet of fuzz. I dressed up as Art Garfunkel for Halloween two years in a row. I became a teacher in the mid-1980s. I made silly-looking hair part of my presentation. Students called me Mr. Frizz. I cultivated the persona.

The first poem I ever published was about the time I got my hair cut at a salon during my first teaching job in Connecticut. Up until that point, with the occasional and disastrous boarding school exception, my mother always cut my hair. She kept it cropped close to the skin. When I lived in my first apartment and worked full time, I made an appointment at a local hair care place in Farmington. I was completely out of my element. I happened to go on Halloween. A woman in a bee costume directed me to the shampoo station. I had never seen an industrial shampoo station before. Instead of sitting in the chair and tipping my head backwards, I faced the sink and bent over as if I were about to bob for apples. The woman in the bee costume laughed. This was not my last embarrassing moment in a hair salon.

While in one sense I made my peace with funny looks, a part of me always wanted to appear cool and slick. After I moved to Hawai'i in 1992, I took another stab at conforming to hair fashions. At the Fantastic Sam's on the edge of lower Makiki, a half-decade after the bee costume incident, I asked the hair cutting professional to cut my hair short, the same length all the way around. She must have had time on her hands. She asked me if I wanted to look stylish. Against my better judgment, I asked her what she had in mind. She turned me away from the mirror and said she would give me a stylish haircut. If I didn't like it, then she would cut it all short, the same length, just as I initially requested. As this seemed like a fair deal, I said okay.

For half an hour she worked. I imagined what might be happening on top of my head. When she turned me toward the mirror for the big reveal, I think I audibly gasped. Imagine a mullet crossed with the spiky hair puff of an ichthyosis patient. Imagine a mullet stuck in a light socket. As I stared at my reflection in the large salon mirror, I imagined that is how I would look if a cat had crawled on top of my head and died of electrocution. I told the woman to shave my head as quickly as possible. She jabbed at the mullet-puff with resentment. "I guess you don't want to look stylish," she said.

"I don't look stylish," I snapped back. "I look like a serial killer."

The truth is that I have always wanted to look stylish, but I thought that stylishness eluded me. In retrospect, I believe that I eschewed attractiveness. On some unconscious level, I feared attracting others because I feared the nuances of my own asexuality. I wanted to convey anything other than sexiness. If someone wanted to have sex with me, I wouldn't have known what to do. Back then I assumed this was because of some humiliating deficiency. Now I regard that indifference as part of my asexual identity.

I was comfortable wearing my hair in a way that made people laugh. I did all kinds of experiments on the hair on top of my head. I died it blue. That's an intentional spelling mistake. The store-bought chemicals caused most of my hair to fall out. When it grew back, I slicked it down with Vaseline. During one regrettable time in the last part of the 20th Century, I stocked up on a mail order product called Knotty Boy Dred Wax and styled my hair into homemade and clumped whiteboy dreadlocks. I'm certain I looked ridiculous. I suppose ridiculousness was an aesthetic I had learned to cultivate.

It was during that clumped and matted time of my hair evolution that I came out of the closet to my mother in her Redlands home. When I told her I was gay two days before Christmas in 1999, the first thing she said was, "I still love you." The second thing she said was, "I hope you're planning to keep this quiet like they do in the military." The third thing she said was, "Won't you please let me cut your hair?" The conversation that followed was a difficult one. I tried to explain to her that my hair was a conscious way to telegraph my difference. I used my hair as a way of getting people to understand that I wasn't exactly like them. I told my mother to think of my hair as a metaphor.

In the first months of the new century, I told my principal at school that I was gay. He told me what I did in the bedroom was none of his business. I dyed my hair rainbow colors the next Saturday. A month later at a school chapel assembly, I told a story to the entire student body about the time the woman in the bee costume laughed at the way I bent into the shampooing station. I mentioned in the story that I was gay, kind of as a side comment. After I stepped away from the microphone, I realized I had just come out publicly to my school community. I used hair stories as a Trojan horse to house my queer coming out narrative.

As I aged, I settled into a routine with my hair and beard. I'd shave everything off in the summer, let it all grow unfettered until New Year's and then shave it all off again. During the early days of the pandemic, I taught classes from my computer screen at home. Time folded in on itself. I didn't tend to my hair at all for two years. When I finally shaved my head and beard in that apparent lull between the Delta variant and the first Omicron wave, a friend told me she was relieved. She said I was starting to look like the Unabomber. I'm keeping my hair short now. I'm cleanshaven as I write this. My hair is evenly trimmed. I look like an actor who played a suitor for one of the Golden Girls back in the eighties. No, I don't know why I said that. I'm programmed by personal history to make self-deprecating hair jokes. My hair is the feather of an island

SEVENTEEN

IN APRIL OF THE LAST YEAR OF THE PREVIOUS MIL-
lennium, I traveled by myself to Amsterdam. My plan was to be a tourist,
see Van Gogh paintings, take legal psychedelics and smoke weed openly
in coffee shops. The trip was transformative and awkward. I entered the
Museum of Film to watch a new print of *Superman II* and accidentally
ended up in Theater 5 where I peaked on two cannabis gummies during
a Yehudi Menuhin documentary. I was a cliché, really. I was punctuating
epic midlife changes with a trip to Amsterdam to do drugs and read
Siddhartha alone. I had this weird encounter with stoned Russians on top
of a houseboat. I barely avoided mugging on at least six occasions.

Almost a quarter century into the next millennium, that Amsterdam
trip looks different to me now. I associate the entire trip with finding free
access to bathrooms. I was drinking wine and beer, espresso, ingesting
mushrooms, and smoking constantly. I needed to pee a lot. I learned to
walk through hotel lobbies toward bathrooms with confidence. Perhaps
because of my unfortunate hairstyle, I got stopped by toilet guards a few
times. If I really had to go bad, I'd pay them a gilder and shrug. I was
there before the Euro. It was obviously a long time ago.

The story I've told most often about my Amsterdam trip is my
Homosexual Agenda origin story. I'd purchased a bag of mushrooms
that sold legally under the "Philosopher Stone" brand name. I spent
my morning coming on to the mushrooms while drinking espresso and
listening to a French Horn player at a café by a canal. At some point I
added alcohol and THC to the caffeine and psilocybin coursing through
my bloodstream. I carried my laptop everywhere. I have already described

myself as a cliché, and yes, I indulged fantasies of being a writer, sucking in inspiration with all that legally illicit assistance. As I sat on café patios with my computer open, the line blurred between writing down thoughts and eavesdropping.

While I typed on my keyboard, I became aware of a woman behind me. She spoke loudly in English to whoever she was sharing her table with. I heard her say, "I'm not prejudiced. I only hate Serbians." My neck snapped around and she caught me staring. I moved my eyes back to my laptop and continued to work on a new story. The idea for that story had occurred to me while taking a shower after another bout with Philosopher Stones. I had started to contemplate that phrase: The Homosexual Agenda. I used to hear this phrase at home and in Florida Orange Juice commercials on TV in the 1970s. My dad spotted the homosexual agenda in women's tennis, *Yentl,* and the turtleneck shirt industry.

After I had been out of the closet for only a month, I understood how ridiculous the phrase was. I also began to understand how deeply I'd been immersed in propaganda equating homosexuality with desecration of the family and the end of civilization. Perhaps it was the Philosopher Stones, but I had an epiphany: the way to undo the power of self-destructive myths is to tell new tales. In my writing, I began to make fun of gay panic. I created this Super Anti-hero named The Homosexual Agenda, an ironic amalgamation of every homophobic stereotype I'd ever heard of. They hung outside of high schools and tried to entice girls into joining softball leagues. When the woman who expressed hatred for Serbians caught me glancing at her, she stood up from her chair. She came around a table and stood behind me. I could feel her eyes on my computer screen. She thought I was writing about her. She aimed to catch me in the act. When she read from my laptop, she saw that I was writing about The Homosexual Agenda.

In 2017, I published a book of prose poems with a small press in Hawai'i. My editor wanted to call it *The Homosexual Agenda*. I was okay with that title. The book designer didn't like it. He thought it evoked stereotypical images of rainbows and pink glitter. In some sense I had thought that was the point, but in another sense, I knew what he meant. The other title I liked was *Atoms of Muses*, the name of one of the poems in the collection. We went with that. The book came and went. I balanced stories of this comical embodiment of stereotypes with narratives about queer youth suicide.

Three years after the publication of my prose poem book about The Homosexual Agenda, I was asked to read at an event sponsored by the Hawai'i Printmaker Association. I admired the other writers who had been invited to participate. I decided to write something for the occasion. I wrote about the return of the Homosexual Agenda. The reading went okay, but as I stepped away from the podium, I promised myself that I wouldn't keep writing about the same character over and over. Covid struck six months later. I didn't do any more readings of any kind for more than two years.

I am not traveling to Amsterdam this summer. I am traveling to Denver. I can eat cannabis chocolate with my Denver Omelet in public in Colorado. This will be my first trip to Denver since the pandemic began. The last time I was there, I drank delicious microbrew in this bar where Jack Kerouac used to hang out. I embrace my tourist status. I will sit outside of the revitalized train station in the public plaza. I will work on my book about truth and my bad yoga experience. The Homosexual Agenda may or may not make an appearance. If I did reanimate this anthropomorphic distillation of other people's prejudices, I would want the Homosexual Agenda to be aware that in many parts of the country, it has become illegal for school librarians to share books about queer families to kids in queer families. Trans kids face death threats when they need to pee or when they want to play sports.

As a boy of the 1970s, I was aware that the anti-gay rhetoric coming out of Florida was troubling and threatening. In the late 1990s, I must have thought things were changing. Today in the mid-2020s, hatred and prejudice persist. For as long as I have a functioning memory, I will mine the same creative terrain, over and over. I may not resurrect The Homosexual Agenda, but I am comfortable holding this character in my consciousness, considering how every new story is an attempt to rewrite the old story. The old stories don't go away. Rather, they attach themselves to a new batch of language and emerge from hibernation like locusts. Or bears.

EIGHTEEN

MY SMARTPHONE TELLS ME I HAVE A NEW MEMORY.

From my bedroom window, I occasionally see fireworks. I imagined for a while that these aerial displays came from official celebrations on beaches near me, but when I gaze out my bedroom window, I face Tantalus, not the beach. I face other apartments, too. The fireworks must come from rogue pyrotechnicians. From my bedroom window, an hour or so after dawn each day, hundreds, maybe thousands, of green parrots fly from Makiki to Nuʻuanu. An hour before dusk they fly back. They are beautiful, but parrots can be like zombies in the way that they crunch and crush, cause havoc and disturb.

I post ocean photos on Facebook, and people in Texas tell me I live in Paradise. With many ways to respond, I find myself negotiating that territory between trying to say the right thing and trying not to say the wrong thing. I comment back that yes, in many ways I do live in Paradise. I always add a line about gratitude. Sometimes I say that Paradise is a social construct benefitting the colonizer.

Staring out the window, I don't see Paradise. I see dim apartment light or the soft tint of sunset in November as condominium windows cast glimpses of shadow and reflection. From my rocking chair, I see square boxes outside my square box. There is the green tilt of waning sunlight. I am sitting quietly and rocking gently. My silence breaks with a pound on my door, successive taps. When someone knocks on your condo door, they most likely live inside the building. Otherwise, they would buzz up or tape notes to your car windshield. Call me, maybe.

If someone who lives inside the building knocks, it might be about plumbing issues, that wet spot on the ceiling, noise complaints, or maybe they've figured out that my inability to clean well has contributed to the cockroach problem. A knock on a door can jolt me out of my private Makiki. I go to the door and see my neighbor, Nainoa, the EMT who has arrived with a package. FedEx accidentally delivered it to his floor. I ask him about his newborn. He apologizes for any crying I might hear. I hear no crying. I am compelled to apologize for the sounds of my pet parrots. We exchange best wishes. I apologize for not wearing my mask. "Bro," he says, "You're in your home. That's fine. That's why I'm standing over here."

The sky outside my window is window-tinted and concrete-tinged, blue like some sweet one's baby blanket. The day is passing. I swerve into my pre-bedroom routine. Eventually settling into bed, I prop myself up against pillows, planning to read a paperback and doomscroll through my Facebook feed. My phone pings from my bedside table. I look at the message so that I can forget I received a message.

My iPhone says I have a new memory. If my phone tells me I have a new memory, then I should write about this in my memory journal. As soon as I begin journaling, I realize that my phone has told me what to write. A machine controls me: I would not be writing this if my phone hadn't pinged. I listen for other creativity triggers. A gecko cackles. When I hear that familiar, sharp chirp, I flash back to the meditation retreat thirty years ago. I've described that trip already, the occasion of the vagina-shaped soul-pot and the woman, Dewi who channeled the spirit of a medieval monk named Epiquo. In my previous telling, I set the retreat on Hawai'i Island, but in actuality these events took place at a repurposed monastery off the Pali Highway on the way into Kailua. Such details surface when I hear the gecko chirp.

I have made fun of New Age spiritual practitioners for much of my life, perhaps because of a defensive tendency to reject spiritual communities before they reject me. As the psychic at the retreat contacted her dead cleric mentor, a reptile sounded. In her channeling voice, the woman at the retreat said, "Hello, Gecko." She drew out the first word and spit out the second. Whenever I hear a gecko's cackle cut through Makiki noises, I say to myself, "Hello, Gecko." I channel her voice by remembering her voice. My phone has prompted me to write about this. My technology implanted a new memory without my consent. I wonder if I can come up with my own memories prompted by recollection and not by phone notification. A pair of stories comes to mind having to do with wet pasta.

My brother, Caleb, and his friends kidnapped me in Aurora, Colorado in 1968. They were second graders. I was five. The specifics of the story are hazy. The emotional residue persists. My brother ordered me to follow him over to his friend's basement. Excited to leave the living room of our townhouse, I ran behind the older kids. A Pixie Stick had been promised. At that point in my life, I would have done anything for sugar. I trusted Caleb. He is my family member. He led me by the hand across a courtyard and into a home where I'd never previously set foot. He told me to wear a blindfold.

We sat on a couch, apparently unsupervised. I heard a girl's voice tell me to put my hand in a bowl of monkey brains. "Do it!" she said. "Put your hand in the bowl!" I hadn't even finished kindergarten. My eyes were covered with black fabric. In a stranger's house with my brother at my side, I would do as ordered. Terrified and crying. Screaming. I now understand, fifty-five years later, that Caleb and his friends were tricking me to believe that benign food items were objects of gore. They told me the grapes dipped in mayo were eyeballs. I put my hand into cold pasta. They told me I was fondling monkey brains.

I know a woman named Keisha Zan who ate her own placenta. I'm not judging. I'm using this detail to pinpoint her as a person with a specific attitude about motherhood. Keisha and I have a mutual friend named Elle Tobago. Keisha's daughter, Olivia, was in daycare with Elle's daughter, Jane. Keisha invited Jane to Olivia's sixth birthday celebration. At the party all the children were invited to stick their hands into bowls of cold, wet pasta. Soggy rotini. Sheets of limp lasagna noodles. Angel hair. Clumped, moist orzo. The activity was called Sensory Noodles. Elle told me that a few days after the party, all the parents got phone calls from Keisha about possible exposure to hoof and mouth disease.

NINETEEN

AT SUMMER CAMP, I NEVER COULD TELL A GOOD GHOST story. Turns out at summer camp, I lived through my own ghost story. Camp Ebb and Flow in the California mountains above Palm Springs in the 1990s. I call this story, "The Fiend." It's so funny, too. I don't mean the Fiend story is funny—though I'm sure it is in some ways. I mean it's funny how as a kid at summer camp, I'd sit by fires on campouts shivering with fear when the counselor told stories about killers with meat hooks loose in the woods. If I ever tried to tell a ghost story myself, I could never avoid the most ridiculous cliches: *Humans can lick hands too.*

The scariest stories exist in my memory more than in my imagination. Horror stories are fun to make up, but not so fun to live through. Telling my father on the day after he sent in my last college tuition payment that I was gay: that was a horror show. Telling my friend Quantum that I never wanted them to call me again, not until they had been clean and sober for one year: that was kind of horrific also. Facing the mirror can be scary. But if I am focusing specifically on ghost stories and that terrifying Halloween kind of dread, then I would have to say my scariest story is my Fiend story. That story has some layers to it. Each layer evokes its own kind of horror.

After three years of being a Camp Ebb and Flow camper, I was invited to return as a counselor-in-training (C.I.T.) in 1989. I was sixteen years old. The first layer of the story is the literal layer. Assigned to the youngest campers, I did my job. I assisted the two head counselors with making sure the nine-year-old campers got to their swim classes and their horseback riding lessons. I'd typically start the fires on campouts, and if anyone needed a credible voice to lead patriotic singing at the Sunday sing-along, I could do that. If I ever had downtime, I'd wander by the oldest camper cabin and see what the fifteen-year-old boys were doing.

The oldest campers at Ebb and Flow were closer to my age than the twenty-something counselors I had been assigned to work with. After dinner and before lights out, I generally found myself walking down the trail to the furthest cabin in the woods. A guy named Eddie Spiro told dirty jokes. A kid named Marvin Cashman had a stash of Ritz Crackers and Cheese Whiz that he would share rather generously. A line existed between my role as counselor-in-training and the campers' role as paying guests. It was a thin line. I had been them a year ago. I enjoyed talking to those guys in the oldest cabin. I enjoyed exchanging cassette tapes and talking about bands. I enjoyed listening to the shirtless punks in Cabin 15 tell salacious stories about sexual conquest back home.

The head counselor in Cabin 15 was Willie Clackford, a biology major at USC. Willie ran the riflery program. In the late 1980s, it was no political statement to teach teenaged boys to shoot guns at paper targets festooned with NRA logos. Or maybe it was, but it wasn't presented that way. Camp Ebb and Flow fancied itself as kind of a back-to-nature camp where boys could become men and men could act like boys. Elvis Presley owned a home on this same mountain in his early movie days.

Back in the 1950s, some Western movies had been filmed on what became camp property. The camp director, Mr. Bittman, wore Wrangler jeans and the kind of leather hat Clint Eastwood could have worn in a spaghetti Western. Willie Clackford knew how to point and shoot a gun, but he had other interests too. He knew a lot about seventies porn. If you got him talking about his biology major, he'd tell you more than you ever wanted to know about the roosting patterns of ravens and crows. He knew how to do this trick where it looked like his penis was talking. He could recite proverbs from the Bible from memory. Early into the summer session, one of the fifteen-year-olds under Willie's supervision asked me if I had heard about the midnight rock throwers. I didn't know what he was talking about.

This is about where the second layer of this horror story should get a little bit of attention. This kid who first told me about the rock throwers was from Florida. Most of the Ebb and Flow campers came from Southern California, from San Diego to Santa Barbara to San Bernardino. We had a contingent from the Bay Area, and if someone told you they came from Oregon, Arizona or Nevada, you probably wouldn't be all that surprised. But a camper from Florida was an anomaly. Why would anyone travel clear across the country for summer camp when there must have been plenty of options for outdoor recreation back home?

The Florida kid wasn't a super close friend. He was a camper, and I was a counselor. He and I got along. He wore a puka shell necklace all the time and everywhere, even when he wore nothing else in the outdoor showers, cold water only. We swam together. Mostly, he'd swim while I watched him move his skinny body. I was a lifeguard during free swims at camp. He was one of the few kids in Squirrel Lodge, the cabin for the fifteen-year-olds, to come to free swim. While the younger campers seemed to value opportunities for structured socializing, the older boys valued self-regulation. No one from Squirrel was going to go to an organized activity unless they had to. The fifteen-year-old from Florida in the puka shell necklace came to free swim every day. I noticed him noticing me.

I'll name my narrator, "Chet," and make him younger than I am, so I can set my ghost story in the 1990s. Maybe I said before this happened in the '80s, but let's make it the '90s. I'll say that I, as Chet, came out as gay to friends at the end of my college years. When I was a 16-year-old camp counselor, I was so full of inner-conflict that I didn't even know I was full of inner-conflict. I deflected the horror of my late adolescence by trying to be funny all the time. In seventh grade in Yucaipa, the small farming town at the edge of the so-called Inland Empire in Southern California, I was literally voted Class Clown by the student council. We all pretended it was a compliment, but I knew it was a loaded one at best. When I was around the bony fifteen-year-old from Florida at Camp Ebb and Flow, I recognized the same kind of character. He was the clown of his cabin. People liked him, but only when they were laughing at something he said or did. He wasn't invited to those poker games where the other boys sat on each other's beds in their boxers.

Here comes another layer of meaning in this horror story. There is a reason for the pop culture stereotype of the evil and predatory clown. Performance is exhausting. If people are laughing, maybe they are laughing at you. Florida kid and I made some kind of unspoken decision not to treat each other that way. We didn't make each other laugh. Instead, we tried to scare the shit out of each other.

I'd stick with bad ghost stories around the campfire. This is kind of embarrassing, but my go-to ghost story was some kind of retelling of the plot of Brian DePalma's *Dressed to Kill*. I am not proud of that. This is no story to be telling around a campfire. I really was not a skilled ghost story raconteur. The Florida kid was great at scaring me. After the afternoon free swim on the third day of camp, he walked up to me by the high dive and asked if I had heard what happened in Squirrel Lodge last night.

"No," I said. "What happened?"

The skinny Florida kid brought his hand up to his puka necklace. "You haven't heard about the Porch Walker?"

The Florida kid threw me my towel. I slung it over my shoulders and sat on the bench by the Buddy Board. He slipped his shirt back on. "There's been this incident happening in the woods at night outside our cabin."

"What kind of incident?"

He leaned into his story: at night a stranger is throwing rocks on the front porch of Squirrel Lodge. The rocks land on the porch and roll toward the front door of the cabin. The rocks, then, must be coming from the woods. Twice the invader has walked across their porch in heavy boots. Four or five people have seen his shadow. A few folks think he walks with a cane.

I was astonished. I ran from the swim dock up the trail to Bunny Rabbit, my own cabin. I can't remember what I said to the Florida kid, nor can I remember his facial expression as he described their forest intruder. I remember the sound of his voice. I remember the slope of his scrawny shoulders. I remember telling one of the Bunny Rabbit Lodge co-counselors what the Florida kid described. The co-counselor shrugged and said something shitty about the Florida kid.

On the fifth night of the ten-day sleepover session, the story of the rock throwing porch walker went viral across the camp grapevine. That is a stupid way to mix metaphors, but it says what I mean. Everyone at camp was on hypervigilant alert for intruders. No one had heard the camp director and his wife, the Bittmans, say anything about the rock thrower, but word in the trees had it that each of them was suspicious of an inside job. Counselor began suspecting counselor. The known pot smokers and the presumed homosexuals took the brunt of the accusation-based abuse.

The kid from Florida held my hand in his lap. He was reading my palm. He claimed psychic abilities. I did once see him make a radio go static with his mind. We had been listening to a station from Palm Springs that played "Smells Like Teen Spirit" one time too many. "I'd rather listen to static than hear this song again," I had said. With his eyes closed, he rubbed his temples with his fingertips. Static replaced music. He looked at me and smiled. He was giving me that same look again now as he rubbed a crease in the palm of my hand. In fortune teller mode, he asked me if I wanted the good news or the bad news first. I said, "Give me the bad news." He told me my hands were sweaty. Drawing my hand back, I said, "Are you for real?"

The camper from Florida said the bad news was real. He said I was going to be blamed for the porch walker's mayhem. I asked him what the good news was. He kissed me on the lips. I felt his tongue make contact with my skin. I pulled back and screamed. We were sitting at the bench by the Buddy Board again. I leapt up, looking around in all directions. The Florida boy told me to relax. He told me no one saw anything. He said he was sorry. I told him it was okay. I said I was going to go back to my cabin. I was the sixteen-year-old. He was two weeks from his sixteenth birthday. He seemed in charge. We each stood there and stared at each other without speaking.

By lunch the next day, everyone in the dining hall was talking about a specific cassette tape. While the campers in Squirrel Lodge had all been on a mandatory horseback ride up to Knotty Point, someone had slipped an unmarked cassette into the tape player owned by Riley Gavin, the assistant counselor in Squirrel Lodge. Riley had been expecting to relax to some Run DMC, but when he pressed play, he heard a deranged and breathy voice say, "I am the Fiend. I am the Fiend. I am coming to kill you all."

It's been decades now since this happened. I don't know if I'm getting the details down as they exactly occurred. The porch walker threw rocks that rolled toward the cabin, so they had to be coming from the woods. Now there was an intrusive and threatening voice on a Run DMC tape. Mr. Bittman, the camp director, still hadn't made a public statement but the rumor going around was that he was about to get the county sheriff involved. All the boys in Squirrel Lodge came together like fingers in a tight fist. I suddenly felt like an outsider. I walked over to tell them to stay strong. None of my friends invited me inside.

The tape must have been placed when someone knew the Squirrels would be out on their trail ride. Every Squirrel counselor and camper went on that horseback ride. This means they were all clear. The call was not coming from inside the house. The timing also suggested, however, that the Fiend was no vagrant from the highway. Whoever put the tape in the assistant counselor's boom box knew the camp activity schedule. Signs pointed outside the walls of the cabin, but inside the walls of the camp.

On the night of the Fiend tape discovery, Mr. Bittman took most of the younger campers over to Idyllwild on a school bus to visit the Idyllwild Playhouse to see a live, local version of *Company*. As I was C.I.T. with the nine-year-old campers, I went along as a chaperone. By "Ladies Who Lunch," it was obvious that something was happening back at camp. News didn't travel as instantaneously in 1989 as it does now. Somehow, though, word had moved from Camp Ebb and Flow to the Idyllwild Playhouse. We whispered to one another in our seats. We gossiped at intermission. A shooting back at camp: that's what the story was. We were to stay with the youngsters until the end of *Company*. An older counselor claimed to speak for Mr. Bittman who was already on the road in his BMW, driving back to camp with his wife. The senior staff had apparently decided that if we brought the young kids back to a chaotic situation, it would only make things worse. Mr. Bittman would calm things down before the end of the musical. People kept talking about a shooting victim.

Obviously, it was impossible to enjoy the amateur Sondheim show. We put the campers straight to bed as soon as we got back to camp. The kids in my charge knew something was happening. They had heard of the Fiend. Some of them thought he might be loose. A couple nine-year-old boys were crying. News was hard to come by. No one was allowed to go out of our cabin for the night, but some counselors gathered secretly to report news and spread gossip. Eventually, I heard the shocking news: Willie Clackford, the riflery instructor, shot Butch the Goat, the camp mascot, by accident.

On the night of the shooting, the denizens of Squirrel Lodge had come up with a plan to catch the porch walking, rock throwing Fiend. Tying fishing line to trees all along the perimeter of their cabin, suspending three horse harness bells to the fishing line, they would wait for the invader. When the line was tripped and the bells rang, they would catch the Fiend in the act. No one knew Willie Clackford would actually take to the porch at sundown with a .22 rifle.

It happened before the sun even went down. Willie was picking his vantage point on the porch. He needed to decide whether he would sit in a chair or lie down on a blanket. He was a better shot on his stomach, but he thought maybe if he shot from floor level, he'd miss his target. He was only meaning to practice. He wasn't going to pull the trigger. Apparently, Willie snuck back to the cabin while a number of campers and counselors watched *The Never Ending Story* projected onto a sheet tacked up on a wall in back of the Dining Hall. He had his gun, but only for the purpose of establishing his positioning and his sightline.

When the bells rang, Willie couldn't help himself. This was the warning system they had devised. Willie was keyed up on Folgers instant, Pringles and cheap banana pudding. There was a shot and a squeal. In the version of the story I heard, Willie knew he messed up as soon as the bullet left the barrel. When the shot was fired, campers and counselors came running. The boy from Florida was the first one to discover the gunshot victim. "It's Butch the Goat!" he announced. The camp mascot was bleeding out under a spruce tree. No one could believe what was going down.

On the way to breakfast the next morning, I was stopped by Mr. Bittman as I stepped onto the main path to the dining hall. He grabbed my wrist. I pulled my hand from his grip. He spat out an order to follow him to the woodshed. He literally was taking me to the woodshed? I didn't have any choice but to comply. As we entered, I saw Ms. Bittman standing behind a table with a tarp over a lump. Maybe it was the smell: I knew immediately what was under the tarp.

Butch the Goat. Mr. and Ms. Bittman wanted me to look at the rotting corpse of our beloved camp mascot. I did like that goat. Even though it had horns, it was gentle and friendly. Mr. Bittman pushed me forward. When Ms. Bittman pulled the cover away, I closed my eyes as fast as I could. It was too late. I saw the gore. I felt terrible. I really liked that goat. I didn't have anything to do with Butch's death.

They made me sit on a chair where I could see the dead goat's body. Flies swarmed. I was afraid to open my mouth to protest. Mr. Bittman began his inquisition. It turned out he was holding the very same cassette that ended up in the assistant counselor's tape player, the one that said, "I am the Fiend."

"Do you recognize this, Chet?" Ms. Bittman asked.

"That's not my tape."

"It's a Memorex, Chet." Chet is the name I've given my character in this story. I suppose I am trying to establish distance from my point of view character, but it's not really working. When I tell this part of the story, it all comes back as if it happened last week. "We've taken a look at the cassettes you display on the shelf above your bunk." He seemed to be pausing for dramatic effect. "All of your tapes are Memorex."

Was the Camp Director joking? "A lot of kids have Memorex. It's like the most popular brand. I don't know what you are trying to prove."

Ms. Bittman laughed and said, "It's funny you should use the word 'prove', Chet." The Director opened the woodshed door and motioned for me to walk out. So relieved to leave the corpse of Butch the Goat, I followed. I thought of the play *Antigone*. We had read it in English that year. I hoped someone would see to it that Butch received a proper burial. Mr. Bittman led me to his office, a wood paneled room on the other end of the main dining hall. He looked at me. I looked at the floor. In a ten-minute monologue, he lay out his case. The doctored cassette had come from my collection. I had been observed hanging around the fifteen-year-olds' cabin. I knew their routines. I had not been on the trail ride. The camp director was giving me an opportunity to confess. He clearly thought I was the Fiend. I was kicked out of camp without being given a chance to clear my name. My parents didn't even believe me when I told them I had been set up. I hadn't been given time to say goodbye to my friends. I never got to say goodbye to the Florida boy. None of it seemed fair.

A year to the day that I was kicked out of camp, I got a letter in the mail from the kid from Florida. He said he got my address from the camp directory. He asked me if I remembered that he had predicted I would be accused of causing all the trouble at summer camp. He wrote in clear block letters in blue ink. He told me how he had orchestrated everything. From his top bunk near the window, he'd throw rocks he had smuggled into the cabin and hidden under his blankets. Somehow, he'd lean out the window and throw toward the door. He had marked me as his fall guy. In his letter, he was telling me that he knew I didn't do it. He did it. He had only been kidding around when he started the rock throwing. It got blown out of proportion, and he didn't want the police to catch him. He said he didn't want to set me up. He had no choice.

"I knew you had secrets," he wrote. "I figured I could exploit them."

He knew I didn't look at him the way other boys our age did. It was a thing he had over me. He was a camper in the fifteen-year-olds' cabin. I was a sixteen-year-old C.I.T. We had kissed. He knew I was gay. He got me in trouble because he could get me in trouble. I never figured out why he wanted to harm me. Maybe he was gay and his behavior grew out of confusion. Maybe he hated gay people and his behavior grew out of a need to bully. Self-preservation couldn't have been his only motivation. He was a smart enough kid to have figured out some other way to cover his tracks if he had wanted to. The question of intent is the scariest part of this whole story. That's the layer of horror narrative I'm still trying to understand.

It kind of embarrasses me to say that I still dream about this Florida person. I don't have these dreams very often, but I think it happened the other night. I was dreaming that I had been hired at Camp Ebb and Flow as an adult. In the dream, I ran the swimming program. The kid from Florida sat on the porch of Squirrel Lodge, still looking like he did when I last saw him decades ago. I woke up and had no idea what this dream indicated, other than the fact that I still carry those Fiend characters inside myself. I recognize that I haven't forgotten the past. That right there is the deepest level of interpretation for the Fiend story: I recognize I am haunted by memory.

TWENTY

ONE WAY I WANT TO SEE YOU IS WITHOUT GLANCING sideways. I am not being literal, though I do live with the aftermath of retina surgery. When it comes to the left eye, my peripheral vision is most reliable, though not that reliable. I can't see more than shadows. My father is not on social media, but he prints racist fliers and posts them in the elevator of his nursing home anonymously. If I tell stories of his casual hatred, people look at me sideways. Surely, I am exaggerating. I say that I love him because I do. I know love can be a trapdoor as much as it can be an open window.

One self-serving thought: if anyone has read this manuscript this far, they will understand that I may indulge in writing that swerves away from the strictly narrative. I want to write a prose poem section. I believe that life becomes story, but it doesn't happen as story. Life happens as moments, events colliding into events, joys and terrors manifesting simultaneously and in complex relationship.

The English teacher at boarding school was so popular that the eventual king of a Middle Eastern nation praised him for his pedagogy at a graduation ceremony. In 2016, after the teacher was dead, an official inquiry uncovered decades of that popular teacher's sexual abuse of teenage boys. I am still so vague when I refer to a specific person who sexually harassed me when I first came out of the closet. No one believed me at the time, and no one believed me when I tried to talk about it a couple of years ago. What do we see when harm walks into the room? Flowers in pretty vases distract the eye from focusing upon the hand that cut the stem.

One way I want to hear you is with ears that listen for revelatory kinds of silence. It is difficult to get anyone to consider that asexuality can be anything other than a way to justify the existence of the broken parts. One way I want to see you is without glancing sideways. The sportswriter's tribute to Junior Seau, the deceased Hall of Fame football player, said the man "committed" suicide. Even though I generally avoid the comment sections on sports websites, I decided to write a note about how "died by suicide" made more sense as language construction.

People commit murder, sin, crimes. Suicide is most accurately described as the way the terminal disease of depression—and in Seau's case, chronic traumatic encephalopathy—ends life. The writer on the sports website thanked me for my comment, changed his text. A few sports-fan commenters questioned my masculinity. I told them I question my masculinity all the time. My masculinity has told me it has no problem with these kinds of interrogations. After I read through the comments on the sports site, I went to a museum, looked at art, then sat at a beer joint and read some.

When I travel, big books help me mark time. I read the pages in the Pessoa biography that describe how the Portuguese poet's best friend poisoned himself slowly with strychnine. Fear is a slow roach working a blood stain, feasting on loss. In the art museum, they hung the Van Goghs and the Monets in the room adjacent to the psychedelic Grateful Dead posters. I respond positively to the juxtaposition, the invitation to connect the seemingly unconnected.

Let's go abstract, maybe a little. Fear kills to claim what could never be gathered. Joy is wind, sacred vapor. Joy is sand. To sift is not to fist. To grip is to own. Fear's a land grab. Joy prompts me to wander through fields of experience like a canyon fox. Feed need. Chase butterflies. Forget to want. Sometimes vulnerability is a kind of strength. Sometimes vulnerability is an unlocked door.

The story I'm trying to tell is not exactly a story. The story I am telling is sitting in the big wooden chair angled toward the window at the brew pub in the town I visit but don't live in. Beer is on the table. A guy nearby sits with his friend. Each holds a phone, and while they pause every now and again to talk about sports, they mostly sit quietly and look at their screens. The story I am telling sees something in its screen that I can't see in my screen. We sit side by side. My story asks me if this is going to be about masturbation again. I tell my story I am not writing about masturbation. The story I am telling asks me if my father still lives in Fargo. I remind the story that it already knows my father lives in Fargo, and my story shrugs, goes back to its phone scroll.

The story I am telling is not interested in how ironically I wear my pink Converse. If the story I am telling could ask me why I can't commit to a beginning, middle, and end, I would look at the guy in the brew pub with the green hair sticking out of his cap. I dyed my hair blue three days before I came out of the closet in 1999 at the age of 36. My follicles protested and my hair fell out. My teacher in graduate school sent me a copy of his book on asceticism. In my rambling thank-you email, I told him I thought it was possible for asexual people to have sexual fantasies. Mine usually unfold in the third person. I thought we were having a serious conversation. He ghosted me, never wrote back. Was it because he thought I was coming on to him? I wasn't. My other friend thinks maybe my former professor ghosted me because I said I was asexual. Maybe he wanted to come on to me. In the bar in the town that is not Fargo, I think about the time my father made the racist joke about the white buffalo.

This is not exactly a story of one thing that happened as much as it is a story about all I can remember when I think of what happened when I started calling myself asexual. The story I am telling rolls their eyes and moves their thumbs super-fast on their phone screen. The beer-drinking friends are talking about cribbage. The story I am telling isn't even trying to hide the fact that they are eaves dropping on these cribbage folks.

Make it funny. Make it nice. Make it up to me. Make it go away. Make it over. Make it about shame again. Make the humiliating story about the drive over the Pali into a poignant reminder to be grateful for opportunities to learn more about self-preservation. Make it stick. Make it like they do in the restaurants. Make it sing. Make it work better. Maybe try new batteries. Maybe it makes most sense to learn how to make mayonnaise with a bowl and whisk. Make it more viscous. Make it a poem about a sex crime. Make it a memory thing. Make it about that time in creative writing class when Stephen Dunn, the famous poet, told me I seemed like a person with interesting life experiences who knew absolutely nothing about writing poetry.

Make it murder. Make it happen in boggy marshland on a wet and foggy night. Make it play the song about the long black veil. Make it more horrific. Make it order the smoked octopus. Make it more of a science fiction thing. Make it a loop in the continuum. Maybe the father is his own grandson because he went back in time and had sex with his mother's mother. Make it repulsive. Make it clear that if you're going to refer to Leviticus, then I'm going to refer to Oedipus. Make it less about more and more about less. Don't feel like you must resolve the note. Make it sound like chocolate tastes. Make it resonate like a plucked wire.

Somewhat typically, a student in my high school English class asks why we are reading this Emily Dickinson poem today. I have responses in my head that circle around questions about the nature of truth. I've responded to questions of "Why are we studying this poem?" in the past by suggesting that poetry is both useless and essential. We don't use poems to respond to legal obligations nor to form shopping lists, but we'd have trouble finding a human civilization that didn't have a culture of chant, song, lyric, and/or rhyme. Verse craft as evidence of being alive: that's the kind of defense of poetry I mount these days. I sell the idea that to shape words on the page is to mimic the way our tongues form sounds in our mouths.

Poetry asks me to bring words inside and conform them to the shape of my skull, the contours of my Dutch room. I don't own words. I don't rent them. Words exist as common property. Words are sentient life-forms with their own autonomy. As soon as I speak or produce the page, the words stop belonging to me. I wrote a letter to this friend I've been struggling to communicate with lately. In the letter, I tucked in a page of a poem I'd written that day. I never heard back from her. At first, I thought my specific poem offended. Then I wondered if the offense comes, not from my metaphors and images, but from my assumption that poetry is an appropriate way to repair friendship. I consider the analogy of prayer. If I tell a conflicted friend that I will pray for them, the friend may look at me and wonder if this is an act of compassion or condescension. Write poems to reflect, not to deflect. I intend to write about asexuality. Any time I tell someone this, they look at me like they feel sorry for me.

The activist writer leaves a legacy of sacred exhortation. We must create big fictions or poems that bulldoze rather than poke like dull sticks on thick skin. Point the camera at the vulture. Point the camera at the dead flesh the vulture circles. Don't point the camera at the beautiful tree. Stop making piano jingles. I wake up with a dream in my head, contorted recollection of some kind of contest I was losing. In college, I drank my housemate's cranberry juice. She'd been rationing it to treat her yeast infection. Once I was swindled by a carny. Perhaps the preferred term is carnival worker. I lost forty bucks at a ball-throwing game. During worldwide pandemics, I stay on my couch. June, 2020. George Floyd is murdered. Societal confrontation with entrenched racism? I stay inside and read old Russian novels.

I sent my friend a text about lunch. I couldn't meet in the park because my car battery died. If you give me a bullhorn, I will lose it in the backseat under the clothes I meant to take to Goodwill. My creative lens points inward more than outward. The act of getting out of bed is as routinely private as the act of eating an oyster. I do care about polluted waterways. One time I stood at the raw bar for an hour without ever tipping the shucker. Over the riot noise, I hear the sounds of my own regret.

I know high school writing teachers who think it is important to talk with students about audience. Who are you writing this for? I don't think it's a terrible question. I also believe any reader can pick up anything and, if the thing is well-crafted, or even if it's not, find some opportunity to be moved. What's the difference in implication between the questions "Who are you writing this for?" and "What are you writing this for?" For a brief time at the turn of the century, I ran a lot. On one visit to The Running Room, a shoe store on Kapahulu, I told the salesman I didn't like to run competitively. I just liked to run. He silently laced up my Adidas.

A year later I was running a marathon. Eventually I developed foot injuries. I ran for myself because I live in a body. I ran with other bodies because I live amongst other bodies. I challenged myself to move faster because I noticed what other bodies do. I hurt my feet. I write about asexuality because I live in human skin in worlds made by human language. I have interacted with other humans with bodies and skin. I suppose the word "interacted" is doing a lot of work in that sentence. I use language with other humans with bodies and skin. My back hurts now more than my feet. My voice feels strong and tired at the same time. I exist because of intercourse, but I don't think that intercourse is the purpose for my existence.

To write to justify my faults and shortcomings is to write something more boring than dream recollection or the argument the church lady from St. Andrews wanted to have about gay marriage with Jack at the *Rigoletto* intermission. My strengths are my weaknesses, and my weaknesses are my strengths. I am balancing a beautiful glass orb on top of a pile of cigarettes. To float atop a stack of flimsy death tubes, the handblown globe must defy gravity. To surface above a cloud of perceived doom, I must defy anxiety.

Awareness of weakness helps eliminate weakness, but awareness of strength can diminish strength. When, for example, I know I am trying to be funny, fewer folks laugh. On the other hand, if folks laugh when I wasn't trying to be funny, I become offended. Oh, do I amuse you? Heat rises. When hot weather comes, I want to stay low. When I donated my old car to the Kidney Foundation, I came to understand that the decision to get rid of my old vehicle did not get rid of my old vehicle. Including awkward phone calls and notarized documents, the end of my relationship with that car necessitated participation in rituals of transition.

Ending involves removal. Decision. Incision. Excision. Six weeks after they hauled it away, I saw that Honda Element parked at Ala Moana Beach Park with my old plate numbers and someone else's cap on the dash. My shortcoming is not so much one thing as it is a folder full of tendencies. I tend to write about the deaths of people I don't necessarily have permission to write about. All over the Covid map, bodies pile inconveniently. I tend to end my poems with concrete imagery.

Squeezed at the middle like a toothpaste tube, like that mustard bottle in the door of your fridge, you wake up hard to empty sometimes. Weight of worry is your way sometimes. You pull your belt tighter each morning. This is not metaphor. In the morning when you wake up, you thread the only necktie in your closet, the Three Stooges novelty tie, through the beltloops of your khakis. Weave through, loop into loop into loop, pull and knot. You have not owned a real belt since before quarantine. The leather belt you bought at Liberty House in 1998 separated at the buckle just as you started working from home. How can a belt separate at the buckle? Are you asking me this? It's a parrot thing. They chew rough. They are also attracted to shiny objects. I don't really want to get into it.

During online learning and pandemic times, you became a square of a face in a screen. You taught your classes, talked to your mother, took meetings with supervisors, all from the neck up, face only. You tied your pants with a Three Stooges novelty necktie on the days you wore pants without drawstrings. How were you supposed to buy a new belt anyway? Goodwill was closed. The mall was closed. I have too many boxes from exploitative shipping conglomerates in my closet already. I have switched over to first person. I replaced you, left the old self with the broken belt on the floor of the old car. I don't drive much right now. Nowhere to go, and I stopped wearing glasses. They fog up when I wear a mask. Only one eye works anyway. I wear a mask all the time now. Standing at the corner, squinting, standing on the beach, toes on the verge of submergence, I wear a polyester Three Stooges novelty tie through my belt loops. Squeezed tight at the waist, I'm just waiting for the joke to land, waiting for the light to change, waiting for the tide to rise.

Someone should write a book about how arrogance can be mistaken for bravery. To remind the world of your own existence is brave if you are often made to feel invisible. To remind the world of your own existence is less brave if you often make others feel invisible. Someone should write a book about how wanting something from others affects the way we look at others. I met someone once who had self-published a book full of old-timey ice cream soda recipes. He told me that if something he said offended someone, that was the other person's problem, not his problem. I think that is how he defined free speech for himself. He was free to offend. He made his money in the funeral industry.

Someone should write a book about ways straight-cis-white-men with money use language to cultivate power. Someone should write a crime thriller where the impoverished driver of the getaway car is forced to choose between killing or being killed. Someone should write a book of prose poems investigating links between genre and gender. Someone should write a book about how having a sexuality is not the same thing as having sex. Someone should write a book about halving what one has. Some-. one should write a sexy book about asexuality. Only an asexual person should write a book that views asexual people through a sexual lens.

Actually, I'm not sure I believe that has to be an inviable rule. If a meat-eating person shares a vegan recipe, the recipe is accepted. If a vegan person shares a meat recipe, the validity of the recipe is called into question. Someone should write a book about vegan desire. Someone should write a book about vegan desire without making carrot or peach or eggplant jokes. Sexual vegetable humor is low-hanging fruit. If, on a scale of sexiness, I had to rank the voyeuristic act of watching an attractive person take the skin off a banana with their fingers or take the skin off a roast chicken leg with their teeth, I'd probably go with the lips on the greasy drumstick, to be honest.

Yesterday I opened Desiree's letter, red envelope with white paper inside like fists inverted, the blood and then the knuckle. She writes of how she taught poetry to elementary school kids, then sat on the floor after they left and cried. Today I played "Here Comes the Sun" to high school students, the Nina Simone version. I had some notion that reading poetry could be like listening to music. My error in judgment: I have no idea how my students listen to music. That old thing: the way we see the wheelbarrow depends so much upon what's in our heads as we gaze. The new thing: maybe that's not it.

The week before Wolfman died, he sent me his Nina Simone box set through the mail. I didn't know at the time that he was going to swallow and drink what he swallowed and drank. I thought the music was a gift until I heard the news of his suicide. Maybe it wasn't a suicide. Maybe it was an overdose. I had stored the box under my bed. Pulled it out. Played the song. Here comes the sun. Here comes the sun. When I run at night, I can't see where I am going. My fear manifests as a twitch in my little finger. My hand is moving, but I'm not gripping. Maybe I'm grasping to make memory into archetype. Not every poem is about grief.

Not every song is about learning how to lose. The space under my bed is less metaphorical than abandoned. Remember that time when you said you could drink a gallon of milk in one sitting? Remember how each new day was a promise or a prayer? Zombie stories are grief stories too. Memory feeds dead life. Rough crunch. In the dream, I ate my computer like a cracker.

Neon Bates Motel lights. No one knows how much I love *Psycho*. The first time I saw it, my mother was too frightened to watch with me, and Dad was angry, if not drunk, so I viewed it in the den by myself as part of some kind of Hitchcock marathon week on 1970's, off-network, syndicated, L.A. TV. Scared. I'm watching it on my phone now in bed alone. My hobby is stuffing things. A man should have a hobby. I am quoting from the movie. Hard to quit once the movie begins. A boy's best friend is his mother. Okay, I'll stop.

Also, I acknowledge the difficult validity of arguments about *Psycho* and gender identity. When the horror movie villains are played by male actors in dresses and wigs, are we supposed to ignore the perpetuation of harmful stereotypes? Are we supposed to associate the character's evil with dominant culture's own fear of difference? My mother, what is the phrase? She isn't quite herself today. That's a *Psycho* quote too. Hitchcock's misogyny is another whole topic. We all go a little mad sometimes. We all can make metaphor out of the Bates Motel. I've become self-conscious about the fact that I started this paragraph ten days before Mother's

Day. The scene when Marion Crane discards the scraps of paper in the motel bathroom? That was the first time a toilet had been shown in a Hollywood movie. The shower scene comes.

So many cuts, from the drain to the eyeball, rotating. Mother, Oh God. Mother. Blood. Blood. What have you done? Anthony Perkins, the actor who brilliantly plays Norman Bates, was cursed by his success, by the way he could never be seen as anyone other than Hitchcock's monster. I thought he was great in *Friendly Persuasion*, a part he played before *Psycho*. Hitchcock led him through a dark tunnel. Bird fetish, methodical cleaning skills. His smile cuts too. Some bugs infest the jalapeno flowers on the only plant on my balcony. We all kill things sometimes. She was standing back there with a sandwich. That's another quotation from the movie. Cut. Copy. In my care, stuff dies.

During the first pandemic year in quarantine, I surrendered to sourdough, Dickens, and balcony meditation. After two years, the collective cultural consensus suggests it's time to emerge. I get the vaccine. I feel the egg crack. I conceive of breaking through the protective membrane. The mummy wakes to feed in a world it doesn't understand. Tell me I'm not the only one not having fun yet when I go out in groups. Every moment that might feel spontaneous feels fraught, like if I don't enjoy this fucking margarita, I'll never breathe again.

My one friend, Jasper, spent his first night out, after more than a year of pandemic quarantine, without me. I want to be alone in crowds. I want to disappear as the anonymous guy with a book in the coffee shop. If I were a shiny bead, I would roll toward the lens end of a kaleidoscope. Magic, turn, turn, light, turn, light, magic, magic, light. I pull the mask out of my pocket. Breathe into cloth. My beard got so long in quarantine that I felt compelled to read the Whitman biography. That's corny, but true. I walk outside without a mask, without a yawp. I project no luminosity. Each atom belonging to me perhaps shouldn't also belong to you. Last summer they had murder hornets. This year they have cicadas.

I am not feeling an itch at the base of my skull on the left side. I am thinking about getting another tattoo, but I am also thinking about not getting another tattoo. I am thinking about whether or not it's strange to pay someone to poke my skin with needles and color. I am thinking about how the best way to extract an eggshell from liquid is to use another eggshell. I am thinking about the time the teacher told me I was an earnest writer. My friend in Durango told me that same teacher allegedly impregnated his student and allegedly made her pay for the abortion. The story is gossipy. I am thinking about how skin reacts to touch.

I am not thinking about the article I read about the professional cuddlers who were forced to take their businesses online during peak Covid times. I am not thinking about respirators. I am thinking about asexuality only because I am thinking about love. I am not avoiding the topic of sex, but I am not at this time going to write about how in high school I took money to write sex poems for boys on the track team. I am not writing about everything I am thinking about. I am thinking about everything I write about. I'm not bragging. I'm confessing.

I am thinking of writing as others think of skiing: surrender to the mountain, to gravity. I am thinking of writing as others think of skinning: surrender to the blade and the bleeding. I am not thinking of the book *I Am Thinking of Ending Things*, and I am not thinking of ending things, but I am thinking of how things end. I am thinking about how I felt when I wore a sleeveless tee shirt with pockets in public. I am thinking about the words we use to describe violation.

In documenting my day, I'll begin with that moment when I drank instant coffee over the sink. I became jittery, then sent my homeroom students to another WebEx room for virtual assembly. In a mask in a classroom with masked sophomores in front of me, I teach the *Antigone* lesson. The sixteen-year-olds seem to enjoy the play, but I sense a split. Some want this story to reflect modern reality; maybe we should speculate about contemporary implications or dive into situational ethics. Others read this book the way they watch Marvel flicks or study the extended universe of the *Conjuring* movies.

They want to know who affiliates with which God. What happened in the last story? How does Aphrodite connect to Oedipus? Is there more than one Euridice? I frequently lose control of the conversation. The son of a friend of mine asked me the other day if I liked the *Star Wars* prequels. I said I did not so much. After this thirteen-year-old explained how important those movies were to greater *Star Wars* mythology, I told him I did not care about greater *Star Wars* mythology. I watch those movies for the space ghouls.

My friend's kid told me I was a disgrace to the *Star Wars* community. I'm pretty sure these sophomores in my English class think I am a disgrace to the *Antigone* community. I am thinking about how in the United States we are trying to go back to football stadiums and concert halls without masks. In India, cities dispose of bodies in mass burnings. In New York City a year ago they ran out of mortuary space. Refrigerated trucks served as morgues in California. The disposal of flesh is the story. My day ended with a plate of chicken meatballs, a THC gummy, one gin martini and organic bedsheets I ordered from the internet.

This is association-centered and not plot-centered because I'm not building to the moment of greatest tension. Michael asked if he should take me home via Kapahulu instead of the Ala Wai. I'm not withholding information in order to create suspense. When I create narrative about someone else's misfortune, I become a vulture. The car in front of us waved Michael around. The reason this is not plot-centered is because I witnessed someone else's humiliation the other night, right where

Kapahulu meets the H-1 intersection. This was the same Saturday night we saw the pig on the leash at Kapiolani Park.

When Diana makes cookies, she uses just the right amount of chocolate. Michael makes some noise, not so much of disgust or surprise, but more a squeak of discomfort, like he knows we should not be watching this man's surrender in the middle of the road. Another reason this is a collection of sentences and not a plot-centered narrative is because I am not reflecting on how someone else's pain made me a better person in the long run. And then I reread what I'm writing. What if I am doing that?

Michael states the obvious: a man is taking a dump in the middle of one of the busiest intersections in town on a Saturday night. Traffic snarls around him. One last reason this is not a story is I haven't figured out exactly when meditation and reflection can become exploitation and theft. Let's engage in some wordplay to deflect the awkwardness embedded in the anti-linearity. Sacred. Secret. Secretion. Desecration. Discretion. Surrender to surreal kinds of rendering. In the locked room where they keep the antique doll houses in the Dutch museum, I scream.

Most of my supernatural encounters involved drugs, so they weren't supernatural encounters. The Chicago airport featured blinking strips of neon over moving indoor sidewalks in the 1980s. Wolfman and I would drop acid and good sense to go out there on weekends. Back in the days before the terrorists won, you could find places in airports to entertain yourself during recreational psychedelic journeys if you were male and white and if your parents had money. On the el(evated train), trekking from Roger's Park to O'Hare, Wolfman and I collectively heard God command us via intercom to look out the window at the exact moment we passed a gigantic frog mural.

In Amsterdam, I overheard a woman in a bar say Britney Spears was a better singer than Bob Marley. That night in the shower I was visited by a fat angel who called themself The Homosexual Agenda. They didn't ask me to worship them, but they asked me to write a novel about worshipping them. Most of my supernatural encounters involved drugs, so they weren't supernatural encounters. Did I say that already? I have dead friends who covered their addictions with ritual. A hole in the ground is a tunnel that hit a dead end. The woman in the movie *Cat People* was from Serbia. I love the scene where she flays the lecherous psychiatrist.

TWENTY-ONE

I LIKE A GOOD COOKIE. MY FRIEND, DIANA, MAKES THE best tahini shortbread. I was looking for something equally tasty, but perhaps more evocative of flavors from my youth. The *New York Times* published a recipe for peanut butter rounds with Hershey's Kisses in the middle. I baked a batch. Mine looked kind of lopsided. I posted the photo on Facebook anyway. Some gay guy I know made jokes in the comments about how I obviously had an areola fetish. The cookies with kisses looked like nipples to him. This was in public social media space. My teenaged niece had liked the cookie picture. A former eighth grade student commented that she was going to make a batch with her kids. In my head I wrote the guy to tell him he didn't have consent to turn my cookie photo into a sexual joke. And then I worried I was prudish and humorless. I've known gay men who use sex humor to reveal hypocrisy and disarm the powerful. I've known other gay men who use snarky, bawdy comedy reflexively, as though they had become conditioned to substituting humiliation for love.

I love my father, but I couldn't spend time with him when we were both adults. Now that he has turned ninety and lives with constant nursing home care, I can be around him the way I can be around a sick patient in a hospital. I want to lift his spirits. I have trouble seeing him as anything other than a collection of his medical conditions. In February 2024, I took six family leave days from school and flew to Fargo to be with Dad as he recovered from pneumonia. Caleb, Dmitri, and Hattie flew in too. We met with his "care team" and helped pack up boxes of possessions he no longer needed. The first thing he said to me when he saw me was "You look better without a beard." I had a beard as I stood there by his hospital bed.

I look through the lens of my twice-detached retina. So much of what I see seems abstract and poetic. I speak in bird imagery. Only after careful rumination would I consider opening the door to the black raven room. Crow mythology belongs to others. Crow iconography has been used against others. Jim Crow is the obvious example. Gothic raven imagery provides one way to face loss. Nevermore. In Frank Capra's *It's a Wonderful Life*, a big black bird hovers around Uncle Billy in the Building and Loan establishment. I used to listen to music by The Black Crowes, a rock and roll band formed by long-haired white brothers who hated each other. The door to the black raven room is not a closet door.

My dad flows in and out of lucidity. I don't think he is suffering from dementia. I think he is choosing when and when not to pay attention to all that is falling apart around him. He is aware of his entropy. He cannot put his socks on by himself. He cannot feed himself. He cannot go to the bathroom by himself. My brothers and sister and I pack up his apartment and arrange for him to live in the place where he will receive 24-hour care. Caleb spends time sorting through Dad's finances. I am grateful to my brother for doing what I can't. Dad tells me to pick a flannel shirt from his closet. He says he wants someone to help him change his socks in the morning. How can I not love this person? I choose the blue plaid. At home in Honolulu, I push up the sleeves and wear it whenever the temperature drops below eighty degrees.

The Dutch Room hosts hallucination, locked space in my head, the room at the bottom of the museum in Amsterdam with all the miniature doll houses. Unlock the locked door to find open windows. In the room with the rocking chair, there is a linen curtain waving, wind struck. The black raven never screams. No painting of the black raven room could capture the science of various vortexes. Flash. Vector of light beam. What a fruitful mirror.

To make meaning is not necessarily to tell stories. To tell stories is to pretend that every experience translates into plot. Words don't have to line up for narrative. Words can be objects placed in piles like bricks on the floor in the sculptures of minimalists, Carl Andre and the like. I am not a minimalist because I aim to write about everything, and I think Carl Andre allegedly did something murderous that I obviously don't want to endorse. I would be a minimalist if all my sentences could exist only as shapes with ninety-degree angles. The rhythm of this paragraph is the rhythm of breath in an asthmatic buffalo.

Why can't I stop thinking about the time I drove with my father to the buffalo museum? I suppose that is the last time I saw him as my father. We passed the sign in rural, Eastern North Dakota that said God, Guns, Trump. Dad spoke unironically about how pure and peaceful the sentiment made him feel. I said, "There are opposing perspectives, you know. I'll give you mine if you want to hear it." We felt like father and son then. Conflict and attempting to connect.

When I visit Dad in the care facility in Fargo in February, I see him as an old man I want to assist. I think of the time in Redlands in the 1990s when I last saw my father's father. My dad and his dad were not speaking. Grandfather Lester ended up in a nursing home in the town where my mother lived. My mother and father were divorced. My mother visited her ex-father-in-law because she wanted to alleviate his pain. When she took me with her to bring him blankets, he didn't recognize either of us. My mom still called him Dr. Dyke. He was a man she took care of because she has always been a caregiver. She lives carefully.

Either one is never supposed to look a black crow in the eye, or one is always supposed to look a black crow in the eye. I can't remember which. I read in a parrot book that if you give parrots your side-eye and coordinate your blinks, your birds will be less afraid of you. My breath musters up phlegm pebbles as parables. Look out. Here it comes. The indulgence becomes a vice. The vice becomes a habit. The trouble starts. There is no reason to enter the black raven room. There is the shocking section at the end of the Flannery O'Connor story about the Misfit who shoots the praying woman because she wouldn't stop talking.

Leg. Computer. Television. Oops, I lost. The game is to quickly name nouns without repetition. Each noun must be unrelated in meaning to the noun that came immediately before. You can say, for example, cow and computer side by side because unless you are nitpicking at the most absurd level, those two words have no connotative or denotative similarities. If you said cow and milk, you'd be out. Cereal. Abstraction. Lettuce. Cup. Oops. I've eaten lettuce cups before. That's a connection. Lost again. Cowbell. Assertion. Head. Pig. Wonder. Chocolate. Ball. I didn't exactly lose that time, but I distracted myself with a memory. When I was five years old, my parents both worked in hospitals. They hired a nanny from England who took my siblings and me to the supermarket to buy candy. She said I could get a chocolate bar, but I didn't understand the concept of British accents.

I thought the nanny said I could get a chocolate ball. Imagine my disappointment when the picture of some sweet sphere in my head met the reality of routine checkout line candy. Potato. Manscape. Oops. I lost. Manscape's not a noun. And if it is, I don't want to think about it. The more I think about it, of course manscape is a noun. I just don't want to picture shaved male crotches right now. Cremation. Umbrella. Snack. Alligator. Tongue. Oops. That one is debatable. I would argue that an alligator is defined by its dangerous mouth, tongue included. I have never dreamed I have been devoured by an alligator, but I have gone to bed worrying I will dream I have been devoured by an alligator.

Sustain the game. Anxiety. Prayer. Nightmare. Memory. Regret. Oops. Lost again. Memory and regret are obviously related.

My very first memory: I watched a televised football game with my father. I've heard that it is hard to remember anything that has happened to us before we are five. If this memory actually happened, I would have been two or three. It's possible I have created a story in my head and have convinced myself it is a recollection. The memory is more a photograph than a movie. I am sitting on my father's lap in an apartment in Baltimore. I see red brick walls, blue shorts and a white button-down shirt. My dad is talking about Johnny Unitas. We are watching the Baltimore Colts. I am a queer passivist poet who loves the admittedly morally ambiguous National Football League. This memory serves as my football fan origin story.

In her book *Minor Feelings*, Cathy Park Hong tells stories about how the English language humiliated her as a child. She finds ways to break back, ways to use the barriers of imposed language to make art. I don't want to claim that I understand her experience. I don't want to steal or mischaracterize her argument. I mean to say she inspires me to consider the language of cultural expectation.

Before my parents got divorced, they had large, framed wedding portraits of each of my siblings hanging over their bed. There was a space for my framed photograph. I was never going to have a wedding portrait. On one occasion, during the years after college when I grew old enough to know what I pretended not to know, I asked my mother if she would ever put a portrait of me by myself in that spot. She said no. She never really gave me a solid explanation as to why not.

The ways I learned to talk about sex and love left silence and empty space. How do you answer the old friend from summer camp who asks you if you have a sweetie? Knowing him, you accept he assumes your sweetie would be female. If you tell him that you place yourself on some kind of asexual edge of some gay sexual spectrum, he's going to stare at you or laugh at you. The page is a cage or a canvas.

The demands of a paragraph are coffee cake crumbs, residue of what's left of an experience after consumption. My breath is coming out funny again. The space on the wall begs for one kind of picture in one kind of frame. In the most sacred spaces of the home I grow up in, I see signs of my erasure. Oh, how the bugs have prompted me to growl. Okay, now you are beginning to bug me. Let's climb on the topiary sculpture. I become aggressive when I ax to mulch of myself. I retreat to word play when I'm not sure what to say.

In another early memory of my father, I am sharing a room with Caleb in Denver. If this memory points to an actual experience, it would have happened in 1967 when I was four years old. On the other side of the bedroom from the bunk beds I share with my older brother, a chalk board hangs. Dad tucks us in and then draws us a picture. In my memory it is a cartoon dog and a flower. I remember finding a box of paints and a pallet knife in a drawer when I was seven. I asked my mother who this belonged to. She told me my father used to be an artist. I wonder whatever happened to the man who tucked me in by drawing flowers.

Follow the line the word makes. Track the movement from sound to meaning to implication to emotion. Cheese is not to breeze as music is to chocolate. There, their, they're. To, two or too. Follow the line the word makes. Notice where the mark fades, smudged. Paint evokes light without emitting light. Pixels evoke marks on a page. Emotion emission. Crimson and black dominate. Attract vampires. This is no sick sucking saga. Swish. Sway. Sashay. Not that sucking is sick. Seek freedom from secrets. One vampire wants so much to taste sunshine. Soak in the power of revealing light. Die from exposure. Follow the line the word makes. Narratives are blood if not bloody if not brooding.

The light-seeking vampire writes fantasy breakfast menus. One morning Dracula and Lestat will take their Benedicts on the lanai. In the dark I am less willing to surrender. Silence is less aggressive than swimwear. Follow the line the word makes. Through forests there are castles made of yesterday's promises. In the happy ever after, everything has ended. Sliver ballot. Vote for the proper conclusion. In the vampire's coffin there is a window. Streak through the heart. Follow the line the word makes. In the vampire's kiss, there's an essence of caraway.

My friend, Arturo Gonzales, can't understand why I don't visit my father more often. His dad died in a fire when he was fifteen. He tells me he'd give anything to spend just an hour with his father, Horacio again. Every time I have a vacation, Arturo asks me if I am going to see my dad. Mostly I say no. I tell him the stories of the racist fliers in the elevator. I tell Arturo the story about how my dad screamed at me over my admiration of Barbra Streisand. When I tell him about how Dad made me take down my Martina Navratilova picture, he nods. I can tell Arturo thinks I have rejected my father for ideological reasons. Such is the era we live in; it's easy for people to hear my stories and assume my dad's behaviors signify adherence to Conservative American values. My dad's behaviors go beyond political disagreement. He once left dog shit on the kitchen counter for my mother to find because he didn't like the way she had been cleaning his section of their shared bathroom. He votes for Trump, and Arturo seems to think this is the reason I have trouble being around him.

I tell my friend, Arturo, that we moved every two years because my father could not keep a job for longer. My father was educated at Exeter, Yale, Duke and Johns Hopkins. As a white, heterosexual, cisgender man with a sterling resume, he was easily a top candidate for jobs across the country. When he entered a workplace, he would alienate his colleagues. The first time I visited my father after the pandemic, he told me about the story of losing his job at the Omaha hospital. I won't tell that one. I'm still trying to understand it.

"Was he ever diagnosed with a mental illness?" Arturo asked. I answered this question honestly. "Did it only manifest when he was older?" I told him no. For some reason my closest friends have a hard time understanding that my difficulty with my father is rooted in something other than disagreement. For some reason, my closest friends don't want to believe our estrangement is not my choice. They think I don't get along with my father because his certainties offend me. To tell the truth, I worry at times that they are right. Truth is a social construct.

Virginity is a social construct. That's no new revelation. The word "virgin" can serve as suffix to words as distinct from one another as martinis, Appleby's, *Rocky Horror Picture Show* and anal. If virginity were not a construction of language, then this sentence wouldn't make sense. This sentence does make sense: "The night you lost your *Rocky Horror Picture Show* virginity, I lost my anal virginity to a martini virgin the night he lost his Appleby's virginity." Language is a human thing built by humans. Virginity is an act of language. The word asexual is a social construct. I don't think the concept of asexuality is made up. Don't make me pull out that story about the night in boarding school when I rode in the back seat with four other boys to the porn drive-in.

I know it sounds weird that they would show porn on a drive-in theater screen. I am perhaps embellishing the memory. We hid Wilson Whitcomer in the trunk of the car we borrowed because he was just sixteen and couldn't legally see R-rated movies. Wilson was not only the youngest kid in our group; he was also the horniest. He was willing to spend an hour curled up in the boot of a Buick in order to see some boobs on a big screen. The movie was called *Private Nurse.* I've googled. It exists as a campy, soft-core throwback. I can't remember a single thing about the movie other than drive-in sized breasts. I do remember throwing up in the middle of the night after we'd returned.

Wilson Whitcomer found me puking in the third stall. He assumed I'd been freaked out by the essence of sex. I had been freaked out by the essence of sex. I asked you not to make me pull out that story. Don't make me pull out the metaphor of the fennel bulb. Prudish and frigid are not so much social constructs as reflections of misunderstanding. Don't make me pull out. Don't make me put it in. I am not a virgin unless you are. Absence is not emptiness. Silence doesn't have to be a failure of noise. In case the fennel bulb doesn't make metaphorical sense to you, I ask you to consider how much of the flavor of fennel reveals itself in layers, starting with what's buried underground.

I wrote an intimate chapter about the aftermath of Wolfman's death and the family he left behind. I deleted the section. Didn't want to cross a boundary. Didn't want to tell yet another person's story. Silence can be a betrayal or silence can be one way to stop a betrayal. I only kind of remember the sound that came out of my body when I heard the news of Wolfman's death. I was at school outside on my phone. It's the kind of sound you can't remember. At the same time, it's the kind of sound you can never forget.

When Caleb, Hattie, Dmitri and I heard that our father was going to need constant care, we convened at Caleb's house in Fargo. Caleb, his wife Dorothy and their daughter Eleanor have been taking good care of my father for the past two decades. We, his four children, walked into Dad's nursing home room after he had suffered a bout of pneumonia. The four of us live thousands of miles away. He saw us and said, "Uh oh. Is there something I need to know?"

Sometimes I think of poetry as a way to dig into raw emotion and put words to feeling. Other times I think of poetry as a way to put pain aside and into a frame. Said another way, I consider how the power of poetry emanates from both its freedom from form and its adherence to form. Podcasters talk on the opera show about Stravinsky and the *Rake's Progress*. Freedom and rejection. My father has a history of showing up where I live, unannounced. After college I moved to Houston. Dad flew from California. He called from the airport.

While I worked, he stayed in my place, read my diary, and stored up questions about why I was so sad. I wanted to impress him, maybe make him happy, so I put on a Stravinsky CD. He drank his bourbon and told me my salsa had spoiled. In my early twenties I didn't understand that if someone liked some classical music, they didn't necessarily like all classical music. I didn't understand that salsa had an expiration date. My dad cursed, made some snide comment about how terrible the tonelessness was. *Rite of Spring* doesn't bond the mutual-fund-enthusiast -doctor-father to the Streisand-curious-second-son. Podcaster suggests link between the *Rake's Progress* and Johnny Cash.

Podcaster suggests link between weeping and moon worship. For once I'd like to write about a memory without thinking of my dead friends. In school today, I read my students the last ten pages of "Sonny's Blues." My voice can't contain the perfection of written language that echoes with the spirituality of a corner piano played by a recovering addict. Most milk and Scotch glasses cast no halos in barroom light. Podcaster ends with an excerpt from a book about scarred hearts. Sing or weep.

Today my sister-in-law Dorothy texted to ask if I wanted to chip in for a chair that will help my father stand up. What songs do you sing when skin and blood become monumental blossoms? To fade in sun is what flowers do. The countertenor sings in deliberate falsetto. Whenever I try to explain to my friends why it's hard for me to have a relationship with my father—. Oh, never mind. I've talked about this too much already.

I worked for a while in the nebulously defined role of "humanities teacher." I was asked to read a poem in an all-school assembly on the occasion of Memorial Day. I chose an anti-war poem by Denise Levertov. The administrator in charge of the event asked me to choose a more patriotic poem. I understand why people would want holidays to honor heroic soldiers without focusing on the inherent carnage of war. Another Memorial Day, I forwarded an email from an organization that was collecting DVDs and CDs for Veterans Hospitals. It seemed like such an obviously positive cause that I didn't think about the regulation against using professional email for personal purposes. I was told not to send such emails again.

My friend, Randy Everton, served in Afghanistan for the U.S. Army. He believes that the pandemic was a hoax devised to dethrone Trump. He thinks the 2020 election was stolen. I stopped following him on Facebook. We text each other on our birthdays. I consider him a friend. He writes poems about wounds he sewed as a medical serviceman in Kandahar. Memorial Day is the beginning of summer to most. Randy told me it is appropriate to tell a serviceman, "Happy Veterans Day," but it is not appropriate to wish any veteran a "Happy Memorial Day." That day is for remembering the dead. On the first Memorial Day of the pandemic era, I stayed inside for 24-hours. The next year on the Friday before Memorial Day, I read "On Flanders Field" to my English class.

It's somewhat of an obvious choice, but it seemed important to remember the permanence of sacrifice and loss. At that time, some of my students were sitting in front of me in the classroom in masks, and some of the students were sitting at home in front of the camera on their laptops, without masks. After I read the poem, we each watched separate movies using our own earbuds, laptops, tablets, and phones, selected from a list I made up. Several students watched *Spirited Away*. Several students watched *Parasite*. This May, Memorial Day comes in a year when college campuses are exploding with anti-war protests. Should I look for the right poem to read, or is it self-serving to use the suffering of others to feed my curricular needs?

I sit on the bed next to my father in the hospital room in Fargo. He asks me if I am still writing. I tell him I try to write every day. He asks me to send him my book when it gets published. The day before, he told me he didn't think he would make it to the end of spring. Today he says he'll read my book when it comes out in a year. Yesterday he asked us not to take his picture. Today he smiles when he sees the family selfie. He says he will use it as his Christmas card next season. Follow the line the word makes. Dad's favorite joke from my kindergarten days: what's black and white and red all over? It makes more sense if you hear the joke read. My dad's favorite joke from my seventh-grade days: I can't repeat it because it's so racist. The punch line has to do with sex between a football player and Richard Nixon's wife. When I was in high school, I left the dinner table unexcused when Dad started a joke by saying: "One homosexual said to another, my rectum is so well-trained."

TWENTY-TWO

FLOWER. OPEN TO SUNLIGHT. MAKE INSECTS DANCE. Summer movies earn dollars by fulfilling desire. Pour citrus and bubbles into gin this season. Cut flower. Wilted flower. Dried and pretty is the best we can hope to expect from the inevitable decay that comes with exposure to air and sun. Sweat standing up. Soak up cold by watching movies about Scandinavian misery. Embrace the heat by watching *Night of the Iguana* naked and alone. Love the smell of wet sheets. Love the skinner, hate the skin. Love the skin pouches where sweat pools. Summer as tunnel light. Beacon as promise. Promise me you won't confuse technology with photosynthesis. Though envy is green, I still love asparagus.

I am trying to tell you something. I am trying to tell you something. I am trying to tell you something about love. A flower cannot create love, but a flower can evoke love. Evoke tender illumination. The sun is never far from the central metaphor. How do I know a flower can't create love? We are not standing still in a cucumber patch. Flower is not flour, and shins are not shiny as sunscreen glows on bare stomach skin. I clutch paperbacks with my sandwich hand and sit on park benches in summer. In summer, hope is rest. The church down my street hangs Bible Camp banners with flame imagery. As electric as son is, blood is better.

As a child, I wasn't allowed to say that anything sucked. The word was a curse word in our family. My mother told me that her mother wouldn't let her say the word "sweat." She had to say "perspire" instead. That's funny to me. Funny as in odd. I won't say that my writing sucks, but I will say that I hoover up my experiences and turn them into stories.

Was Thoreau the one who said he wanted to "suck the marrow out of life?" It might not have been Thoreau.

After I left my family when my February North Dakota trip was over, I sat in the Fargo airport for three hours. The flight to Denver was delayed. In front of me, a man with two young sons buckled a suitcase. The family was Asian. A woman stood against a post, speaking on the phone in a language I didn't understand. She was Black and wore Muslim clothing. My brother, Caleb would read my description and ask why I had to mention the races and identities of these characters. He would not be wrong to raise questions. It was hard not to notice that everyone else in the airport was white. I have lived in Hawai'i for over thirty years. I'm not used to being in spaces that are not multi-racial. When I finally found my seat in the back of the small jet, I realized I'd be sitting next to the woman of color in Middle Eastern Muslim clothing.

I started writing this section two days before Father's Day. I am not saying it is a Father's Day chapter. I am childless and solitary. I have never been a parent. I can only imagine what it must be like to see your son become the kind of man you never thought you would sire. I read a reported story online today about a man who, as an 18-year-old gay kid, was kicked out of his house after his stepsister outed him to her father. Still a teenager, he slept on park benches and harvested lightly tainted food from garbage cans in the tourist district.

It's an old story. Every time I hear a queer version of the abandoned child tale, I feel pain. My teeth hurt when I inhale. My father's skin puffs under the eyes just as my skin swells when I am exhausted. We are talking on Zoom. In my father's face, I see not so much my face. I see the face of the father I want him to be. When I said I tilted toward asexuality, I was using tilt less in the pinball sense and more in the teeter-totter sense. The homeless teen in the story lives in New York with his husband and writes for a news show today. He speaks to his stepfather now even though his father has never apologized. Crush is to beer can as violate is to aperture.

If I tell people I am an asexual writer with a tendency to go for the poetic, they mumble. Most don't know whether to console me, ignore me, or ridicule me. Ridicule is probably too strong a word. If I tell people I am a poet and asexual, I get a lot of questions. Either that, or I get silent stares. I don't like it when people get fussy on Facebook about how "alot" and "irregardless" are not words. If I mention in a social media post that I am not looking to pair up with someone, I get a lot of hugging emojis. Curious friends have asked me what the difference is between asexual and traumatized. Curious folks have asked me what the difference is between asexual and incapable.

The woman of color in Middle Eastern Muslim clothing sits by the window on this flight from Fargo to Denver. She tries to tie the two ends of the seatbelt together. When she realizes this won't work, she taps me on the shoulder and points to her lap. I speak to her in English. She holds the two seatbelt ends and shakes her head. I ask her if she speaks English. She says no. I ask her if she needs help. She says yes. Much of this interaction is non-verbal. We gesture and emote. I buckle her seatbelt for her, trying hard not to touch her body.

I doze during the flight. As we descend, I wake up and see Colorado out the window far below. The woman turns to me.

"Chicago?" she asks.

"No," I say. "Denver."

"Chicago?" She is staring out the window.

"Denver."

"Kenya?"

The person in the seat in front of us turns around. He catches my eye and looks away.

"We are landing in Denver," I say. "Where is it you want to fly to?"

To talk about not wanting to have sex I must put up with questions about my sexual experiences. People want to know what I have and haven't done. I can imagine an erotic encounter, but I am never involved. I don't call myself a poet unless someone else does first. I've read Ben Lerner's *The Hatred of Poetry*. I've read Matthew Zapruder's *Why Poetry*. I've read *Sister Outsider*. If I tell people who don't read poems that I write poems, they could think I'm pretentious, delusional, or both. If I tell people who don't read poems that I am asexual, they ask me what kinds of poems I write. If I tell people who do read poems that I am asexual, they ask what kinds of poems I write. I have no musical aptitude, but my beard makes me look like I play the mandolin. I would like to embrace my true self, but first I need to work through some consent issues.

North Dakota beer pools in mugs in this Fargo rooftop joint. My brother's friend asks me if he heard me right. Did I say I was an atheist? Now I am talking about a different trip to Fargo. This story happened before the pandemic. My brother's friend has that slim look of a marathon runner. His wife tells me the Fargo Montessori community is super tight. I say that while I have wallowed in and have benefitted from the beauty of several holy stories centered around God or gods, I do believe they are stories. I am a writer, so I accept the sacred potential of fiction and poetry.

In the beginning was the word and the word was good unless it was godawful. Atheism allows me to stop listening to entitled men who want me to give them something vital. Atheism allows me to say no thank you when authority figures try to sell me worldviews built on the foundation of their prejudices. Atheism protects me. My youth pastor was fired for molesting a boy during a healing session. Atheism allows me to walk away when the ample men bring their power out to feast on the spirits of the vulnerable.

In the Fargo pizza joint, I tell the good-looking friend of my brother that my atheism allows me to dance with the demon who can't be a demon because demons only exist in stories to serve up lessons. My brother is a heart surgeon. I think I make him uncomfortable every time I meet his friends. To his credit, he always introduces me. Mostly I think my brother, Caleb is embarrassed by me, but he's not ashamed of me.

The woman of color in Middle Eastern Muslim clothing shows me her Fargo-to-Denver boarding pass. I tell her she is headed in the right direction. She doesn't seem to understand me. I point to the boarding pass and give her an open hands gesture, hoping she will interpret this as a question: where is the boarding pass to your next flight? Her Denver boarding pass is a slip of paper. I ask her if she has another paper. I can't figure out how to communicate effectively. After the plane lands, I smile at her and wish her well. She is way behind me by the time I see the flight attendant at the head of the plane. I tell the flight attendant I am afraid the woman sitting next to me is not sure where to go. The flight attendant says, "I'm not sure the woman sitting next to you knows much of anything."

Demons don't always look like those we demonize. I know one particular demon who wears pink corduroy. He collects hot sauce packets, squirts them on bagels with Velveeta and eggs at 3 AM, more munchies impulse than hangover cure. The fly fisherman in the pizza joint in Fargo asks me why I have to call myself an atheist. Why can't I say I'm agnostic? I say I call myself an atheist because I believe religion is fiction. I tell him I love fiction. Stories reveal truth even if they are not real. He shrugs, orders another round. My brother plays "Ride the Lightning" by Metallica on the jukebox. We drink without speaking for a while.

When I get to the gate end of the Jetway, I look back. I become Orpheus. The woman of color in Middle Eastern Muslim clothing becomes non-romantic Eurydice. She waves at me with a big smile. I stand over to the side of the Jetway and take a couple of steps toward her. When she catches up with me, I ask her if she wants help. Leading her to the gate agent, I report that she and I sat next to each other on the plane. I tell the gate agent that I don't know the woman. I say I worry she doesn't know where to go next. The agent understands. I tell the woman of color in Middle Eastern Muslim clothing that the agent will help her. She gives me praying hands and smiles. I touch my heart with my right hand and tell her I wish her the best.

For the first time ever, I am baking croissants from scratch. During the pandemic, I assign myself projects. As the butter slab solidifies during what I think of as Phase One of a multi-phase process, I take a bong hit, sitting on my bed on a Saturday afternoon. I stare into the eyes of myself at eight-years-old. The picture used to hang in the hall in the house I grew up in. When my mother sold that house, she told me it was hard to part with that picture of me with the guinea pig.

If I had known at eight when someone snapped a picture of me at summer camp in The Nature Area that I would grow up to be a guy in his early sixties who lived with parrots in Hawai'i, who identifies as gay and asexual, who writes prose poems, teaches school, drives a Subaru, and potlucks with specific loved ones, I think the boy-me would have been fine with that. I think the boy-me would understand the tattoos and the hippy hair. I tell the kid in the photo that I have always had his back. He sustains that innocent gaze as his way of letting me know he still likes chocolate ice cream. He thinks I should get the freezer fixed.

By the time I have walked from the C terminal to the D terminal in the Denver airport, I am crying. I am not usually a crier. I wish I was. When I was in boarding school, I discerned that crying would get me beat up, so I trained myself to hold my tears in. These days they don't come easily. In the seating area for my next flight to Phoenix, I am practically bawling. I know others are staring at me. I don't care. I cry because I am exhausted. I cry because my father wants help putting on his socks. I cry because I'm worried I didn't help the woman of color in Middle Eastern Muslim clothing enough.

Wynton Marsalis said, "I don't run from evoking things." To provoke is to poke. I'm not sure what invoke means. To evoke is to stoke promise, potential or possibility. When butter softens on the counter, a mixing bowl comes next. The song about love evokes the memory of the neighbor's tree. Eventually we all meet cancellation. I love how there is no stopping the rising sun. This morning, I will rise with intention. This morning, I will stay in bed an hour longer. My desire evokes desperation. No? Am I misunderstanding what the light reveals? The woodwinds evoke a moment. Sound evokes time. First, we were standing on the corner, talking. Then the light changed. Say it with me now: the longer we stand still, the more dust we collect. Soft butter is not the same as curdled milk.

My day of flying is a long one that begins in Fargo at 6 AM Central Standard Time and ends in Honolulu at 11:30 PM Hawaii Standard Time. At some point during the hours of introspection, I weave an inner monologue around the idea that I fell into the trope of the white savior. I was acting as if the woman of color in Middle Eastern Muslim clothing couldn't have survived without me. It's not so much that I believe confession leads to absolution. It's not so much that revealing leads to revelation. If poems unmask or make truth out of secrets, then metaphors work to show how imagined scenes can reveal truth. Even an image as well-worn as a road not taken tracks new ground when someone's trans daughter raises her hand and demands to be listened to. Can we go back to what we were first talking about? What's the difference between confession and revelation?

Confessions happen when we reveal secrets, while revelations happen when secrets are revealed to us. I used the word reveal in my definition of revelation. Re-veal: to be a baby cow again. Moon and unmooring. Moo. What's the difference between confessing, revealing, and exposing? If daylight never breaks, sleep still comes. In dreams I struggle to read the words on the page. When my friend read one of my poems about asexuality, he told me he didn't understand what I'd written. I must be a little confusing. Obfuscation is armor. I confess that I am more dragonfly than butterfly. I flit more than I flutter.

After my big 50th birthday weekend more than ten years ago, I got pulled over for a lapsed safety inspection. The police response was overwrought. The first patrolman called for backup. I was handcuffed and driven to a substation. The only place to go to the bathroom was in a jail cell. My brother from North Dakota had been visiting. He was in the car with me, paid my bail, took off in my car. He drove to the airport, got on his plane home. His pregnant wife was back in Fargo awaiting his return. I was fingerprinted and given a court date. I walked three miles back to my condo, too full of shame and silence to call a friend or pay for a ride. My brother texted a picture of the parking garage stall where he'd left my car at Daniel K. Inouye International.

Eventually all charges were dropped. An administrative error had marked me as a suspect under a bench warrant. After a judge in court apologized to me, they returned my bail money. My brother and I had a few things to discuss. I was angry with him for abandoning me. He was angry with me for needing him. He called me a little girl. We don't talk about those events much anymore, and we don't talk about religion. He used to live next to an interesting couple. The husband designed productions for Broadway theaters. He mostly worked remotely from Fargo because he liked the flat land and clean air. The man's wife taught religion classes at a nearby Bible college. She and I became Facebook friends. She wrote a book that her publisher rejected because it wasn't homophobic enough. She got a new publisher, posted pictures of herself with tape over her mouth and wrote about how she had been censored. I wrote her an email once to tell her I was grateful for her allyship. I tried to get her to correspond with me about mainstream Christianity's contempt for queer people. She never emailed back. She may have felt like I was baiting her. I wasn't. I was looking for her spiritual affirmation.

To make croissants from scratch at home without appliances other than hands and a rolling pin, I must accept my limitations. First batch was objectively a disaster. On a whim I bought something at Safeway called Amish Butter, neglecting to notice how much salt it contained. When the first croissants became savory bread pudding, they were less terrible. Success at most crafts involves wisdom gleaned through touch. Press too hard on the rolling pin and the butter squirts out. Don't press hard enough and the flour and butter will resist lamination.

When I woke up last Sunday morning, my intention was to run to the store quickly, return, and bake the dough that rested overnight in my fridge. My car wouldn't start. My new car had a dead battery. I called AAA. To call repair service for a new vehicle still wearing temporary plates is to feel shame. I've skipped the fun part of the ownership process and jumped right to that part when possessions nurture insecurities. In the parking lot, my problematic neighbor told me I should drive my car for half an hour now that it's started. Before I knew it, he and his wife had convinced me to drive them to Zippy's Kahala for breakfast. Over eggs and Spam, we talked about the Vietnam War again.

The pastry goes in the oven later than I'd planned. This time my homemade croissants look and taste like what I might buy in a bakery. A mediocre bakery. I still must work on cutting angles with precision. I still must work on proofing and rising. I steal the obvious Maya Angelou line, type it into this manuscript, and then I delete because my usage might be thievery. This triggers a memory of another time in another writing class. Approve the transaction to terminate plans for developing that story strand. I am caught inside several transitions. I stare at the cursor and press return. I hope the woman in the airport arrived safely at her destination. The more vulnerable my father is, the less I resent him. I peak inside the oven and inspect my pastry. I'm somewhat surprised. The croissants have puffed up and turned brown. It was hard for me to show vulnerability when I was a child. The batter doesn't leak as much butter this time. I anticipate an airy rise.

TWENTY-THREE

I FINISHED THE FIRST DRAFT OF THIS BOOK IN FLAGSTAFF, Arizona where I was visiting a writer friend from graduate school, Larry Lin. He told me he wasn't used to seeing me work in paragraphs. I knew what he meant. When I sat in classes with Larry during our MFA years fourteen years ago, I was drawn to prose poetry and braided lyric essays. My brilliant word experiments were neither brilliant nor experimental. I wrote a novella without the letters "E" or "R." I handed in workshop drafts with asterisks and numbers and words all over the pages. In seminar discussions I'd say things like, "The sentence is a jail cell." Cringe.

I don't have any problem with paragraphs. I encourage my students to use them. Possibly because of the way language is formatted on phones and computers today, my students don't indent. They prefer their prose in blocks and fragments. As writing is shaped by technology, it's possible that the indented paragraph will be replaced. Is a hyperlink or a video drop a paragraph? Are we supposed to indent in texts? If AI language programs indent, then I suppose indenting won't fall out of fashion. When is it best to glide smoothly between one topic and another? When is it best to throw the poetic gears into hyper-speed and teleport instantly to another universe entirely? When is juxtaposition better than transition?

One former student, Holly Waimano, published exceptional teen poetry in the school literary magazine. She was the bright star of the school's poetry slam team. When she was in the last semester of her high school year, she asked to read my *Atoms of Muses* book. I lent her a copy. I believe students should make their own book choices. I hoped she wouldn't find the content to be inappropriately off-putting. Two days later, she returned to my classroom and said, "I read your book." After a moment of silence, she said, "You like repetition and juxtaposition."

My mind jumps around, so my words jump around. It would be inaccurate and insensitive to say I have ADHD because I've never been diagnosed. I've wondered, though, whether or not I would find such a diagnosis if I sought one out. My mom scheduled an appointment for me to be screened for dyslexia in eighth grade. I reacted badly. I'm kind of embarrassed by how big a fit I pitched in the car on the way to the testing session, a session that never happened.

In my defense, I had been brainwashed to think dyslexia was something to be ashamed of. My dad told me that "Poor kids are dumb. Rich kids have dyslexia." That was one of his favorite jokes. I don't think of dyslexia that way anymore.

Each of my three siblings had tested into the gifted and talented program in school. In our district, the program of that sort carried the ridiculous name of MGM which stood for "mentally gifted minors." I was the only child in my family who did not get into that program. I had actually seen every MGM musical ever made, and I couldn't get into the MGM club. It didn't seem fair. On the day my mother picked me up after school to take me to the diagnostic appointment, I swirled into a tornado of protest in the front seat of the Buick station wagon. "More Than a Woman" played from the eight-track. My mom retreated. We went home.

Paragraphs provide segues and transitions. Paragraphs imply that one thing will lead to the next thing. I am not writing about every memory that comes to mind. I allow myself to skip over some topics and incidents. I could use paragraphs to negotiate the space between confession and withholding. A plan forms. I imagine ten chapters I have written that I have not written. I conceive of sample paragraphs from each of these invisible chapters. I will write these ten paragraphs and arrange them in an order that appeals to me. I will not worry too much about transitions and segues.

I imagine that each paragraph connects to its yet unwritten short story. These ten blocks of prose below are not connected to anything above. I am not referring in these sections to Larry Lin or anyone else I've mentioned before. These are ten fragments from what I could have written about, but mostly have not.

One: Never was I the sexual aggressor. I never said anything to him about sex. If I was aggressive about anything, I was too intense about my desire for friendship. I wanted him to think I was funny. I wanted him to come out to me. I wanted the two of us to exchange fiction manuscripts. He brought up sex all the time in our private conversations. On the day after Memorial Day, he said that if I wanted to have him, all I had to do was grab him. He put his hand high up his own thigh and gripped his tiny penis. I stammered and stood up. I wanted him to talk to me about his parents and his upbringing. I didn't want him to talk about sex while grabbing his crotch.

Two: The boarding school I attended in tenth grade in Massachusetts occasionally ran buses to the mall on Saturday night so we could see movies. On opening weekend of *The Deerhunter*, Reggie Kelly dressed as Travis Bickel with the army jacket, white tee shirt, Mohawk and shades. Travis Bickel was the character in *Taxi Driver*. He wasn't even in *The Deerhunter*, but Robert DeNiro was. That's all that mattered to Reggie Kelly. I was a little too afraid to go into the same theater as Reggie dressed as Travis Bickel, so I went to see *The Electric Horseman* with Robert Redford. I don't mean that I went to the movies with Robert Redford. I mean that Robert Redford starred as the Electric Horseman, a washed-up rodeo performer.

Three: My woodshop teacher in seventh grade really was named Mr. Wood. Woodshop in public schools in California in the 1970s was gender segregated. I hated being alone with the boys in woodshop only slightly less than I hated being alone with the boys in the locker room. Alex Cromworth used to steal my watch from me every day by bending my arm back. I'd have to buy it back from him for a quarter. I told my mom the extra quarter was for a juice box. Under these conditions, perhaps it's not surprising that I began to steal tools.

Four: At the exact moment when I passed the exit on the interstate that would have taken me to my grandparents, the oil alarm in my car went off. I don't really believe in a literal god, but whenever I try to devote myself to a loving deity, I conjure up that anecdote. Maybe the hand of God broke my car so I would be forced to connect with my grandfather and grandmother the year before they had to move out of their home and into Allegra Village. I think of God as a work of fiction. In the literal sense, this makes me an atheist. I love fiction, though. In this more theologically flexible sense, God has a meaningful place in my life.

Five: My mother and father had occasional neighborhood parties on weekends during my teenage years. When I was thirteen, I was jumping in and out of a swimming pool with two boys my age who had wrestler bodies. Two girls wore sexy swimwear. As Jeff Jeffries pulled himself up the ladder, one of the girls, Tammy Kavanaugh, caught me staring at Jeff's ass. She was staring at it also. We kind of caught each other. She smiled at me. I wasn't sure if hers was a friendly smile. I ducked underwater and swam into the deep end. Later that night our parents busted us in the driveway kicking around tennis balls we had set on fire with gasoline and matches. Mom and Dad were shocked at my behavior. They wanted to know what on Earth I was thinking. I didn't have the means to tell them that the metaphor was pretty literal. I was thinking about balls on fire. I was thinking literally about hot balls.

Six: Vampires are probably my least favorite of the classic monsters. I like some specific vampire characters. Dracula is great both in book and movie form. I've enjoyed *Interview with the Vampire,* again in both book and movie form. I had a Buffy phase. Nosferatu is a cool creation. As a type, most stories of the vampiric undead involve predation on the vulnerable. Vampires use seduction to turn people into night creatures. Legends of vampires reflect cultural fears about dark sexiness. A wolfman myth is more my style, perhaps because wolfman myths involve fear of one's own body.

Seven: I once spent a weekend in a beach house two lots down from where Ursula Le Guin lived in Oregon. She walked along the beach with a companion. I knew who she was. I walked toward her but intentionally didn't make eye contact with either of them. I have learned my lesson about pestering writers. Amy Tan caught me talking about her to my sister, Hattie, at a seafood restaurant in the Ferry Building at the Embarcadero. It was the night of the first Belichick/Brady Superbowl. The restaurant was half full. When she caught me saying her name to my sister, she got up and switched tables. Ever since then, I've tried to be casual around famous writers.

Eight: Tattoos helped me come out of the closet. Tattoos are not a subtle way of claiming autonomy over one's skin. The painful attraction of the needle can be a problem, but containing the pain within the confines of tattoo rituals can be cathartic. My arms are covered with feathers and flowers. I didn't plan out any elegant, inked sleeve. I collected my tattoos one or two at a time. When I traveled, I looked for tattoo shops. After my neck tattoo, I figured I had transformed my body enough at the skin level. I challenged myself to go a little deeper.

Nine: This woman and I got into a kind of comment scuffle on Facebook. I don't even remember how I know this person. I think she and I are just two folks. Self-deprecation is my default mode. My favorite comedian when I was a boy was Phyllis Diller. Her routine involved making fun of herself incessantly. Maybe she was supposed to be a parody of a suburban, white woman who failed to comply with the expectations of domesticity. Phyllis Diller was like a 1970s potential Karen who had refused to become a Karen. This woman from the comment scuffle looked like Phyllis Diller in her profile picture.

Ten: The reason I made the hyena joke is because I was self-conscious about my hygiene. The reason I made that cantaloupe joke was because I didn't know what to say when you told me you contemplated cannibalism on cannabis. The reason I made that pizza joke was because I was ashamed of the weakness of my pee stream. The reason I made that intestine and rectum joke was because I am unaware of my internalized racism. The only reason I made that joke about artificial intelligence is because I'm insecure about my ability to cook artichokes.

TWENTY-FOUR

I FLEW TO PALM SPRINGS TO VISIT MY 87-YEAR-OLD mother at her condo in the desert. This was 2024, the summer of the *Barbie* movie phenomenon. When I posted on Facebook that I'd be seeing this movie with my mom, one of her contemporaries commented with shock: "I would have thought she would rather see *Oppenheimer.*" My mother had no interest in seeing *Oppenheimer.* We watched *Barbie* sitting side by side in an otherwise empty theater in Rancho Mirage at 10:30 in the morning. Because of my vision issues, I couldn't catch a left-side glimpse of my mom as the movie played. I laughed a few times, but my mother gave no audible indication as to how she was reacting to the show.

When the movie was over, I was cautious. "So, what did you think?" As the lights came up, I could see she was smiling. "I thought it was great," she said. "I'm glad it was so feminist." When I was growing up, my mother had never called herself a feminist. When I was in college, fresh out of my semester of Introductory to Sociology at Wesleyan, I heard her tell my teenaged sister that feminists were angry. As we walked out of the theater in Rancho Mirage, I found myself wondering what had changed for her. Why was she now comfortable with the term?

My mother and I communicate well, but it's hard to dig into personal issues with her. When I came out of the closet at the end of the 1900s, I had imagined a long conversation. Perhaps she could tell me about her own relationship to same sex love? After listening to five minutes of my awkward coming out soliloquy, she said to me, "Do we still have to talk about this?" When we walked out of the movie theater in the summer of 2023, I couldn't find a way to ask about her changing attitudes as a woman in the world, so instead we talked about Barbie. My mother was trained as a pediatrician. She quit her medical practice to raise her children. Perhaps that lived experience fits some kind of Barbie ideal. On the way back to her condo in Palm Desert, I asked her if she had felt accepted as a woman doctor in the 1960s. She kept her eyes on the road and told me a story. I asked a couple of follow up questions, but Mom deflected them. Instead, we talked about the movie.

If it's wrong to tell stories about my friends and acquaintances, it's even worse to tell stories about my mother. My mother has always sought to improve her understanding of the world. For decades she has taken classes at community colleges, libraries, and senior centers. She doesn't take these classes for credits. She takes them because she thinks learning is fun. She has told me that she avoids the writing classes. She calls them "touchy-feely." I told her that those are the types of classes I teach.

I told her about the time I taught creative writing to adults, and my friend, a retired accountant, wrote a story about his father's love of musical theater. My mom asked me why I would encourage a man to write his story when obviously he would never publish. I told my mother that storytelling was like exercising. It's good for all humans. She shook her head and laughed. I tell some of my mom's stories as a way of honoring her. I'm worried, though, that we think about this differently. I'm worried she will read my recollections as a kind of betrayal. I worry about this regarding my father as well.

The day after the movie, my mother and I went to the Palm Springs Museum of Art. We have our routines when I come to town to visit. We see a movie. We seek out the glass exhibit and the Duane Hansen sculpture in the museum in Palm Springs. We eat lunch at Las Casuelas. I get the taco-enchilada-burrito combo plate with beans and rice. She gets an ala carte taco. This summer the temperature reached upwards of 120 degrees. We watched news of one of the Trump indictments on TV in air conditioning. We went to the pool. She fed me salads, cold dips and gin and tonics. My sister recently told me that while our mother has a hard time saying "I love you" out loud, she shows her love by making us food and teaching her children to knit. On the day I arrived at her place on this recent trip, she presented me with a ball of yarn and two knitting needles. I sat under the ceiling fan and worked on the skills she taught me. I intended to make a placemat, but when I saw how slow I was at knitting, I changed my goal and aimed to make a coaster. After four days of knitting, I ended up making a bookmark. It looks like woolen bacon.

My mother and I have learned to listen to one another well. I only experienced one moment of conflict during my weeklong stay. I suppose I should know that I'm too old to have my mother do my laundry, but when she asked me to throw my dirty clothes in the hamper, I obliged. I didn't stop to think about how she would react to my cutoff corduroy shorts. I am capable of dressing appropriately for work or social occasions. Because I knew I'd be staying indoors in the Coachella Valley during peak summer heat, I packed for maximum comfort. I look at that pair of shorts with the ragged fringe and a missing button and see the garment as casual, suitable for maximum relaxation. My mother took the cutoffs with the ragged fringe out of the dryer and held them up.

"You really need to throw these away," she said. She showed them to me. I had never noticed that tear by the zipper. My parrots rip my zippers if I leave my clothes on the floor. They are attracted to the shiny metal. If my mother only wanted me to throw away my shorts, I don't think I would have reacted as I did. She dug into her criticism. "How can you wear these? You are sixty years old? When are you going to grow up?" Perhaps she didn't really ask me that question about growing up, but for some reason I heard that. I heard the same tone of voice that I heard when she asked me in 2000 why I wanted to "court rejection" by telling my employers that I am gay.

She said what she said, and I heard what I heard. For the last two days of the trip, I walked around feeling like my mom would never be proud of me. The night before I left Palm Desert and flew back to Honolulu, I wrote her a long note. I told her how hard it was to maintain her approval. I asked her why she judged me by the pants I wore. I didn't send the email right away. I've learned that it's best to save drafts and sleep overnight before sending letters written under emotional stress. After I landed in Honolulu, I waited another day and then sent her the missive.

She called me as soon as she read the email. I noted that this was an improvement. I came out to her by mail at the turn of the last century, and though it only took the letter five days or so to travel from Honolulu to Southern California, it took her two weeks to reply. This time, I found her voicemail as soon as I woke up the day after I flew home. She was apologizing. She sent me an email apology at the same time. "I love you," she said. "I'll always be proud of you." I called her back and we cleared the air. I suppose I overreacted to the comments about my pants. I heard the criticism and attached it to other criticisms from decades ago. By the end of our phone call, everything appeared to be settled. We don't have a long history of talking about our feelings with one another, so as we moved to end the call, we both seemed to strain against an awkward silence. Thankfully, we each thought to mention the Barbie movie. "I'm more Weird Barbie than Stereotypical Barbie," I said.

"That's fine," Mom replied. "You can be any Barbie you want to be."

TWENTY-FIVE

THE SATURDAY BEFORE THE TUESDAY THAT WAS SEP-
tember 11, 2001, I filled up my red car with gas in Kailua. As I
stood with the pump handle in my fist, I overheard a younger man
tell an older man that Hawai'i is not really America. He was a local
surfer kid. The older man may have been a tourist. Exactly a week
later, days after the attacks on New York City, Washington D.C.,
and the field in Pennsylvania, I saw American flags everywhere
across the island. When America is the attacker, people reject
affiliation. When America is attacked, people claim affiliation.

In his essay, "The In-Betweens: On Asian-Americanness," Jeff
Chang quotes Jonathan Okamura who said there were no Asian-
Americans in Hawai'i; there were locals; there were Native Hawaiians,
and there were haoles. According to these influential writers and
thinkers, "Native Hawaiians were always local. Locals weren't all
Hawaiian. Some haoles were locals. And if one had to ask, one wasn't a
local." I'm haole. I have never thought of myself as local, though I have
lived in Makiki for more than thirty years.

Part of being a writer is discovering what to read. When I moved to
Hawai'i from Texas in 1992, I was still figuring out how to take control
of my literary life. As a child, I worried so much that I was not reading as
much or as fast as my siblings. My middle school offered speed reading
classes where we would stare at projected texts on the screen, several
words at a time displayed at varying levels of rapidness. After each flash-
reading session, we would take comprehension quizzes that we would
score and grade ourselves. I cheated relentlessly. We would self-report

the number of pages we read each month from books at home and transcribe that data onto a grading chart. Again, I cheated relentlessly.

I was wearing a pink shirt with holes in it the second Saturday after the 9/11/01 attacks. This would have been during my brief period of life when I dedicated myself to marathon running. I'd been out of the closet for about a year and a half. Perhaps I cared about looking attractive. The shirt was once pale blue with darker stripes, but I laundered it badly. Bleach had turned it pink. That's what put the holes in it too. My hair was also bleached. Who knew what I looked like to the woman who approached me in the Kaimuki parking lot? She recited a long story about how her car had broken down a couple of streets over. She said she worked at the UH bookstore. It became apparent pretty quickly that she was asking me for money.

Reading was a transactional activity for me when I was growing up. If I did it, I got a reward. I learned how to say I read when I really hadn't. To this day, I fight my internalized impulse to lie about books. "Hey Tim, have you read *Infinite Jest*?" I said I read that one for years. Even as I cheated my way through scholastic reading programs that attached reading to prize-fetching and punishment, I fell in love with specific books as a child. A middle grade novel called *The Mock Revolt* by Vera and Bill Cleaver sent jolts through my consciousness. To this day, I don't know what that book was about. I only remember descriptions of skin bubbling on an adolescent arm after the protagonist got a tattoo. The book tapped me on the shoulder and pointed toward worlds I didn't know existed.

Never attracted to Narnia or Middle Earth, I savored Grimms Fairy Tales and *Watership Down* to satisfy my fantasy appetite. In our living room on wooden bookshelves my dad built, my mom collected every Agatha Christie novel in twenty-five-cent paperback editions. By the time I got to them, the pages were yellowed. By senior year in high school,

I had read each one three times. At boarding school, cheating my way through English class, the only assigned reading I loved was *A Streetcar Named Desire*. On vacations I'd read Jason Bourne novels; a guy wakes up on a beach and, despite displaying savage-level martial arts skills and the ability to establish his will over every firearm ever made, he has no idea who he is. That was my kind of novel. When I was twenty, someone gave me *Zen and the Art of Motorcycle Maintenance*. I don't know how that book would speak to me now. I'm afraid to revisit it. When I was just starting to enter adulthood, this Robert Pirsig memoir prompted me to consider what might be possible in life.

My friend, Brenda, identifies as *māhū*. I don't consider myself qualified to define the term, but as I understand it, *māhū* refers to the third gender in local Hawaiian culture, or perhaps the third sex. I think of Brenda as a transwoman. She defines herself that way as well. Brenda served as house manager when I played a butler in a community theater production of Noel Coward's *Present Laughter*. Over the past decade, Brenda and I have kept in touch on Facebook and through occasional exchanges of personal essay drafts. She told me a while ago that she would consider me local. I never see myself that way. She pointed to my decades teaching and writing in Hawai'i and said that I contributed to the well-being of the island. I accepted her words with gratitude.

As the woman in the Kaimuki parking lot told me of her automotive dilemma, a voice in my head warned me that I was being conned. Still, I reached for my wallet. When she snatched the twenty from my hand, I saw her expression shift. I was the sea bass staring into the face of the fisherman who just lured me from the water. She ran away. I had been talked out of my money. Had this incident not happened in the aftermath of 9/11, maybe I would have reacted with more caution. I wanted to believe that I existed in some kind of community. I wanted to believe that we were all Americans, that everyone in that parking lot wished the best for everyone else. Existing in some state of naivety, I wanted to help another local person in need.

The two books I remember loving in college were *Midnight's Children* by Salman Rushdie and *Tar Baby* by Toni Morrison. I wrote many essays in my English major on books I never read. Occasionally I got caught. Mostly I didn't. When I moved to Honolulu, I was only beginning to develop a reading life independent of what others wanted from me. My teacher friend subscribed to *Harpers* and *The New Yorker*, so I followed that lead. *Harpers* published "Pafko at the Wall," the first section of Don DeLillo's *Underworld*. I was too new of a serious reader to understand *Underworld*, but I loved "Pafko at the Wall." In 1993, the magazine published the now-famous David Foster Wallace essay about the Illinois State Fair. I honestly thought that was the funniest thing I'd ever read. He had a footnote that was only an exclamation point! A year later, *Harpers* published his cruise ship essay. When his first nonfiction collection was published, I taught something he wrote about metafiction and TV. I ordered *Consider the Lobster* for a high school elective I invented called Vision and Voice.

When I told my friend Harlo that I had been talked out of twenty dollars by a woman in a parking lot two weeks after 9/11, I spoke with great shame. I didn't want to admit that I'd trusted a stranger who wished to take advantage of me. Harlo laughed. He told me things like this had happened to him more than he cared to admit. There was that one time in college, for example, when a fast-talking, middle-aged man talked him out of his athletic shoe. Right there on the street, the man told Harlo a story about wanting to photograph his sneaker for a design project. Harlo surrendered his shoe, and then as the man ran away, my friend realized he was never going to see the sneaker again. More than likely, the man was going to use Harlo's Saucony as a sex toy.

When the writer, Jeff Chang, came to speak to my high school English class, he read a passage from his essay on Asian-American identity. In a subsequent discussion, one of my tenth-grade students asked me if I thought of myself as local. I said I did not, but for some reason, I felt the need to say that my friend, Brenda, told me I was. I passed along her compliment. It was kind of an insecure display on my part. I communicated her notion that one becomes local by contributing positively to the local community. A boy with a shark tooth around his neck on a chain told me that with all due respect, he wouldn't call me local. Local doesn't have to do with what you do. Local, according to this intelligent fifteen-year-old boy, has to do with who you are.

Sometimes I dwell upon the time the woman conned me out of twenty dollars in the Kaimuki parking lot in the aftermath of 9/11. I don't dredge up the incident to wallow in pity or to live in the past. I think about the way my friend, Harlo heard my story as an invitation to tell his story of the time he was swindled by the foot-fetish dude. Whenever something bad happens to me, I tend to want to keep it a secret, to withhold my misery because I am ashamed of how I allowed myself to get into a miserable situation. I appreciate the casual way Harlo commiserated with me. He reminded me of some lessons so obvious they are almost cliches. Still, they are useful cliches: there is no shame in being imperfect. Everyone stumbles through life.

As I settled into living in Hawai'i, my reading life and my teaching life converged. In the nineties I taught Denis Johnson, Mary Gaitskill, *Fun Home, Maus, Persepolis* and *Saturday Night at the Kohala Theater* by Lois Ann Yamanaka. Reading and teaching were invitations to explore the worlds of storytelling, poetry, and art. The books I encountered invited me to explore my own passions in creative writing.

My first published poetry collection was a chapbook called *Awkward Hugger.* I wrote the title poem after I returned to my grad school campus two years after receiving my Masters. In line to get into a Spanish restaurant, I recognized an old classmate, Angelina Murillo. She recognized me and said my name as I approached. I said her name back and opened my arms for a hug. As I leaned in, she pushed me away. My hug was rejected. For the rest of my time on campus, I wondered why Angelina didn't want to embrace me. We had hugged at graduation. Did I smell like urine again? Maybe she never liked me as much as I thought she did. It took me about twenty-four hours to work the shame and anxiety out of my system. I went home and wrote my "Awkward Hugger" poem. Essentially, I was arguing that we humans shouldn't be so quick to punish ourselves and feel guilty.

I take a lot of writing classes. I teach a few too. I like the way a writing class gives me a chance to meet other people quickly. In the 1980s, I sat in a car with a woman from a writing workshop who wanted to play me a new CD she had recently become enamored with. This woman from the writing class played me "Fast Car" by Tracy Chapman. The song was a new release at the time, far from its eventual elevation into eternal classic status. I never saw the woman again after the class ended. She had written about an abortion. I wrote poetry attempting to name my conflicted feelings around sexuality. A writing class gives me a way to know someone's personal story without knowing someone personally. I try not to enter writing classes with a voyeuristic attitude. Instead, I look at writing classes as opportunities to share brief connection and learn more about human nature.

People who talk about writing eventually talk about the struggle of getting work published. There is that trope of the elevator pitch, this idea that the plot of a complicated story should be summarized in a concise and pithy way. During a summer writing class in New York a decade or so ago, I ended up in this literal situation: alone in an elevator with a literary agent. We entered the car at the ground floor of the Bryant Park

Hotel. We rode up thirty-six floors, just the two of us in the enclosed space. We both were on our way to the part of the conference where aspiring writers pitch their projects to agents who, if interested, might help the writers sell books.

It was nearly impossible for me to conceive of myself as a person who might one day publish a book. I idolized so many writers. I could never imagine myself in their professional company. I put David Foster Wallace on such a high pedestal that I went to the University of Arizona to get a Masters in Creative Writing. Just like he did. As soon as I got there, I started to understand that this was a ridiculous reason to choose a graduate school. Fortunately, I had great teachers who taught me to read more widely and to learn something from every book I encountered. After graduate school, I tried to bring that attitude with me back home as an English teacher. When I returned to teaching high school in Hawai'i after getting my MFA, I insinuated myself into the school's chapel program. After reading something from the altar to the incoming ninth grade class about *Star Wars* as a queer text, I noticed a tiny person standing in front of the podium. I said hello. This person shoved a piece of paper in my hand and ran away.

The paper said, "Thank you for saying you are gay in chapel. You will be hearing from me in the next four years." I did. The young student was a good writer who took my class senior year and worked on an independent study project with me the semester before graduation. We kept in touch as this aspiring artist studied dance and poetry in college. Upon graduating from an Ivy League school, this young person transitioned her gender and changed her name. She and I stayed in touch. She teaches dance and choreographs productions focused on gender identity today. I consider her to be a close friend. A month ago, she texted to recommend Kelly Link's *Book of Love*. I texted her last week to tell her I devoured it in fewer than five days. I loved it.

I don't need to call myself "local." I feel most comfortable in spaces where I am permitted to settle as an outsider. I suppose that makes me a reluctant colonizer. Maybe in being from nowhere, I aspire to be from anywhere. I never feel like I had a hometown. Born in Baltimore in 1963 while my parents were studying medicine at Johns Hopkins, I moved with my family to Augsburg, Germany, New York City, Denver, Birmingham, East Grand Rapids, Omaha, and then Redlands, California, all before I was twelve. I've mentioned this already. In summers I'd go to Christian Back-to-Nature Camp in Tennessee. By tenth grade I was sent to boarding school in Massachusetts. I went to college in Connecticut, worked in the state a year after graduating, and then moved to Houston. This was all before I was 25. People ask me if my parents were in the military. The Germany stop was army-related, but other than that, we weren't moving because of national service. We were moving because my dad had trouble staying in one place for more than two years.

When I was 47, I left Honolulu for Tucson to get that creative writing degree. The first class I took at the University of Arizona was called "Poetry of Place." This would have been 2010. The news media had reported a slate of stories involving queer young people who had killed themselves. There was a report about a tree in a backyard in Texas. There was a report about a bridge over a gorge in New Jersey. From Facebook I learned of an initiative to stand up against suicide of queer youth by wearing purple clothing on one specific day.

In the elevator to the top of the Bryant Park Hotel, I recognized the name on the badge of the young man in front of me. He was a literary agent at a prestigious firm in New York. In twenty minutes or so, I would have an opportunity to stand in line in order to sit down in front of this very same person to pitch my novel. This was that apocryphal moment. I was literally in an elevator with a man who might be able to help me secure a publishing contract. He was staring straight ahead at the elevator doors. He was not holding his phone. He just stood there. Undistracted. I stared straight ahead. Then I stared at him. He looked at me, caught my eye. Half-smiled. I looked away and stared at the elevator doors again. Silence can be so loud sometimes.

When I was in fiction and poetry school, I asked one of my professors if he thought there was a link between writing a good story and being a good person. He openly laughed at me. He told me he knew plenty of assholes who were geniuses. Memory has a way of simplifying narrative. Perhaps epiphanies are not really epiphanies when we humans go through them. Perhaps those single moments of insight are not really occurring in single moments. Sitting in the class on the poetry of place, discussing Italo Calvino's *Invisible Cities*, I counted the number of people at the table wearing purple shirts. Mine came from the Goodwill near my apartment on 6th Avenue. Thirteen other students in class wore theirs.

I can't say I was thinking about Italo Calvino. I was thinking about this one news report I read about a dead fourteen-year-old in Los Angeles. I could almost feel my ego as a physical presence. I wanted so hard to feel good about myself for wearing this purple thrift shop shirt in solidarity with deceased children. Then I felt disgust. How was I doing anything positive? In what way was public performance of empathy solving any kind of societal problem?

For thirty-six floors, I stayed silent in the elevator of the Bryant Park Hotel. I had an opportunity to pitch the novel I'd started in graduate school. I'd been working on it for four years. I think it was almost finished—like, for real, ready-to-be-published finished. I stared at the doors in front of the elevator. I didn't even make small talk. I could have told the agent that I liked his tie. It was purple. I could have told him it reminded me of the time I wore a purple shirt in graduate school, how that moment started me on a journey of writing about queer teen suicide. I could have said that the reason I told the story in intentionally disjointed passages was because in writing about LGBTQIA+ youth suicide, I wanted to respect the stories of others by making clear that no one's life unfolds as neatly as literary fiction. Could I really have said any of that? It didn't seem like it would have made any sense.

From my rocking chair in Makiki, I look out my window and see other windows. Each pane reflects a story. I published my book on gay youth suicide as a collection of prose poems. My prose poem book has a purple shirt on the cover. I regret there is no number for a suicide hotline on the second to last page. From my rocking chair in Makiki, I start to tell a new story.

Not every queer tale is a sad tale. The 9th grader who handed me the note thanking me for saying I was gay in chapel? She became a dancer. She talked to me about ballet shoes and gender dysphoria. She infuses her beautiful spirit into her art. I write about joy. I write about death. I write about that time I was mistreated. I write about that time I mistreated someone else. Imagine and recall. This journey from shame to acceptance: how should I speak of something so complicated? I contrive for myself an origin story. There was this yoga class. I didn't contrive the class or the memory, but the story I set down on the page is shaped, crafted, and manipulated. There was this bad yoga teacher. There were these nights in Makiki thirty years ago. Every poem is about place unless it is about time. Then again, time is a place.

I've read essays and blogposts where writers say they wrote their memoirs because they were tired of keeping family secrets. Chosen families keep secrets too. I tell two friends I might publish a story based on an experience I had with my bad yoga teacher. Each friend worries that this is going to ruin some relationships. I don't want to ruin any relationships. I travel to Flagstaff on spring break to write the last chapter of my memoir draft.

The sports bar in Flagstaff provides me with a metaphor. All around me there are televisions without sound. Bad country music blares from a stereo system. On one screen is a commercial for a phone plan. On those two televisions over the pinball machines, there are basketball games. Someone is watching women's lacrosse on the TV over the bar. The televisions are tuned to specific stations, volume at zero. Each specific station shows specific people playing specific games, enduring specific dramas, or selling promises. The images imply some kind of storytelling, but the coherence remains elusive because the sound is off and because every one of these stories plays side by side all at once.

If I were to ride up thirty-six floors of an expensive hotel in an elevator alone with a literary agent today, what would I say about this book I am writing? Would he, she, or they understand if I told them my book is like a sports bar in Flagstaff with several storylines broadcasting at once? No, that would be a terrible elevator pitch. I'll try to come up with some better ones.

Hypothetical elevator pitch 1: I'm writing about this thing that happened to me once and how the way I look at it now is different from the way I looked at it then.

Hypothetical elevator pitch 2: I'm writing about the difference between knowing people and writing about people.

Hypothetical elevator pitch 3: I'm writing about not having sex with a yoga teacher who seemed like she wanted to have sex with me. I'm writing about not being ashamed of memories that have caused me shame. I am writing about asexual identity.

Hypothetical elevator pitch 4: I am writing a series of stories that take place in Makiki, the most population dense district in Honolulu, Hawai'i. I am writing about the way light bounces off the windows I see from my sliding glass door. I am writing about how hard it is to know other people. I am writing about how thousands of folks can live together in the same neighborhood without appreciating who anyone else is. I am telling ghost stories and metaphorical stories as a way of telling my own story.

Hypothetical elevator pitch 5: I write about memory to understand how stories distort lived experience. I am writing about how every narrative is about place unless it is about time. I was going to call my book *Some Deft Segue*, and then I decided to change my title to *Makiki Postmodern*. At some point, I rejected that title too. "Postmodern" seems like a moldy word, and though I live in Makiki, I'm not local and thus am insecure about speaking for my neighborhood. For a while I was calling this manuscript a work of fiction.

If someone said it was autofiction, I would agree. Now I prefer to refer to it as a memoir with lies in it. My name is TIM, and my mode is TMI. I look out the window and see other windows. The man in Makiki Park who tried to speak to me of Jesus has become a memory ghost. I think about the difference between reflected and deflected. I think about what it means to turn skin into fiction or nonfiction. I think about love.

If I were to ride up in an elevator with a literary agent today, I might just ask them if they ever think about love. I might ask them if they ever dodged a phone call from someone who needed them. I might tell an agent in an elevator that every story becomes its own simulation: the people in the book don't know they are in a book. The people who create the fiction question whether or not they are responsible for their characters.

How about I don't tell the agent in the elevator that I am writing a story? I could say I am a high school English teacher. This is enough for me to be. Now that I am not trying to sell them anything, the pressure is off. Perhaps I will engage this literary agent in some elevator small talk. Would they be drawn to philosophical questions? I might ask whether or not they trust their memories. There is a scenario in which I wouldn't take this ride at all. I'd stay on the ground floor. Or I'd take the stairs. I'd climb and climb, step after step. I'd keep climbing, and when I got tired, I could find some dark landing where I could seek solitude for a few moments.

In 2022, I took my first vacation trip since pandemic quarantine began. My friend, the former student and current dance teacher and artist, lives in Denver. A pal from grad school lives in that city too. I can smoke weed there with impunity and shop for books at the Tattered Cover. I'm a member of the Denver Art Museum. I like the city's public library system. The flight from Hawai'i took a day and a half. When I landed, I felt ready to check into my hotel and sleep. Tucking myself in, I expected to disappear into slumber. Cacophony woke me. An alarm rang. A mechanical voice implored "Exit the building now! Do not take the elevator!" Groggy and panicked, I jumped into clothing and grabbed my phone, keys and wallet.

The stairwell was not empty. Behind me I heard footsteps. Running down the staircase in an emergency, I didn't know if there was any kind of passing etiquette. I stepped aside and let a man and woman gallop by. They were in their twenties, friendly. They asked me if I knew what was going on. I didn't. Turns out it was a false alarm. At the bottom of the staircase, the man and his girlfriend hugged me. We had bonded together as we descended our staircase of mystery. Maybe I should have told the agent in the elevator at the Bryant Park Hotel that my book is a descent on a staircase of mystery. I could ascend that same structure. Taking it slow, I'd step up two stairs at a time. After fifteen or so floors, I'd stop on a shadowy landing and recline onto the cold concrete floor. Why would I do that? Not sure. It makes as much sense to me as coming up with an elevator pitch.

A sophomore student asked me once if I would rather be rich and unhappy or poor and happy. I could have told the student that I have already answered that question by how I've lived my life: I'm more poor than rich; I'm more happy than unhappy. I told her that I mostly want to be loved. Was that the right thing to say? Should I be saying things like that out loud to teenagers? What is the relationship between confession and absolution? What hurts more: the story we can't remember or the story we can't forget? I live to express love. What else is the point? I write to save my life. I write to save time. I write to name the broken parts. I write to claim the beautiful parts.

I have written myself into the dark of a cement landing on a staircase of mystery. I imagine how my own tale might end. I once took a fiction writing class where the teacher told us we weren't allowed to kill any of our characters. While his edict amused me, he had a point. Beginning writers use death in their stories to fabricate drama. He wanted us to find drama in the everyday moments of life. Today I saw a butterfly on my way to work. A student showed me a chapbook of poems she made herself. She sewed the binding with white ribbon. I read this essay online by a man who dropped off his only child at college for the first time. In reflecting on his own good fortune, he expressed gratitude for being his own boss, living with his wife and kids and owning a big screen TV. I can't claim any of those circumstances. I don't think I want the last scene of my story to take place in some metaphorical stairwell.

I am back in my rocking chair, staring out the window of my Makiki apartment. Light bounces off glass and metal. I wait for fireworks, and then I decide that I don't want to see fireworks. I am not looking for lost luster. I don't have parrot wings or angel wings. I don't have regrets as much as I have memories like molten feathers that fall from my body and float toward the ground, spinning. Aiming for a soft landing. I suppose it's time to close my eyes now. There's a very good chance I'll die alone. I'm okay with this. It's fine. There are vision problems in my left eye. So much depends upon the way we see the red wheelbarrow. Let's not chase after those white chickens. I breathe. I sway gently in my rocking chair. I'm not planning to do a backbend here. In this quiet, there will be no grunting, no lift from the hips. Inhale. I seek something still. Exhale. I still seek something.

ACKNOWLEDGEMENTS

Perhaps because I am a teacher as well as a writer, I place a high value on learning. I have taken a lot of writing classes in my life and am grateful for everyone who has ever taught me and collaborated with me in those formal educational settings. More than ten years ago, I enrolled in summer writing classes with The Writers Hotel where I met Shanna McNair and Scott Wolven. This experience eventually led to my connection with High Frequency Press. I am ever grateful for all I have learned and continue to learn from Shanna and Scott.

From 2010-2012, I studied at the University of Arizona and worked at the Poetry Center in Tucson. All my teachers and colleagues from those years have influenced the way I think about reading and writing. I am indebted especially to Aurelie Sheehan; she left this plane of existence (or this plain of existence, or this plain existence) in 2023 and is missed by many. Aurelie was one of the best teachers I have ever known. She encouraged me to write about everything.

While creating this book was often a solitary experience, I benefited so much from select readers. Thanks to Frankie Rollins, Susan M. Schultz, Melissa Gutierrez, Lawrence Lenhart, Anjoli Roy, and Tom Gammarino for conversing with me about writing during my early drafting stages. I'm grateful for my friendship, literary and otherwise, with River Selby. Thanks to Paul Hamamoto, Heather McMillen, Diana Fontaine, Allison Hedge Coke, Michael Bosley, Asha Appel and Mark Maretzki who listened to me read the first ten pages of *Backbends* out loud in a back yard off Diamond Head Road in the summer of 2023. Thanks to Elle Hong for talking to me about writing, going on decades now. Perhaps I need to acknowledge Frankie Rollins a second time because she read my book again as I neared completion. Through her writing coaching business, The Fifth Brain Collective, I was able to get her help with proofreading and editing. I am grateful for my writing friends. Every conversation I've ever had about my book has helped me understand what it is that I am trying to create.

In the book, I refer to writers whose literary output has inspired me. I want to acknowledge the work of Jeff Chang, Art Spiegelman, Robert Lowell, Mary Oliver, Tim O'Brien, Richard Powers, Cathy Park Hong, Ben Lerner, Matthew Zapruder, Audre Lorde and Jonathan Okamura. I mention all of them in the pages of my book, and I acknowledge all of them as inspirational writers whose work has challenged and enlightened me.

Bamboo Ridge Press published an earlier version of the mango story. A version of the poem referred to in the book as "Gentle Tool" was published in *Foglifter* journal. Very early versions of stories involving the goddess within and The Homosexual Agenda were published in work I did for Tinfish Press. I am grateful to the editors and writers who worked with me and gave me those opportunities.

Writing a memoir (with lies in it) involves telling stories about friends and family members. I acknowledge that this can be uncomfortable for my loved ones. I am grateful for those who have supported me as I have written about them. Thank you to my siblings and in-laws: Mac, Molly, Peter, Sarah, Chris and Michele. Thanks to my mother and father. Thanks to Eli, Heather, Claire, Michael, Dan, and all the members of my chosen family in Hawai'i. I have talked to my nieces and nephews about art, books, and life. I am grateful for those conversations and for them.

There are so many other people who have supported me, read my work, talked to me about my memories, and listened to my stories. If Scott Turpin hadn't told me that he liked reading the prose in my social media posts, I may not ever have considered that anyone might want to read a book full of my personal writing. It's kind of amazing how much a small bit of sincere encouragement can do for one's creativity.

Speaking of creativity, I must acknowledge Kelly Van Eaton for the artwork on the cover. I am grateful for Kelly's talent and friendship.

I hope that as a teacher I have been sincere and encouraging to emerging writers. It's not original to say that teachers learn as much from students as students learn from them, but just because that has been said before, doesn't make it less true. I acknowledge all the young people who have sat in my classrooms and have talked with me about literature and writing. Thanks to all the colleagues I have worked with in schools since I first started teaching in 1985.

I acknowledge my queer friends and mentors who have taught me to be proud to be part of the wide and diverse LGBTQIA+ community. I acknowledge Smith Galtney, Jack Canfield (in memoriam), TC Tolbert, Sam Ace, Trace Peterson, Mardi Jaskot, Kamden Hilliard, Mark Pangilinan, Kaelin Tancayo-Spielvogel, The Bills, Michael "Thin Man" Bosley and many other brave and hilarious folx who have taught me a whole lot about what's up.

I have learned so much from all of you.

Timothy Dyke is a teacher and writer who lives in Makiki, Hawai'i. He is the author of the Tinfish Press prose poetry collections *Awkward Hugger* and *Atoms of Muses* and the book-length poem, *Maga*. His stories, poems and essays have been published by *Drunken Boat*, *Santa Monica Review*, *The New Guard*, *Bat City Review*, *Bamboo Ridge Press*, *Ho'olana*, and other publications. He received his BA in English and his MA in Liberal Studies from Wesleyan University. He earned his MFA in Creative Writing from the University of Arizona. Since 1992, Timothy has taught English to young people at Punahou School in Honolulu.